Timothy Argent, best-selling author of travel books, is following an old wagon trail across America's West, charting his progress with laconic postcards to his publisher. Suddenly all communication stops, and after six weeks the desperate editor persuades Melinda Pink to go out and find the man.

She tracks her quarry to Dogtown, a ghost town that people are restoring in an effort to attract tourists. There are 'the boys' at the gourmet restaurant, the horsey owner of the Grand Imperial Hotel (complete with Modigliani nude above the bar) and the striking if raddled couple collecting for their museum. Way up in Crazy Mule Canyon is a recluse who prefers animals to people and emphasises the point with a rifle. And there is the caretaker at a ranch, who lived with an exquisite coloured girl until she disappeared – around the time that Timothy Argent came through.

As the heat-wave tightens its grip on the Sierra foothills Miss Pink unravels the mystery of Argent's disappearance from a welter of evidence. Evidence that could accumulate only in wildest California: a place of breath-taking beauty, of laid-back innocence and stark savagery.

In this atmospheric tale author Gwen Moffat, herself a wilderness traveller, has again created a 'first-rate mystery that is impossible to pre-guess'.

# RAGE

## Gwen Moffat

For Shirley from Gwen
Best wishes.

Largs, April 6th 1990.

**MACMILLAN
LONDON**

First published in Great Britain 1990 by
MACMILLAN LONDON LIMITED
4 Little Essex Street London WC2R 3LF
and Basingstoke

Associated companies in Auckland, Delhi, Dublin, Gaborone,
Hamburg, Harare, Hong Kong, Johannesburg, Kuala Lumpur,
Lagos, Manzini, Melbourne, Mexico City, Nairobi, New York,
Singapore and Tokyo

ISBN 0-333-52343-1

A CIP catalogue record for this book is available from the
British Library

Typeset by Matrix, 21 Russell Street, London WC2

Printed and bound in Great Britain by
The Camelot Press Ltd, Southampton

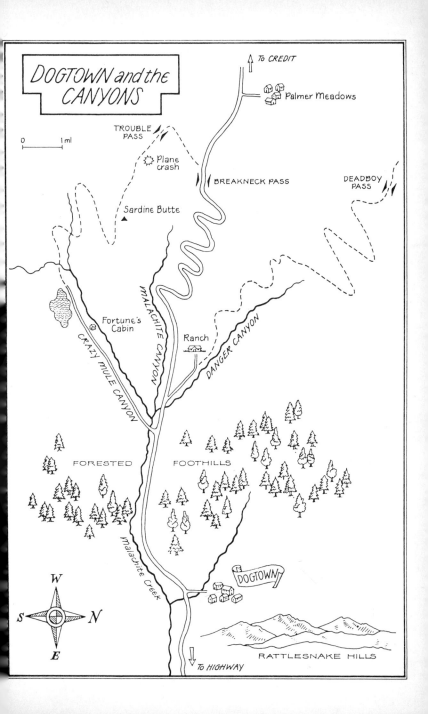

# Introduction

After the man died the body hung motionless. The legs were in shadow but when the cottonwood leaves shifted in the breeze, sunshine flickered over feet that were bare and delicate and covered with small burns.

The sky was cloudless, bleached pale by the heat. On the far side of the river the mountains rose in tiers of cliffs to a crest like torn brown lace. The river ran through a desert where there were no side streams.

The water was wide and shallow. Not far from the grove of cottonwoods was a ford marked by hoofs and tyres. Closer to the trees and on the same bank was a pool, its surface a few inches above the level of the river, its outer rim reinforced by concrete. At ten o'clock in the morning the surface of the pool was glassy: a part of this hot bright world where the only movement came from the river, the cottonwood leaves, and an armadillo scavenging under the hanged man. Suddenly the armadillo checked and listened, its snout twitching, then it ambled away into the undergrowth.

People were coming along a path towards the pool. They were all elderly, some quite old. They wore shorts and bright clean slacks, and their flesh was tanned to the colour and texture of old leather. The men had bulging paunches or skeletal frames and the women had long ago given up the struggle to resist rich food. They moved purposefully and with a confidence born of familiarity. Reaching the pool they separated as if under direction: men to one clump of willows, women to another. After a few moments they reappeared, their ageing bodies revealed, and even flaunted, by psychedelic swimwear.

7

They eased themselves into the pool until they were sitting facing inwards: a circle of disembodied heads, all their attention concentrated on the sensation, real or imaginary, of warm mineral water soothing arthritic joints and various unidentified conditions.

'What was that?' grunted Frank Ward – an old pharmacist from Illinois – thinking he'd heard his wife gasp. He adjusted his hearing aid and looked to see what had attracted Bett's attention.

'Gross,' she exclaimed without feeling. 'Alien, like flying blood, you know? Only a redbird,' she added quickly, before anyone could say something snide about ghouls or Alzheimer's.

'Redbirds are cardinals,' intoned Frank with all the weary patience of a man who has been correcting his wife for half a century.

'Cardinals have crests.' In her seventies Bett still had good eyesight. 'Besides, this bird was brighter'n a cardinal.'

Frank peered towards the trees, raised his clip-on shades and squinted against the sun. 'I'll be doggoned,' he breathed.

'There's someone up that tree!' Bett was affronted. 'Someone spying on us. So why doesn't he move?'

Indignant and fiercely protective of their own special place, deriving confidence from numbers, they climbed out of the pool and trudged through the sand to the grove. Ahead of them a vermilion flycatcher flitted away to the last cottonwood.

They were too old to be appalled by death but they found the manner of this one intriguing. 'Suicide,' someone said heavily.

'He's Mexican.' Bett was staring at the man's feet. After the first glance they avoided looking at the face, but the feet were in bad shape too. It was Joe – who had ranched for forty years in Montana before retiring to the Sun Belt – who walked round the suspended body and studied the back of the neck and the branch above. 'That's wire,' he said. 'Barbed wire.'

Incongruous in their scanty clothing, they moved to

his side and stared upwards. They had drawn closer to each other and their silence was eloquent.

'Alive?' Bett whispered after a while. 'They hung him *alive*, with barbed wire?'

'They burned him first,' Joe said. 'Look at them feet.'

Reluctantly they did look, then away, avoiding each other's eyes and then, as if manipulated by strings, they all turned and looked through the willows and across the river into Mexico.

'Why did they have to do it on this side?' Bett protested. 'He's Mex, isn't he? Mexicans have to have done this; Anglos couldn't have.'

'Maybe they meant some Anglos to see,' Joe said. 'Like, a warning?'

# Chapter 1

At two o'clock on a summer's afternoon the air in Soho was warm even on the shaded side of the street; on the other side it must have been sweltering. Over there a massive black man in dreadlocks was haranguing a trio of Japanese tourists. Two Indian women in saris crossed the road to avoid the group. A turbaned Sikh lingered in the doorway of his mini-market observing the scene with wary contempt.

The woman at the restaurant window turned back to her companion. 'At one time,' she observed, 'you would have said that half the people in Soho were foreigners; now you and I are the only Anglos in sight.'

'Don't forget the other customers. Anglos?'

'Caucasians. Whites.'

'That's what I thought you meant. But at one time you would have said "English". You're suspended between cultures, Melinda: a displaced person – although more inclined towards the other side of the Atlantic than this one, I think. What are you going to do next?'

'I've only just got off the plane!' Miss Pink's tone did indeed owe something to jet lag. Her agent's expression remained one of polite inquiry. She avoided his eye. 'I'm going to the Aegean,' she murmured. 'I propose to spend the winter in a villa in the sun, and swim in the wine-dark sea.' At that she beamed, as pleased with her wording as the image it evoked.

'Byron? He wasn't under contract – and won't the Aegean be a trifle cold in winter?'

She sipped her cognac. 'There are plenty of other places that are congenial in winter.'

'Such as Arizona, or California.'

'I've just come from the Southwest. I can't go back.'

'Why not?'

'Well – logistics . . . And I have no money.' Behind the designer spectacles the eyes sharpened momentarily. 'What are you suggesting?'

'Another travel book? Pioneers – the opening of the West?'

She sighed and her tone was indulgent. 'If you can get – ten thousand for me, as expenses, not an advance, then I'll go anywhere that's warm and dry.'

Martin Jenks's face didn't change. 'That might be arranged.'

Only a person who knew her well would have seen that Miss Pink had stiffened. 'I was forgetting the kind of vehicle that I would need in the wilderness,' she said. 'And of course you would want me to go to a wilderness area.' He blinked at her. 'Fifteen thousand,' she said calmly.

'Let me make a telephone call.'

'There's a catch in this.'

'No catch, I assure you.'

'Who's going to pay fifteen thousand to a writer of gothics whose travel books just break even? That kind of money means something illegal – or dangerous.'

'Jet lag is clouding your judgement. I'm not going to kill the golden goose.'

'So who – ?'

'James Dorset.'

'Definitely a catch. The Dorset Press has Timothy Argent. He's a brilliant writer, and he comes over very well on the box: a charmer, in fact.'

'Certainly brilliant, but they don't exactly have him.'

'What? He's left Dorset?' He said nothing, watching her work it out. 'And they want *me*?' Her astonishment gave way to speculation. 'You're not asking me to compete with him,' she went on slowly. 'I know my field.'

'Oh, no one better, Melinda. I don't think there's any suggestion of your competing.' He became brusque. 'Go along and have a word with Dorset. I'll call him and confirm the meeting.' He wasn't asking permission but telling her.

As she watched him make his way through the tables she wondered if James Dorset had stayed in his office over the lunch hour or come back early anticipating her agent's call. Why couldn't his secretary take it? The book had to be important, if it was a book. Something was important. Fifteen thousand. Her eyes glazed as she visualised her house in Cornwall: like an expensive horse eating its head off without any work to do; a big old house that she hadn't managed to let over the coming winter, but the bills having to be met all the same: rates, electricity, oil, maintenance, the gardener's wages, those of her housekeeper, Chrissie Clarke . . . She had to admit that the Aegean was wishful thinking. There was no money for her to go anywhere; she must remain in damp grey Cornwall through the winter, writing yet another gothic romance – unless she were paid to go elsewhere.

'Did you mention money?' she asked as her agent returned.

'I'll leave that to you.'

'It's your job to draw up the contract!'

'Of course. I thought you meant expenses. You know better than I what you'll need in that line. You mentioned fifteen thousand.'

'I was speaking off the top of my head. There's something going on here.'

But he was signalling the waiter and affecting not to hear.

'I've been an admirer of yours for years: sound escapist literature, meticulous observation. I'm talking like a reviewer but then you'll know your own worth.'

Publisher and author exchanged practised smiles as they took each other's measure. Miss Pink saw a lanky young man in peg-top trousers and a white silk shirt without a tie. His thick blond hair was expertly cut and squeaky clean and he had the mid-Atlantic accent and the ingenuous look cultivated by today's youthful achievers in the media. She accepted his welcome as small talk rather than flattery but she was pleased that he kept talking. Despite appearances this man was nervous.

As he talked, James Dorset was trying to relate what he'd heard about her to this large, solid figure on the other side of his desk who reminded him of a maiden aunt, a countrywoman, a dog-lover, a lady. She had turned sixty and she looked it; she was plain but she made the best of her good points and she had taste. Her grey hair was as carefully layered as Dorset's, her spectacles with their thin blue frames matched her soft leather bag, both in a darker shade than her linen dress. The effect of monochrome was relieved by a gorgeous scarf in shades of red and mauve knotted bandana-wise against the chill of Dorset's air conditioning.

They discussed travel, heat, humidity. She told him that she found it easier to accept high temperatures in deserts than a heat wave in London. He registered boyish incredulity. 'Really! Fascinating. I understand you've just come from a desert. How would you like to go back?'

'That would depend on what you had in mind.' She blessed her agent for having prepared her.

'Do you know Tim Argent's work?'

'I read *The Boer Trekkers* but not the Australian book.'

'So you know what he's about. Well, last May he set out to follow a wagon train to California.' He glanced at a pad on his blotter. 'These people left Council Bluffs – on the Missouri?' She nodded. 'They left in 1849. Timothy was to trace their journey all the way to the Pacific and produce a book.' He indicated a file on his desk on which there was a postcard. 'He kept in touch with us – not regularly, but I'd say no more than two weeks went by without word. Usually it was postcards, but I had a letter from Council Bluffs, and a phone call when he reached Salt Lake City and before he started across the Great Salt Lake Desert.' He rolled it off his tongue with relish. 'He survived that evidently – of course he did; the last postcard was from Gabriel, California.' He raised an eyebrow but Miss Pink shook her head; she didn't know Gabriel. 'That was six weeks ago.' He handed her the postcard.

It depicted three shabby buildings with false fronts, an

expanse of grey dust in the foreground, a beige mountain range in the distance. She turned it over. The small print told her that this was 'Gabriel, California. Romantic Ghost Town of the Wild West'. The writing of the message was in a rounded scrawl: 'This isn't even a wide place in the road. There's no road – but the Joplins came by. Leaving tomorrow thank God. Dying to get into the mountains. T.A.' It was dated July 10th. The postmark was July 14th. Miss Pink tried to decipher the postmark. 'It's Endeavor,' Dorset supplied. 'Our map people worked it out. The difference in dates probably means someone forgot to mail it: either Tim or the person he asked to post it.'

'Funny place for emigrants to be, so far south. Usually the overlanders entered California further north, going over Donner Pass, or Carson.'

'They were late and apparently the central passes were blocked so they were working their way down the eastern side of the Sierras trying to find a low pass that was clear of snow. The details are all there in the journal kept by the wife of the chap who led the train: Captain Joplin.'

'Tim Argent would be following the route with the diary on the seat beside him? What would be his next fixed point after Endeavor – or Gabriel?'

'It looks as if he intended shortly to be in the Sierras. Endeavor is at the foot of the mountains. One assumes Gabriel is too, although it's not marked in the *Times* atlas. We just don't know.'

'You haven't heard from him since you had this card?'

'That's right: not for six weeks.'

'What about friends and relatives, all his professional contacts: accountant, agent and so on? Didn't he have a clearing house?'

'We were his clearing house, and the only mail waiting to be sent on is junk stuff and his VAT form. He doesn't use an agent, and he doesn't have much to do with his accountant. I did get in touch with the chap and he's heard nothing at all since Tim left for the States, but then he wouldn't expect to. He has no relatives, that is, no one

14

close enough to keep in touch with him. His two closest friends are no closer to him than I am really. All the same I did call them but they've not heard from him for over six weeks either. Before that they had the odd postcard – with innocuous messages. They don't attach any significance to his silence.'

'But you do.'

Dorset passed a hand over his face. He looked unhappy. Miss Pink indicated the postcard. 'Did you try to find someone on the telephone in Gabriel – or in Endeavor?'

'No.' She waited. After a moment he went on: 'We haven't approached anyone yet, not even our representative in Los Angeles.' He aligned his blotter carefully. 'Timothy had a drink problem. He is – had been dry for two years. He had a lapse between the African and Australian trips, but he underwent treatment and he beat it, again. By last spring he could go to parties, drink soft drinks and even enjoy himself, or at least give the appearance of doing so. I thought this time he'd really beaten it – ' He trailed off and studied her face.

'You're afraid he's succumbed again, out there in the desert. It's wild country on this side of the Sierras.'

He started to retract. 'There could be other explanations. He was driving a Jeep, he was expecting the worst kind of terrain.'

'But he was accustomed to rough driving! You can't think he had an accident. And surely if he'd gone on a long drinking bout, even for a week, he'd get in touch with you when he sobered up. Apart from this problem, he has integrity. His writing reads that way.'

'He has great integrity but then there's guilt, you see. Shame, humiliation, the sense of disloyalty: letting me down. What might he do then?'

'In your place I'd expect a letter that was abject, or defiant, or rationalising; I'd expect some kind of communication. Even if he continued to drink, an established author would surely make an attempt to go on with the job, however erratic he might be.'

'True, but he could have been side tracked. I mean, again. Drink wasn't the only problem. Well, not to say *problem* – ' as her jaw dropped, ' – a failing, like an Achilles' heel? He was, I mean he *is* a charmer. Girls adore him.'

'I see. What age is he, in his mid-forties? Yes, a dangerous time. So you think he's holed up with a lady, and drinking.'

Dorset spread his hands. 'They say deserts do strange things to people. And I don't pretend to understand Tim. There have to be pressures, otherwise why the drink? One gets the impression of a brittle crust. He's prickly and impulsive . . . However, there could be a perfectly reasonable explanation which I just haven't thought of – well, reasonable from his point of view.' He became incisive. 'And no way am I going to have strangers trying to trace him and force him back to the fold – let alone the police. He has to be handled with kid gloves or we could lose him. He *is* our best author, and there's the future to think of – ' He checked, then added defiantly: 'If I were familiar with the country I'd go myself.'

'You need a private investigator.'

'That introduces a stranger. And I'd have no rapport with an American in this context, while an English investigator would have no rapport with the country. But you are discreet, knowledgeable, and extremely experienced in tracking people down.' Miss Pink said nothing. 'You'd have a perfect cover,' he persisted, sensing resistance. 'You'd be travelling with Permelia Joplin's diary and you too would be writing a book. In fact, if Tim had dropped out, for whatever reason, we would ask you to take over.'

'To write the book you commissioned him to produce?'

'We can work something out – but that's the last resort. I mean – ' he was flustered, ' – it's the most pessimistic angle, isn't it? Not that we wouldn't love a book from you but what I'm saying now is: use a book as a cover. The first thing to do is find out what's happened to him. We'll pay all expenses, of course, over and above the rate of a private investigator.' She waited, politely attentive. 'Ten thousand and first-class air fares,' he added smoothly.

'That would last only a month. I'm going to need a reliable off-road vehicle and they come expensive. Another ten thousand should cover it, with insurance.'

'Leave us the name of an American bank and I'll have twenty thousand telexed this afternoon. You shall have the plane ticket tonight. Can you leave tomorrow?' Before she could protest he added softly: 'Money eases most problems, you'll see. You can take Tim's file but return it to me tomorrow. I don't think it can tell you anything. Whatever happened, happened out there, and he didn't see it coming, or I'd know about it – I think. I'll send a copy of Permelia's diary with the ticket. That you can read on the plane.'

# Chapter 2

'Nights are getting colder. This morning we wakened to find all water froze in the pans. Temp was 20° and husband speaks gravely of mountains ahead. Baby's cough no better. When I rise to build fire for coffee – we still have coffee – I put her to bed with Mary to keep warm. The cow's milk has dried now she is yoked to pull waggon with the oxen. The deep sand is hard on the animals. I feed Baby a gruel of steeped corn and boiled water but she is losing weight . . . '

Miss Pink laid aside Permelia Joplin's journal and looked below for relief. She saw a white expanse smeared with cloud shadows, and bright crumbs on a dark floor. The coast of Labrador, she assumed, or even further north; the flight was non-stop to San Francisco.

The cabin was light and warm. Lunch had been delicious; champagne had flowed, and as they flew westward, extending the long afternoon, she had dozed, and listened to Mozart, and divided what remained of her attention between Permelia and Timothy Argent's Australian book: *Penal Colony*.

For a few moments now she considered the icebergs thirty thousand feet below, then she withdrew her gaze to find the eyes of this other author, the subject of her quest, regarding her from the back of his book jacket. He had been looking directly at the photographer who was, she saw by the credit, a woman. That didn't surprise her. There was a sensuous light in Argent's eyes, a sheen on the neck muscles, a warmth to the skin. He was amused, confident, excited; he's going to take her to bed, thought Miss Pink.

Her head rolled and jerked upright. She opened her eyes to find the sunlight in a different place and this man still observing her but quizzically, she thought, asexually. What question was he asking as her aircraft droned stolidly and with deceptive sloth above the polar icefields? If she knew the answer – her eyelids drooped – she would solve the case. There is no case, said an inner voice, but the word had been introduced, had been fed into the computer-brain.

Below her the continent unrolled: snow, forests, plains, the Rockies. She was suddenly wide awake, seeing his face again and properly. All trace of sensuousness had gone. The hint of a smile remained but she thought it was unconscious, that his lips would often lift at the corners, even when he was angry. The mouth curved upwards but the eyes that observed Miss Pink were merely observant. Of course, she chided herself, the situation was subjective; she was bound for a land which she adored, she was excited and receptive, her mind seduced by the sense of adventure.

What had happened there as she dozed was that it was she who was asking questions: wondering if she was starting in the wrong place, should have flown to Omaha, where he had landed. But Gabriel was only a few hundred miles from San Francisco . . . He had been fit, bored but looking forward to the mountains when he was in Gabriel. 'Leaving tomorrow thank God.' Could he have been drinking when he wrote that? Taking his last postcard from her briefcase, she studied the dilapidated store fronts. They might have been studio furniture, throw-outs from Hollywood, tourist gimmicks. If there was a bar or a motel in Gabriel they were behind the photographer. On the other hand Argent could have brought his own liquor with him, could have slept rough – but what had attracted him to Gabriel in the first place?

'It's just a collection of shacks, it'll blow away one day in a high wind.' Irving Dodge spoke absently, his attention on a *mamillaria deserti* on the greenhouse shelf. 'Wide place in the road,' he murmured. 'Silver mines, not gold.'

'It's close to Nevada,' Miss Pink said. 'It would be silver, wouldn't it? All the gold's on the Pacific slope, in California.'

'Not always.' Grace Dodge straightened from her weeding and looked in at the open window. 'There's gold on the east slope of the Sierras too. Bodie was gold, and that's way out in the desert. So was Dogtown. Gabriel could have been either. Is it important?'

'I wouldn't think so. My feeling is that Tim Argent's silence relates to something personal, and something more recent than an old mine.'

'Unless he fell down a shaft,' Irving said, suddenly intrigued.

Grace Dodge's pleasant face registered protest but she caught their guest's expression and hesitated. Irving's smile faded. 'Not to be taken seriously,' he assured them.

The Dodges were old friends of Miss Pink and she had taken them into her confidence. She could trust them not to spread word of her true mission (already, among their circle, she was using the cover of a new book to explain her presence in California) and she needed their help. Who better to fill her in than a botanist and an amateur naturalist who travelled widely in the Southwest?

The Dodges didn't look like great travellers: elderly and rotund, they would never walk when they could take a car – but they had the facts, they provided a launching pad. Now she considered Irving's last remark. 'Everything's to be taken seriously,' she said. 'I can't believe the problem is drink or a woman, or even both of those. He'd have got in touch. But experienced explorers don't fall down mineshafts.'

'Unless he was pushed.' It slipped out. Grace hadn't meant to say it and her hand flew to her lips. 'I read too much crime,' she said.

Miss Pink and Irving emerged from the greenhouse, a marmalade cat weaving about their ankles. Miss Pink frowned. 'As far as I can make out, the Joplins went over a pass to the west of Gabriel. But there's no pass marked on the map.'

'No road,' Irving said. 'There's Breakneck Pass further south, and west of Dogtown, but nothing approaches it from this side. No road, I mean. There's a Forest road serves the Pacific slope. The loggers use it.'

'There's a ranch road coming over Breakneck from Dog-town,' Grace said. 'It's the way they take the cattle to Palmer Meadows.'

'And then you've got a stretch of high country,' Irving told Miss Pink, 'with the odd dirt road – pretty primitive, and hopeless without four-wheel drive. We were up there once looking for condors but we were in a big party on a Sierra Club excursion; you'd be mad to risk it alone, even in a Jeep – '

They exchanged startled glances. They'd all had the same thought but it was Miss Pink who voiced it: 'In a place like that he might have gone over the edge and no one would know?'

Irving shrugged. 'Anything could have happened. Don't go that way, Melinda. Cross the Sierras by Tioga Pass and approach Gabriel from the north. And if you do come to suspect he's had an accident in the high country, contact the police. Don't tackle that area of the Sierras on your own.'

'I want to avoid the police.'

'Then hire a guide,' Grace urged. 'There are lots of packers on the other side who take hunters in the moun-tains in the fall. You'll be safe on a horse and with a local man.'

'A local man could be just who she shouldn't take.'

'Irving, for Heavens' sakes!'

Lying in her bath, a Tio Pepe on the side, Miss Pink reflected on the conversation and found it bizarre. The coastal foothills south of San Francisco are a lotus-land, for climate and culture, and ahead of her was an evening of good food and wine, friends, the opera, and the drive home from the city above the sable light-sprinkled bay. It was a lush sophisticated world where the name Timothy Argent meant a book on the coffee table, an exciting personality on the box, not a black hole out there on the other side of the Sierras.

The opera was her send-off. Next day she crossed California, west to east, from the Pacific Ocean to the Sierra Nevada.

The afternoon found her climbing through Yosemite's forests to Tioga Pass, her hired Cherokee pulling well on the long gradients. The sun was behind her and ahead was the granite crest of the mountains. Beyond them were the deserts.

The Cherokee drifted across the high meadows where the Tuolumne River ran clear and shallow between low banks and rock domes reared like mammoths above the conifers. She came to Tioga and started the long descent to Mono Lake. Around ten thousand feet the air and the light were exquisite, tempting her to stop. But there was no point in stopping unless she were to stay there – and she had taken the king's shilling; there was work ahead. She looked at the dim blue smear of Mono Lake and grimaced. Down there, three thousand feet below, the temperature would be around a hundred Fahrenheit.

She was wrong. The deserts were sweltering in a heat wave and even beside Mono, on the fringe of the Mojave Desert where the lake shore was fretted with salt pinnacles, it was 110 degrees.

She turned south, running parallel with the tall escarpment. As the miles unrolled she caught glimpses of towers and minarets at the heads of deep canyons, and she stopped regretting Yosemite; the Sierras continued for a hundred and sixty miles beyond Tioga and somewhere in that high country of timber and granite was the Joplin Trail.

Shadows stretched across her road and the air, which had seemed stagnant in the sun, began to move. It was still velvety, not sparkling as it had been on top, but with the windows and sunroof open there were air currents inside the Cherokee. She needed them. After three hundred miles of hard driving she was running out of steam, but with shade and a breeze she thought she might reach Gabriel tonight.

Near Endeavor, not a hundred miles from Mono Lake, she found herself bumping along the sandy shoulder. There was a derisive blast from a horn, fading as a pick-up passed. She allowed the sand to stop the truck and she switched off the ignition, trembling.

When she had recovered, had walked round her vehicle once or twice and leaned on its far side, breathing deeply and absorbing the lovely line of the mountains, she climbed back behind the wheel and drove on to find a bed in Endeavor.

Her cover story was accepted without question. Waking with a clear mind she realised that she was already on Argent's trail, had struck it after coming down from Tioga. The Joplins came this way, pushing south, searching for a pass that was clear of snow.

In the local library she was received with courtesy but without surprise. They were accustomed to visits from historians and Western buffs following the old trails. Even English people were not unknown at the library; there had been one from London back in the summer: Timothy Argent, the travel writer. Miss Pink was fascinated; was he researching a book?

The librarian, plump and middle-aged, beamed. 'The Joplin story, isn't that something: to be written up by Timothy Argent! He knew Permelia Joplin's journal by heart. What he didn't know was which way they crossed the mountains. I was able to help him there.'

'It was Breakneck Pass – surely?'

'No, not at all. They went up Danger Canyon and over Deadboy Pass.' Seeing Miss Pink's bewilderment the other was indulgent. 'It's only tradition says they went over Breakneck, because the road's there, but the road was put in fifty years after the Joplins came through. Deadboy Pass is named for the child in the Joplin train that died of pneumonia.'

'I see.' Miss Pink was thoughtful. 'Was this Argent's theory?'

'It's not a theory, it's what happened. It was me told Timothy. He was impressed, said he'd go that way. I had to warn him, other people had *theories*, he'd meet plenty of those where he was going – ' her voice took on a sinister timbre, ' – Timothy just didn't know what he was getting into. They'd be on to him like buzzards. I warned him – and he loved it! Said so. "I love it," he said.'

'Warned him about what?'

'Why, all those crazy ideas about they went up Crazy Mule Canyon – and like you said: over Breakneck. *He* said: "I'll try all the routes and that way I'm bound to hit the trail some time." I told him: "You'll be wasting your energy," I said, and that's not right, is it? Time's money to an author.'

'I shall follow your lead,' Miss Pink said firmly, adding in a lighter tone: 'Who are these people who'd try to lure me into Crazy Mule Canyon and up to Breakneck Pass? Such evocative names.'

'Crazy Mule leads to Trouble – that's Trouble Pass, of course. Danger Creek comes down from Deadboy. You'll sort them out. As for the people, they'll find you, you won't be able to avoid them. You have to go past Dogtown: that's a ghost town in the Rattlesnake Hills. But then you mustn't miss Dogtown; they have a lot of old mining artefacts, and all the houses are the original buildings from the time of the gold diggings. They're restoring the place for a tourist attraction, not so much restoring as preserving: arrested decay, they call it.'

'They?'

'Individuals. A bunch of people moved in from all over: San Francisco, LA, the deserts, you name it. They think they're going to make a fortune out of the tourists. Could be, at that.'

'Like Gabriel?'

'No, Gabriel's finished. Obviously you never saw it. There's nothing left even to vandalise. Dogtown's on the upgrade; it's more like Bodie except Bodie's a state park and Dogtown's private.'

'People stay there?' Miss Pink was concerned. 'I take it there's a motel?'

'You'd be far better to stay in Endeavor. There's what they call a hotel in Dogtown but the rooms aren't ready yet. Most people following the Joplins camp. The Trails party that's coming by bring recreational vehicles and tow Jeeps.'

'A Trails party?'

'Every summer they follow a different trail. So this year it's the Joplins. You'll run into them, you stay long enough – although where you're going to stay's another matter. They might rent you a cabin at Dogtown, full of snakes and roaches, I shouldn't wonder. Best thing you can do is stay here.'

'Where did Tim Argent stay?'

'He camped. At least, I always assumed he did, but he'd be used to it.'

Although she was in Levis and a plaid shirt, Miss Pink's advanced age might suggest to a layman that she'd never been closer to a wilderness than on a Nature Trail in a national park. Now she said: 'You didn't see him again? He never got in touch to tell you which way he decided the Joplins went?'

'No.' The librarian was puzzled. 'I'd expected to hear from him, know how he got on. He said he would write. Of course, it will be in his book, maybe he'll mention Endeavor. That's the trend: what the author did and saw, who he spoke to at the same time he was following an old trail.'

Miss Pink picked up her bag. They were sitting in the librarian's office. 'Now I follow him,' she announced inanely. 'Or can I? He'd be more accustomed to rough roads than I.'

'What are you driving?'

'A Cherokee.'

'You'll need it, but don't go alone. Timothy had a Jeep: one of the basic models – pale blue. He was embarrassed by the colour: baby-blue, he called it. "Not really me, is it?" he said when I went outside with him. And then he drove away.'

'Alone?'

'Oh yes, there was no one with him.'

'I mean, he went on to cross the Sierras on his own.'

'I wouldn't – he didn't say he was meeting anyone.' Her eyes sharpened. 'Why do you ask?'

Miss Pink was flustered. 'I just thought: if he went alone – and a Cherokee is more powerful than a basic Jeep?'

The librarian suppressed a smile. 'But he was a man. I mean: young, powerful – ' she brightened, ' – able to fix things: broken fan belts, punctures, all that stuff. You wait for the Trails people. They're fun; you'll have a good time with them.'

'Perhaps I should do that.' Miss Pink nodded sagely. 'If I were to explore while I'm waiting for them I could hire a horse and take a guide.'

'Well, yes, just be careful who you take, is all.'

# Chapter 3

It was well into the afternoon when she reached her next fixed point. It was three o'clock before she tracked down the rancher who owned the land where Gabriel once stood, still stood if a few piles of planks and some old foundations warranted a name. She was directed down a dusty track to a reservoir and on its bank she found all that was left of Gabriel. Even the three store fronts depicted on Argent's postcard had collapsed, but he'd been here, camping in the sage; the rancher told her that much.

He'd told her little else, or nothing significant. As in the library she hadn't needed to ask about her predecessor; information was volunteered simply because Argent and she were both English, both following the same trail. She wondered how long it would be before people started to think that her arrival might not be a coincidence.

Argent had appeared on an afternoon in July. He hadn't come to the house; the rancher – a leathery old fellow, not over-clean – had been alerted by the stranger's dust trail as he drove down the track. He wasn't bothered; tourists were always going to see the old ruins. However, when the Jeep didn't come back and he figured the visitor planned on spending the night, he went down in his pick-up just to be sure the guy wasn't up to mischief.

He'd found Argent reading and stayed with him a while, charmed by him: 'A well-educated gentleman, knew more about these old trails than I do.'

Miss Pink, registering interest in her compatriot, did push it a little then but learned scarcely more than she knew already. The rancher hadn't picked up much about his visitor; it was evident that Argent, like any good writer, didn't talk so much as listen. She learned that he was alone, that he slept at the site of Gabriel, that he left the following day. Nothing was said of his drinking nor that he had asked for a postcard to be mailed from Endeavor, nor could she think of a way of eliciting this information without exciting suspicion. She did assure herself that he had left the site. Recalling that the Joplins had followed the course of the river from Gabriel she wondered aloud how she might do this, as Argent had done.

He shook his head. 'No, ma'am, that's all private land, and fenced. You got to come back to the highway same as he did, pick up the Joplin trail again near to Dogtown.'

'What a pity. It's quite impossible to go exactly the way they went?'

'Believe me, if it could be done, that Englishman would have. No, he come back to the highway not long after sunrise; I was out early too, shifting a bunch of cows before it got too hot. He waved.'

For form's sake she poked about the piles of timber that were the remains of Gabriel, talking loudly, not to herself but to warn the snakes. Sustaining her cover she took a few pictures but there was nothing to claim her interest in this dull desert, for desert it was, the river having dried up since its headwaters had been diverted by the Los Angeles aqueduct.

She returned to the highway, the mountains a lavender line in the west. Argent would have seen them too, but hard and bright in the sunrise – and he'd longed to be up there; he'd said so on the postcard. Where had he bought that? She hadn't seen a replica in Endeavor although she'd looked. She hadn't dared to show the one in her possession to the librarian.

The sun was sinking when she saw a sign for Dogtown pointing her along a dirt road towards a range of hills the colour of cocoa. It was an arid region, the only vegetation the odd prickly plant and a few grey spires of mullein beside the road. After a mile or two she emerged from a cutting in brown bluffs to a no-man's-land between umber slopes and the forested foothills of the mountains. A creek ran here, lined with cottonwoods, and the road forked. Another sign pointed to her right and she drove through the trees to a lunar landscape dotted with buildings below old mine-tips.

It was a typical ghost town, contriving to appear raw and at the same time old, or old for California. The planks of the houses looked as if they'd been sawn from unseasoned pine straight out of the forest, and under the desert sun the bright brown wood had retained its colour but it had shrunk and splintered. Nails had fallen from their sockets, seams had parted, few walls were vertical. The community looked like cheap clothing that starts to fall apart as soon as it's laundered.

Litter was everywhere: old iron, timber, rusty cars, but here and there, outside houses only slightly less decrepit than their neighbours, stood a pick-up of recent vintage.

One building was of brick, square and uncompromising with a stepped pediment fronting a flat roof. Across the façade above triple arches of windows and door was some illegible print. Beside the door a hardboard panel leaned against the bricks. 'Grand Imperial Hotel' it read.

The front door opened on to a pillared vestibule, except that the pillars were tree-trunks roughly rounded and still bearing traces of paint where someone had tried to achieve the effect of marble. The floor was rough but swept, there were three tables, one not merely scarred, but charred, and it looked like mahogany. There was a brassbound counter top and a framed advertisement for a stagecoach line. Above it hung a large and surprisingly good imitation of a Modigliani nude.

A woman followed Miss Pink through the open door and stopped, silhouetted against the street. The sun had left Dogtown and the interior of the hotel was dim. She was a short woman and she was wearing slacks and boots.

'You were wanting a room?' The voice was pleasant, cultured.

Miss Pink smiled and moved towards a window. 'What

do you have on offer?' She was equally polite. Now she saw
that the woman was about forty, fair but deeply tanned, with
a wide mouth and pale eyes that observed the newcomer
with interest. 'We have cabins,' she said. 'How long would
you be staying?'

'I'm not sure. I'm following the Joplin Trail.'

'Not more than one night then. I can let you have
a cabin for thirty dollars.'

'Perhaps I could see it?'

They went out and round the corner of the building
where big white poppies bloomed in an alley. Beside the
hotel several shacks with tin roofs stood in a staggered row.
There were lace curtains at the windows but the windows
were askew and doorframes sagged. The woman opened
one door and stood aside. Miss Pink mounted a shaky
step and saw a clean bare floor, a brass bedstead with
a white counterpane, a table and chair in chrome and
plastic, a strip light, and a wall lamp above the bed. In
the back wall a louvred door was open to show a lavatory,
a basin and a bath with a shower fitting. She had seen worse
accommodation, although not at thirty dollars, but she took
the room; she needed information.

'You won't get many visitors so far from the highway,'
she remarked as she filled in the registration form.

'I do well enough. "Melinda Pink".' She had no difficulty in deciphering the print upside-down. 'That's neat.
I'm Rose Baggott.' She observed the Dodges' address. 'You
live in California?'

'A forwarding address. I'm from England. Didn't you
know?'

'I guess so. There was an English guy here back in
the summer: Timothy. You talk like him.'

'Timothy Argent. I keep hearing the name. I'm following
him along the trail. Did he stay here?'

'Not at the hotel. I don't think he slept in a bed' – the
generous mouth stretched, the eyes sparkled – 'shouldn't
think he *slept* in a bed all the time he was here. He camped in
the canyon someplace. He was writing a book and he needed

to be on the spot, go up all the different canyons, find out for himself which way the Joplins went. I told him they went over Breakneck Pass but then he talked to the Semples and they swear it's Crazy Mule, and then there's Asa – but you don't want to hear all that stuff.'

'What conclusion did Argent come to?'

'Oh, Breakneck surely.'

'He didn't tell you?'

'I guess he was embarrassed. I mean, he talked to everybody, he was a regular guy, and beautiful manners! He wouldn't tell the others he thought the Joplins had to go over Breakneck because he wouldn't want to hurt their feelings.' Her smile was sly. 'Some people are very possessive about their theories.'

'But you must have discovered which route he'd decided on. I'd like to know so I don't waste time exploring the wrong canyon.'

'It was Breakneck. It's obvious. There's the road, and roads always follow old trails. There had to be a trail before the Joplins came through. It would have been made by Indians and then used by the trappers.'

'That's what he decided?'

'Like I said: he was too well-mannered to say.' She saw something over Miss Pink's shoulder. 'There's Verne Blair. I'll go tell him you're eating at his place. You'll be wanting breakfast as well as dinner? The food's good at the Red Queen,' she added, seeing Miss Pink's hesitation.

'I thought you'd provide food. This is an hotel, isn't it?'

'That's what it was, and that's what it's going to be, but I'm still doing it up. That's what everyone's doing to their property: the restaurant, the museum, me. We're functional, but there's room for improvement. None of us have been here long and we're doing most things ourselves, and it's taking time. There's no money from the state, Dogtown's all private enterprise. You should have seen this place when I bought it. I'll go and have a word with Verne and Earl. Take your rig round to the cabin. I'm afraid there's no key to the door but if you're worried about cameras and stuff lock them

31

in your vehicle. You don't need to though, there's no crime in Dogtown.'

The restaurant took its name from the Red Queen gold mine. At the peak of its prosperity seven thousand people lived in Dogtown; there had been eleven bars, two brothels, and a row of shacks called cribs occupied by the independent whores. It was all on the back of the Red Queen's menu, a stylish piece of printing under a logo incorporating the Queen of Diamonds.

After a good steak ('Corn-fed Top Sirloin Marinated, Broiled, then Teriyaki Glazed!') Miss Pink took her coffee at the bar, served by the part-owner who had introduced himself as Earl Lovejoy. He had waited on her too and by now she knew that the chef was his partner. No one else was in evidence, but then she was the only customer. At the bar she ran a practised eye along the rank of bottles. Observing her lack of reaction, Lovejoy reached below the counter and produced a bottle of Cointreau. They exchanged smiles.

Earl Lovejoy was a pleasing host, and a good advertisement for the cooking. Plump but not flabby, he looked as if he enjoyed his food, and he discussed it with authority. He didn't have much call to do that, he told her, not with most of the customers. He was a dark man, almost swarthy, with thick black hair, a bullish neck, spaniel eyes. He agreed to join her in a liqueur and as they sipped their Cointreau she reverted to the appreciation of good food.

'In time you'll build up a clientèle,' she assured him. 'There can't be another good chef within a hundred miles. The persimmon soufflé was superb.'

He beamed. 'My partner will be delighted to hear that.'

'You should be in San Francisco.'

'But we came from there! Far too many people for us; we're neither of us city boys. Verne's folks were fishermen from Monterey, mine – you're not going to believe this – mine were immigrants from the Dust Bowl in the thirties: Okies. You know: *Grapes of Wrath* stuff.'

'Ah, Steinbeck. A great man.'

'You're like him. I mean –' seeing her surprise, '– there's an affinity. That's what Timothy said: your Timothy Argent, the author. He said Steinbeck was following a trail too, although Steinbeck was actually *with* the Okies, but then Timothy was talking about a trail in the spiritual sense.'

'Searching?' she wondered aloud. 'A life-search?'

He nodded. 'Aren't we all? But Timothy, he was – different. He was an alcoholic, did you know that?' He mistook her hesitation for disbelief and went on: 'He didn't say so, but it was obvious – particularly to us. We see a lot of that: too much emphasis in refusing a drink, you know? And of course, the ladies, they have to push it; women don't see anything significant in that kind of refusal. Ah, here's Verne. Come and meet a fan of yours; she adored the persimmon soufflé. I still say you put too much cream in it.'

Miss Pink shook hands with Verne Blair, a thin balding man in spectacles who put her in mind of an anxious heron.

'We do our best,' he murmured.

'And it's appreciated.' She found herself responding with gallantry.

He sniffed. 'Not often enough. Europeans know what good food is, and Easterners – but not the locals.'

'Timothy did,' Lovejoy told her. 'He went right through the menu. Ate like a woman but he tasted everything.'

'Like a woman?'

'Present company excepted, ma'am,' Blair assured her. 'Timothy didn't have a big appetite, he picked at his food. Of course, he smoked heavily.'

'It was instead of liquor,' Lovejoy pointed out. 'We were sorry for him.'

'We sympathised.' His partner was less effusive. He looked across the empty restaurant. 'Timothy was bored with the West.'

Miss Pink was astonished. 'His books don't read as if he could ever be bored.'

Blair said: 'Ah, but he's a professional. We were talking about motivation one night, about goals. He said something

33

about a man alone on a ship drifting through a warm sea, tying up at islands, exhausting their fruits, and casting off again.'

Lovejoy was gaping at him. 'When did he say that? I never heard him talk that way.'

Blair raised an eyebrow. 'It was the night George and Clint came by. The time they brought the cognac back from Paris.'

'Oh dear. Yes, I remember.' He glanced at Miss Pink. 'Well, French Cognac, what can you expect?' He addressed his partner: 'So you reckon Timothy was implying he hadn't got a goal. But he found one, didn't he?'

'Not really.' Blair regarded the other man fixedly. 'He'd be motivated by the book only as long as it took to write it, then he'd need to find something else to fill the gap.'

'Yeah.' Lovejoy licked his lips. 'Is it the same with you, ma'am? Do you write?'

'Romances,' she admitted. 'Gothics.'

'Are they popular?'

'They have their followers.' She smiled. 'A very different following from Timothy Argent's, of course, but then we have to be very different people: an elderly spinster, an explorer in his prime . . . ' When this produced no reaction she changed tack: 'May I see that postcard, the top one in that rack? I must have some cards of Dogtown.'

'That's Gabriel, to the north of here,' Lovejoy said. 'We don't have a good one of Dogtown yet. Timothy bought several of Gabriel, that same one in fact. He said it epitomised the myth. Those shacks have collapsed now.'

'Odd, for a wilderness traveller to send postcards home.' Miss Pink pretended to read the legend on the back of the familiar card.

'Some people buy postcards just for something to do,' rejoined Lovejoy. 'He only sent one.'

'Now how do you know that?' She looked intrigued.

'Because he gave it to me to mail.'

'And you forgot to mail it,' Blair said. 'I found it in your cagoule.'

'OK, OK. It was just a day or two late. And it was only a few lines to his publisher, nothing important.'

'How do you know it was to his publisher?' Miss Pink asked.

'I read it. He'd put Gabriel at the top as if he'd written it there and he said he was leaving "tomorrow". I forget the name of the recipient but he was at the Something-Press. That would be a publisher.'

'Did he leave here the next day?' she asked.

'No, I told you he worked right through the menu. He didn't stay in Dogtown though. He camped in the canyon, came down for his meal most nights.'

'How long did he stay in the area?'

The partners looked at each other. 'A week?' Lovejoy asked.

'Eight days,' Blair said. 'We don't know. One night he was here, the next he was gone. But I guess that's no more than you'd expect . . . We won't see him this way again.'

Lovejoy looked from his partner to Miss Pink. '*You* will,' he assured her. 'You'll meet in London.'

'I may overtake him yet.'

They regarded her in silence. They might have been considering the possibility of her catching up with Argent but what Blair said was: 'You mustn't leave without visiting the museum.'

'You could spend a day in there,' Lovejoy said. 'You could spend a few days in Dogtown itself. This place is something special.'

# Chapter 4

Despite the Dodges' warning and that of Endeavor's librarian, Miss Pink had every intention of following Argent over the Sierras and, rather to her surprise, people in Dogtown seemed to assume that she would do this. At breakfast in the Red Queen Lovejoy told her she had a lovely day for the crossing and assured her that she would have fun, while Verne Blair emerged from his kitchen to tell her to take care, but it was more of a ritual courtesy than a warning.

Rose Baggott hoped that she would come back to the Grand Imperial and stay longer next time. Only at the museum did she run into controversy, was told unequivocally that the Joplins didn't go over Breakneck Pass and she couldn't follow them anyway: 'Not in a vehicle,' said Charlotte Semple. 'You can go up Crazy Mule to the end of the dirt road – that's the way they went: up Crazy Mule and over Trouble Pass. You might reach Trouble on foot, or on a horse.' Did she sense opposition? She went on: 'We've known this area for years. I've made a specialty of the overland trails; I've followed the Joplins clear to Bakersfield. That's where they settled. It's all in Permelia's diary.'

'Miss Pink is writing a book,' her husband said. 'She knows.' Her cover had been accepted here without surprise.

They were in the dim barn that housed the museum and they moved among the exhibits as they talked, Miss Pink's expression giving no indication that her interest lay in the Semples rather than the Joplins or nineteenth-century artefacts.

There was an air of ingenuousness about the couple, a kind of simplicity common among people only a few generations removed from the pioneers who were their forebears. One of her ancestors had come overland from Missouri in the 1850s, Charlotte told Miss Pink, and settled in the Sacramento valley. Julius Semple's people had been lumber merchants on the Pacific slope for nearly a century. In her fifties now, Charlotte had taken early retirement from teaching, her last position having been in an urban school where violence was endemic. When she retired Julius sold out his share in the family business and they'd taken off for the deserts, gravitating to Dogtown eventually where they founded the museum, a project which they regarded with the kind of proud affection usually reserved for adored children.

Charlotte was a big-boned woman with a mane of titian hair that was rather too bright to be natural. Her skin had started to sag but the agate eyes in their deep sockets were luminous, the lips full and firm. She was still a striking woman, she must have been sensational in her younger days. Her husband was tall and gangling but well-preserved, resembling an ageing Gary Cooper.

'You might hire a horse,' Charlotte was saying. 'That's the best way to reach Trouble.'

Miss Pink was admiring an ornate little lamp. 'Sweet,' she observed. 'Why red glass?'

Julius moved away. Charlotte's eyes followed him. 'It hung in the window of a crib,' she said.

'Oh. They were quite open about prostitution?'

'It was accepted as a necessary evil, and of course, there was no Aids in those days. That makes a difference, doesn't it? All the same the whores had to be segregated; the red light district was at the lower end of town –' she smiled wryly, '– downstream, on the bank of the creek.'

'The unhealthiest part.'

'You could hardly have them upstream. So –' she turned away, changing the subject, '– Rose Baggott has horses but she's not going to rent you one for Crazy Mule Canyon.

37

She *knows* the Joplins went over Breakneck and she's not wasting good horseflesh on someone maintains the correct route goes up Crazy Mule.' She was smiling but her tone was contemptuous. Miss Pink couldn't resist a snort of amusement herself.

'How did Timothy Argent cope – ?' She was tempted to add 'with all this?' but desisted.

'With Rose? He didn't need a horse. He hiked everywhere.'

Miss Pink picked up a wooden object from a bench and regarded it absently. 'That's a snowshoe for a mule,' Charlotte told her. 'It clamps on the hoof, see? Julius is going to replace the straps.'

'Most ingenious. Which route did Argent decide on?'

'Why, Crazy Mule, of course. It's obvious once you relate Permelia's diary to what's there. Timothy was highly perceptive, a kind of historical detective. That kind of nature is essential if you want to follow the old trails.'

'Did you get to know him well?'

'He came here once or twice and we talked about the trail, but trail buffs are kind of single-minded; I guess it's like any other obsession: hunting, cars, making money – people with those interests never talk about anything else. So apart from that we didn't get to know him. He spent most of his time hiking in the canyon anyway and when he came to Dogtown it was just to eat at the Red Queen. He didn't stay long there. He didn't drink. And we mostly eat at home so we didn't see him except when he came over.'

After a pause Miss Pink said: 'You've been very helpful. I'll go up there and look at Crazy Mule Canyon, but it does seem as if I won't get far without a horse–'

'There is one thing.' Charlotte hesitated and glanced towards the back of the barn. 'There's a guy lives in the canyon: a dropout. He's quite old and he's never been known to – that is, he's not violent towards people but – I shouldn't . . . Don't get out of your car and don't stop at his camp. Are you armed?'

Miss Pink chose to ignore the question. 'How does he live?'

Charlotte was embarrassed. Semple appeared from the shadows. 'I was telling her not to approach Asa Fortune,' his wife said. The couple exchanged glances. 'I haven't told her about the crash,' she added.

'Nothing was ever proved.'

'No, nothing was proved.' She turned to Miss Pink. 'A plane went into the mountain three years ago, in the middle of winter. They didn't even locate the site of the crash until the snow melted. When they got there, all the jewellery and cash that should have been on the bodies was gone – there were a few dollars left in billfolds for appearances' sake – and the credit cards were still there – but anything that could be used or fenced was gone. Someone got there before the rescuers.'

'It wasn't any use to the owners. No one survived.'

'Christ, Julius! How do we know?' He looked defiant. 'I like old Asa,' Charlotte told Miss Pink. 'I don't think he did it. And they searched but they never found any of the missing stuff.'

'Of course not.' Semple grinned. 'He hid it in the forest. He's lived here all his life. You gotta believe it: Fortune robbed those bodies.'

Charlotte looked at him, then away. 'But he's not violent,' Miss Pink pressed.

'Not as far as we know,' Semple said heavily.

They ushered her out of a side door to see the larger exhibits. Standing between an old horse-hearse and an ancient Ford Coupé, Miss Pink assured them that she would be back. They responded politely, almost absently; whether she returned or not seemed immaterial to them. She thought that they were collectors rather than curators; the museum, or rather its clutter of artefacts (which she really did wish she had more time to study) fulfilled a need, a gap which might otherwise have been filled by children.

Following their directions she returned to the highway to find the gas station which was a mile south of the Dogtown turn-off. Her tank was filled by a sleepy blonde who had stuck foil stars on her large front teeth. A limpid gaze and masticating jaws gave her a bovine air, strengthened by her difficulty in deducting twelve dollars and eight cents from fifteen dollars, even with the aid of a calculator.

'You must be Mrs Wolf,' Miss Pink said chattily.

'Yeah.' There was no surprise. 'How did you know?'

'The wedding ring. And I stayed in Dogtown.' In the face of a vacuous stare Miss Pink spoke clearly, trying to drive the meaning into the other's brain: 'You'll get a lot of motorists stopping here to fill their tanks before crossing the mountains.'

'I guess.'

'Many foreigners?'

Mrs Wolf blinked. 'Some.' She thought about that. 'How would you know, if they got hire-cars with California plates?'

'They would talk differently.'

The girl shrugged and seated herself gracefully on a stool. Crossing long brown legs she yawned and picked up a magazine. Miss Pink said: 'You had an Englishman here some weeks ago. He was driving a pale blue Jeep.'

'We did? That's too long to remember.'

Miss Pink went back to her truck, took the petrol cap from the top of the pump where Mrs Wolf had left it, and screwed it on the tank. Metal rang on concrete and she realised that the shadowed bay beside the office was a working garage. A man was in there, under a pick-up. She walked over and coughed. He pulled himself out: a heavy, middle-aged fellow, but obliging.

'I wonder,' she said diffidently, 'if you could take a look at my rear light. It may be just a fuse . . . '

He came and looked and found the loose wire which she'd just disconnected. He admired the Cherokee, discovered she came from London and stood chatting as if he had all the time in the world. Trade was slow at the end of summer, he told her; it would take up again after Christmas with the skiers coming through to Mammoth. He wasn't grumbling; he could go hunting in the fall, leave the wife to look after

40

the pumps. It was easy to steer the conversation to the Joplin Trail.

'This sure is a season for the English,' he said. 'They'll have told you about the others?' Her hesitation was minimal but he'd seen it. 'Yeah, they wouldn't be able to help themselves; they're a lot of old women up to Dogtown. Got nothing else to do except gossip about each other.'

'And about the visitors.' She took a very long shot. 'What was she really like?' She said it with the air of one needing to plug a gap and he accepted it as such but he didn't like it.

He shrugged and looked sullen. 'She was quite a looker – pale: light skin, blue eyes, big mouth.' He glanced at Miss Pink. 'She wasn't a slut!'

'Oh no!' She was shaken. 'Argent is a discerning man.'

'Aren't we all?' It was bitter, explosive.

She glanced towards the office where Mrs Wolf was hunched over her magazine. 'Where did they meet?' She was casual and he replied in kind.

'God knows. Does it matter? They're gone.' Bitterness was replaced by hostility and he threw her a startled look as if a thought had suddenly occurred to him. 'Maybe you'll catch them up; you can ask them all about it.'

She drove back past Dogtown on the dirt road that skirted the little community, and headed for the wide mouth of Malachite Canyon. The road began to rise but it was neither steep nor particularly rough and it was followed by a power line. She drove through the little pinyons of the arid lands to big Jeffrey pines, the kind of tree which had provided the timber for Dogtown. Here and there the yellow blooms of blazingstar were bright against the gloom of the forest but most of the flowers were over.

Miss Pink was preoccupied, not so much with the identity of Argent's companion, and only vaguely with the question of where he had picked her up. Even the reason why there had been no mention of her in Dogtown seemed less important than the motive for Argent's silence. Why should a woman – an Englishwoman as Hiram Wolf had implied – not why but *how* – how could she have bewitched the author to the extent that he couldn't even take the trouble to mail a postcard to his publisher? And where was he holed up at this moment?

She thought of the other side of the Sierras: the great fertile valley of the San Joaquin with its farms and bright little towns, the oilfields in the south, but she couldn't visualise him in that kind of environment. Beyond the San Joaquin were the coastal ranges with their steep, narrow valleys; beyond the coast ranges was the ocean.

She came to a fork and stopped without thinking, or rather, she thought about the coast. Big Sur: a rocky, sun-drenched shore, black cypresses, sea lions and pelicans, the blue Pacific. She could picture him there: in a rented house on Big Sur. She looked up the road ahead; by tonight she might have a hint of which way they had gone: west to the coast, north to San Francisco or – there was a further possi-bility, a lure for one kind of writer – or south to Hollywood. That wasn't likely, it would mean breaking his contract – or would it? He was under no obligation to keep in touch with his publisher; he could be fulfilling his contract at this moment, writing the book, doing a screenplay at the same time. She thought about it and shook her head helplessly; he might not be in America at all.

She looked moodily along the fork to her left. Before Hiram Wolf dropped his bombshell she had intended driving up the side canyons: Crazy Mule and Danger, in order to satisfy herself that the pale blue Jeep was not parked at their heads. She was almost certain that it couldn't be; people must have been in the canyons over the past few weeks, although only a local person would have noticed the continued presence of a vehicle; it would mean nothing to a back-packer passing through.

From the Forest map she saw that the road up Crazy Mule was over four miles in length. Better get it over, close a gap. She turned up the track and almost immediately had to engage four-wheel drive. She saw no recent wheel tracks, only the imprint of hoofs: deer and cows. Once she heard a strange, yet strangely familiar sound. She stopped and cut the engine, straining her ears. Unmistakably she heard the chime of a bell, a cowbell. She got down and stalked the sound through the trees until she caught a glimpse of a red and white flank among the trunks. There was a clash as the cow lifted her head. It regarded her for a moment then blundered away.

She returned to her truck and studied the ground thoughtfully. The fact that there were no tyre tracks wasn't conclusive; they could have been washed away by summer storms. She drove on. Some two miles up Crazy Mule a deer and a well-grown fawn crossed the track. A second doe appeared, saw the truck and retreated. Miss Pink paused at the place where a narrow path ran down to the creek. A very old cabin stood there, a stovepipe protruding from its roof. There was a chopping block with an axehead embedded in it and a grey towel draped over the shaft. The chimney wasn't smoking and nothing moved until the second doe appeared further up the track. She slipped across, followed by a skittish fawn.

A mile or so beyond the cabin a tarn showed on the left, reflecting the sky. At its far end the road stopped and a foot-path took off purposefully into the forest. There was no sign of any vehicle other than her own, and only a few empty beer cans and the charred circles of old fires indicated that people came here. The lake had an abandoned look, secretive, even sinister. She was about eight miles from Dogtown and too close for comfort to that log cabin which must be occupied by the man called Fortune. Since he didn't appear to be at home, he could be anywhere, perhaps watching her at this moment. Asa Fortune who robbed bodies. But nothing had been proved; he'd never been known to be violent.

She climbed back behind the wheel and drove down the canyon, a little faster, but that could be explained by its being downhill. And trees were deadly monotonous. She hadn't even got above them. In fact, she wondered if the timber line at this latitude stretched to the summit of the

Sierras, at least to the passes. She knew a moment of panic and longed to be at the top and going down the other side when, presumably, she'd see low ground through the gaps, would see something more than tree-trunks.

There was still no sign of life at the old cabin. Back in the main canyon she turned west but she had gone only a short distance when she came to the fork for Danger Creek, this time on her right, and that was where the power line went. She turned on to a good gravel surface and soon she crossed a cattle-grid to meadows and a monstrosity of a house in bright brown wood with a roof that appeared to be made of tarred felt. It was tall and squarish with windows on two storeys: high windows, arched windows, huge portholes. The corners which she could see were in the form of turrets – angled, of course, but in view of the ostentatious whole, angled only because pine planks can't be curved.

In the rear there were barns, corrals, a neat new cabin. A big pick-up was in the yard. There had been no mention of anyone living in the canyons other than Asa Fortune. She turned her attention to the meadows and observed that from this clearing in the forest she could see the length of Danger Canyon to its headwall and a saddle between granite towers. That would be Deadboy, some five or six miles distant – air miles of course; a footpath would rise in long zigzags increasing the distance. All trails were graded for horses in this country.

She drove through the pasture to a locked gate. Beyond it the Deadboy trail was wide but unmarked by tyres. She turned round and drove up to the cabin behind the house. At the sound of the engine a man appeared at the entrance to a barn. They approached each other with an appearance of nonchalance, Miss Pink disguising her interest behind a front of good humour which bore just a hint of arrogance.

'Good morning. Do you have the key of the gate?'

'It won't do you no good – ma'am. You can't drive through.'

'You mean it's impossible, or it's private land?'

44

'The trail's washed out.'

'I wondered. I saw there were no tracks. I'm following the Joplin Trail – like Timothy Argent.' She'd anticipated recognition of the name, even a disclaimer, but not the reaction she did get. His jaw dropped then clamped shut – she heard his teeth click – and muscles hardened in his cheeks. He scowled. The silence stretched. 'Not everyone's cup of tea perhaps?' She regarded him benignly but her eyes demanded an answer.

His gaze wandered over the meadows and up towards Deadboy. 'I didn't know him,' he said at last. 'I met him, he came by, but he was only looking. He reckoned as how the Joplins went up Crazy Mule anyways.' His eyes lightened a fraction. 'You been up Crazy Mule, ma'am?'

'I have. Was he alone when he came here?'

There was a quality of menace about his stillness, about the time it took him to respond. He was a good-looking young man with dark regular features under an old hat, but in the shade of its brim his eyes were flat, opaque, like a lizard's. There was a snake tattooed on his left forearm. 'I don't know nothing,' he said softly. 'I'm just the caretaker here.'

'I see. Who owns the house?'

There was another pause. She knew that he was considering the impulse to tell her to mind her own business.

'A gentleman from Missouri,' he said.

She smiled coldly, wondering what he was hiding, or if he had nothing to hide and was merely displaying the backwoodsman's suspicion of strangers. She turned and walked over to her truck, aware of a cold point between her shoulderblades.

# Chapter 5

The route to Breakneck Pass climbed the headwall with tight bends where gravel had collected in long furrows. The Jeep loved the climb: purring up the straight stretches and creeping round the bends so smoothly that Miss Pink had to clamp down on a feeling of euphoria, to remind herself that this was a ranch road and not designed for tourists. There was no parapet, no posts, not even a low bank. Indeed, in places the verge had eroded and there was no warning of the break, not even a marker as would be the case on a paved highway. Here the driver's concentration must be absolute; one moment of distraction – glancing at the view when on the outside of a bend, following the flight of an eagle – and control would be lost. One wheel too close to the edge and the truck's own weight would drag it over.

The first elbow was the worst. The road rose slowly out of Malachite Canyon and Miss Pink was prepared for the initial turn because the creek came down the headwall and she could see that there was no track on the far bank – if you can call a slope a bank when it is close to the vertical. But although she anticipated a sharp turn, its constriction took her by surprise and she went too wide and too fast, the tyres scrambling for friction. There was an impression of an abyss below the point of the bend, of dark cliffs above a flash of falling water, then the truck straightened and came back to the correct side of the road.

She was lucky; no vehicle had been coming down. All the same, she took the higher bends with caution, glancing sideways only when she was on a long straight.

She was climbing the timbered spur between Danger and Malachite Creeks. Occasionally there were rock outcrops affording breaks in the forest where she could look east across the desert to a range that must mark the boundary of Death Valley fifty miles away. The depths were blue with distance, the ranges ashen, but near at hand and full in the sun pine needles were a gorgeous green. A few flowers had survived the frosts at this altitude: a sprinkling of yellow composites and clumps of asters like Michaelmas daisies.

Crags gave way to big cliffs that rose clear of the timber, and the trees themselves were tall; there were ponderosas now among the Jeffrey pines. The forest continued right to the pass which was indicated by a sign, otherwise she wouldn't have known she'd reached it. The road didn't dip on the other side and the trees were so thick on the level ground that there was no view.

She stopped and consulted the map. No contour lines were marked on it, only a daunting expanse of green (this signified forest, not low ground). Here and there the green was relieved by white patches of private land, but apart from Palmer Meadows, where there seemed to be some kind of community, there was no sign of habitation. There was a network of tracks but any of these could have been washed out years ago (the map was more than ten years old) and it was difficult to tell which was the way down the Pacific slope.

The first fork she came to didn't appear on the map. She backed up and stopped, studying a surface imprinted with old tyre tracks. The gravel had ended at the pass; here there was only dust. She marked the fork on the map and continued.

She came to a stretch of open grassland. A few cows were grazing along the fringe of the forest where they could get some shade. The altitude was nearly nine thousand feet but the sun was strong enough for her to be glad of shade herself as she ate a belated lunch. The Red Queen had put up corn bread and chicken for her and as she lingered over her meal watched by chipmunks, lulled by the soft chimes of cowbells, she reflected that today was a day to be remembered – at least, this part of it. The morning was a different matter, a very different atmosphere. There was Asa Fortune who, if not at home in Crazy Mule Canyon, could be anywhere, and that in a wilderness she had been thinking of as empty. But it wasn't empty; there was Palmer Meadows, an unknown quantity, and there was the man who looked after the house in Danger Canyon, who became angry at mention of Timothy Argent. She considered that reaction. Argent, the seasoned traveller, wouldn't suffer fools gladly, might speak his mind about locked gates, or about anything that riled him. Would he bother to complain about a locked gate? He was on foot; he'd just climb over the obstruction and continue to Deadboy Pass if he felt like it. But he could have had a confrontation with the caretaker elsewhere: in Dogtown, on the road. The travel writer explores people as well as places; after all, he's going to put them in a book. Miss Pink frowned. She had the feeling that caretaker would not take kindly to being put in a book. Suddenly the day was less halcyon, peopled with speculation, calculation, indecision. Deliberately she honed her mind and concentrated on the place where she was at this moment. Her attention returned to the meadows and she regarded them with technical interest.

Explorers converge. Where there are no trails they gravitate to lines of weakness, where there is water and shelter they sleep; they eat where there is shade. She rose, scattering the chipmunks, and started to look for human traces.

She found nothing. Apart from the boldness of the chipmunks there was no sign that anyone else had eaten food in this place, and only deep ruts in the dried mud of the road showed that people came here at all, and they were ruts that had been made a long time ago, in rain. She drove on, seeing buildings on her right, coming to a board that told her this was Palmer Meadows. On an impulse she left the road and drove the half-mile or so to a cluster of cabins and barns, complete with corrals. There was no sign of human occupation; the cabins were shuttered and no chimney smoked. All the barn doors were closed, and the only animals about were ground squirrels. When she stopped and switched off the engine she found the silence profoundly disturbing.

She returned to the 'road' and continued west, following the route which had in the past carried most traffic. She passed junctions and forks, sometimes making wild guesses as to which was the major fork. She had stopped marking her map; she was going in the right direction and the way seemed simple enough, even safe once the climb to Breakneck Pass had been negotiated. Admittedly the road would be a quagmire in the wet, but this afternoon there were only a few fair-weather clouds above the divide. The night would be fine.

She came to a belt of lodgepole pines through which the road climbed to a crest where a few old junipers grew, scarred by lightning but still alive. There was a saddle and the track dipped to run through alpine meadows where marmots lolloped over scree below a big rock tower. And now, westward, the Pacific slope declined in dark folds to a confusion of foothills. Beyond them lay the great central valley of California, full of hazy sunshine.

The old passion came surging over her: the need to stop and watch the sun set beyond the coastal ranges, but she resisted the temptation; she hadn't come here to indulge herself among sunsets and the creatures of the night. She picked up the road map to try to discover which town Argent would have come down to back in July, some place where she might find a person who remembered him and his mysterious companion, a person more inclined to talk than the inhabitants of Dogtown.

All routes appeared to converge on a place called Credit, and they converged because this slope was in the process of being felled almost to the timber line. Her track had become a logging road and as she navigated bends above awesome drops she was for once grateful for clear felling; she could see if trucks were coming up. She couldn't believe that heavy wagons climbed this mountain, would have thought that logs were lifted out by helicopters, until she passed a stationary and loaded vehicle, evidently left for the night. It was four o'clock and operations must be over for the day. She relaxed

– as much as she could on that road; at least she would have a clear run to the bottom.

The town of Credit was still in the hills: a small straggling resort by a lake in the pine woods, but she was less concerned with its aesthetic properties than its amenities. There were two or three motels, a gas station, stores, even a police presence. A black and white car stood outside a timbered cabin.

The receptionist in the first motel was a slim Vietnamese dressed like a high-class courtesan and moving like a model. Behind her counter sat a little brown man whose freshly laundered shirt hung in folds from skeletal shoulders.

The girl was polite but noncommittal. No, they didn't have many English people staying, and it was difficult to tell the difference anyway. Addresses were no help; visitors gave false ones. When Miss Pink suggested that this might be, at the least, illegal, the girl merely raised her exquisite eyebrows at such naïveté. The old man's eyes remained fixed on a corner of the counter as if he were lost in his memories: listening to the sounds of a jungle or of an Asian street.

'There is a colleague ahead of me,' Miss Pink said: 'a friend. He came through about two months ago, with a lady. They were in a pale blue Jeep.'

'Not here. Maybe another motel.'

But no one at the other motels or the restaurant had seen an English couple in a pale blue Jeep. Miss Pink spent the night at the place run by the Vietnamese and in the morning she tried the gas station but without much hope. An experienced traveller would have started over the Sierras with a full tank and wouldn't need to top up until he reached the central valley where petrol was cheap. But there was just a chance that he stopped to talk, and a gas-pump attendant is an accessible contact.

The woman on the pumps was a spinster in her forties, and inclined to gossip, but she'd seen neither Argent nor his vehicle. Miss Pink was more frank now, no longer disguising the fact that she had a specific interest in the author although she kept quiet about his disappearance, and she did embroider her story. This morning she dropped hints that she was looking at the Joplin Trail from the point of view of a television writer, the implication being that she had a professional connection with Argent.

'So you're working on a production together.' Having arrived at this conclusion the woman became wary. 'Why don't he keep in touch with you then?'

'It's I who am out of touch,' Miss Pink said smoothly. 'Of course, we phone our clearing houses, but if they don't inter-communicate – if only one computer is down – and with the time differential . . . London is eight hours ahead –' She trailed off.

The attendant nodded sagely at this rigmarole. 'I'm writing a book too,' she said.

'Good.' Miss Pink was brisk. 'Everyone should write a book. All that's needed is application. So I go on to the next town. They had to stop somewhere for gas.'

'They?'

'He had an assistant, a kind of PA: secretary, driver, general dogsbody – gopher, you'd call it. He engaged her here but she was English.'

'An English *girl*?' There was a flicker of fear quickly swamped by excitement. The woman sensed drama. 'What did she look like?'

'I never met her. I haven't seen Mr Argent since he left England.'

'She was black?'

'He didn't say –'

'She was very light-skinned, but she was black all the same – I mean, she wasn't white.'

'So you did meet them.'

The woman started to say something then checked. She avoided Miss Pink's eye and looked down the road. 'I never met her, I never saw either one of them.' Her expression was eager again. 'I know who can help you though. The police.'

'I see. They called at the police station.'

'No. Wait while I see if Floyd Bailey's home. He's the sheriff's deputy. He'll want to talk to you.'

The deputy was very large and very neat with an over-blown face and a toothbrush moustache. Miss Pink had pulled away from the pumps and parked in the shade of an oak at the side of the forecourt. The police car nosed in beside the Cherokee and the driver emerged ponderously, introducing himself. She noted that after only a few hours in the resort, her vehicle was already known to him.

He didn't comment on her story concerning her link with Argent but he was interested. He stopped her when she mentioned the author's assistant.

'What was her name?'

'I don't know. I didn't know he'd engaged an assistant until someone mentioned it to me in Dogtown.'

He looked sceptical. 'Why "assistant"? Why not just someone he picked up on the road?'

She wasn't put out. 'Because he is a serious man, a professional. He's more likely to join up with someone who would help him with his research than to waste time on – ' She shrugged and left it there.

'On a hooker – if you'll forgive the expression.'

'Good gracious –' and she was surprised at her own thought, '– you mean she *worked* that road, between Endeavor and Credit?'

If she was surprised, he was amazed. 'What makes you think that?'

'We seem to be flying off at cross-purposes. I thought you implied it. What makes you say she was a – By "hooker" I take it you mean a prostitute?'

'I do, ma'am.' He was firm. 'And I'm saying she was a hooker because she behaved like one. She took one of the loggers for all he'd got, and once they reached Bakersfield she split.'

'A logger operating on that road?' She glanced at the slope above the town.

'Right. He picked her up on the top – no, she picked him up. She was on foot! She'd been with some guy – your friend, would that be? – and he'd hit a deer and put it in the

52

back of the Jeep, she said. Then they'd had a fight because she'd got blood on her and she said the carcass was no good to them and it was poaching anyways, and he threw her out of the Jeep, told her to walk.'

'Where did all this happen?'

'Somewhere on top.' He jerked his head at the skyline. 'She spent the night up there, in a logging rig. Forced the window with a coat hanger. When the guy arrived next morning to bring his load down, she came with him and – er –' he coughed, '– spent some time with him. He gave her all the cash he had on him.'

'What happened to Argent – the man who was with her originally?'

'Well, she wouldn't know, would she?'

'How did you discover all this?'

'It got around, and I take some of my meals at the same place the loggers do, so I talked to the guy who picked her up. I was interested in that blood on her – what she said were deer blood.'

'Yes, you would be. Did she say where she was going?'

'She told him she wanted to go to San Francisco, catch a flight back to Europe, but Bakersfield's a sight nearer LA, and with those looks LA's a more likely bet.'

'You met her yourself?'

'No, it was what this guy told me. He said she was sensational. Did you know she wasn't white? Not completely. She told him she was from Paris, France: Algerian mother – that's African – white father. He said she was sorta golden with long black hair and eyes like asters.'

In the pause he fidgeted under Miss Pink's scrutiny. 'Well, that's what *he* said,' he mumbled, then suddenly, defiantly: 'So what happened to your friend, ma'am? All that blood.'

'There was a lot?'

'There had to be originally. There wasn't none on her shirt and only a bit on her jeans. But there *was* blood: on her –' he gestured, his meaty hands smoothing his barrel chest and waist, '– camisole?' he ventured.

'You mean lingerie, underwear?'

'Right. The blood had soaked through: here.' He placed a hand on his chest. 'Nothing on her shirt, she'd changed that. She was carrying stuff in plastic bags.'

'Travelling without a suitcase? Not even a proper bag?'

'She didn't even carry a purse. I asked all those questions – because of the blood. I didn't like that. And where's your man now, this colleague of yours?'

'I suppose we are talking about the same girl. What name did she give?'

'You said you didn't know the name. This one calls herself Fay. Just that, no last name. She didn't say much about herself and none of it need have been true, like the name. But she was a coloured girl and she wasn't American. Like I said, this guy, this logger, he took a shine to her and he wasn't interested in what happened before they met. Anyways, you can't talk much in one of them trucks, they just kept to essentials. But I'll tell you one thing, ma'am: your friend never come down here, not with a deer in the back. He wouldn't risk it; season don't start for another coupla weeks. And maybe it wasn't a deer at all, maybe he beat her up. Another reason for him not coming down this way where she could have reported it.'

'A good point.' She was thinking that Timothy Argent would never have thrown a woman out in the wilderness and left her to walk to civilisation. The whole story was completely out of character. She saw no reason to doubt the deputy's veracity but every reason to doubt that of the girl who called herself Fay.

'How long ago did this happen?' she asked.

'About two months back.'

She nodded. 'He didn't return to Dogtown. Is there another way out of the forest? There's a whole system of tracks on top.'

'I know, but there's only the two ways in and out; that is, with a vehicle. But he didn't have to go back to Dogtown, he coulda gone past to the highway and no one any the wiser.'

'Or he could have broken down and come out this side on foot without anyone noticing him go through the town, particularly at night.'

'Then he'd have to find a wrecker, go up and salvage his Jeep, and I would have heard about it. But if you crash up there, lady, most people goes over with their vehicle.'

'I can believe that. Then how did the girl escape?'

'Maybe he went off the road after they separated. He'd be in a rage, drunk perhaps, not caring where he was going – ' He regarded her doubtfully, testing the theory.

'I'd like to know,' she said, then, absently: 'After all, we are collaborators – more or less. Where can I find this logger?'

'In Alaska. He got a job with an oil company and left two weeks ago. Are you reporting your friend missing, ma'am?'

She hesitated. There was the blood on the girl – but that was hearsay, not fact, and to alert the authorities when Argent might be in hiding for some personal reason was, to say the least, a breach of etiquette. 'Not at this stage,' she said. 'I'll go back and make some more enquiries.'

He was sympathetic. 'Suppose the girl's story was true, she never said nothing about being with *him*, just a guy, she said. She could have left your friend some time before, taken up with someone else, and *that* guy come down safe, this side or the other.'

She frowned, her mind racing. He could be right, and suppose Argent had met with an accident two months ago, had crashed his Jeep? No action of the emergency services: sheriff, Search and Rescue helicopter, tracker dogs, could save him after such an interval, and nights were bitter at nine thousand feet. But her job wasn't over by any means; she had to find out what had happened.

There were two courses open to her. One was to return to Dogtown by way of Breakneck Pass – and look for signs of a vehicle having gone over the edge; the other was to find the girl – and that seemed impossible. There was no indication of which way she had gone after Bakersfield: Los Angeles,

San Francisco or Europe. Nothing was known about her other than what she had seen fit to tell the logger. However, people in Dogtown had knowledge of her. Hiram Wolf at the gas station had been quite frank – well, fairly frank – and although the caretaker of the house in Danger Canyon had protested that he knew nothing, he protested too much. The others: the Semples, the men at the Red Queen, Rose Baggott at the hotel, none of these had mentioned the girl, although they had all met Argent. What were they concealing, and why?

She would go back then, but when she left Dogtown she'd given no definite indication that she would return. She needed a reason and, having thought about it and calculated that the time in London was now six in the evening, she returned to the motel where she had spent the night and asked the pretty Vietnamese girl for the use of the office telephone.

She dialled her agent's home number. The line was very clear, they both remarked on it. After the ritual courtesies he waited for her to state her business. 'I'm calling from the office of a motel,' she said, 'just to report progress. The fieldwork's turning out to be complicated; there are several canyons involved and the trail could have gone up any one of them. I've completed one route without being any the wiser – I mean, there are no marks, no wagon ruts; so now I'm going back to the east side to try the other canyons. The problem is this lack of tangible and visible evidence. There's plenty of hearsay.'

'Is there indeed.'

'Everyone knows which way our people went –' she gave a deprecating little laugh, '– and everyone disagrees. I see I'll have to go over the ground with a fine tooth comb.'

'I suppose –' he was feeling his way, '– it's necessary to go back? I mean, they crossed the mountains, didn't they?'

'The Sierras are the grand climax to the story.' He would note that she hadn't answered his question, should draw the conclusion that she'd traced Argent only as far as the mountains. 'My book has to have a design,' she said meaningly, then: 'Don't you agree?'

'Of course.' A fractional pause. 'How is the book coming on?'

'Excellent. It's magnificent country. I'm enjoying it so much I forget to take the photographs – which is another reason for going back. The photographs are necessary?'

'Absolutely essential.' Now he knew what was required. 'James was in touch only yesterday, said the book has to be *lavishly* illustrated –'

'I had the right idea. Did he have any other instructions for me? Like one should send postcards back periodically? I mean, people do.'

'No, no postcards.' (Still no word from Argent.) 'Just keep on as you're going would be the message. Are you all right? Anything we can do to – ease the way from this end?'

'Not at the moment. You've given me quite enough, with the instructions about the illustrations. I'm starting back to Dogtown now and I'll call again when I can telephone in comfort. I'm afraid the motel on the other side doesn't have phones in the rooms. A bit primitive actually.'

'There's nothing you need?' (*Why did you phone?*)

'I just called to give a progress report and let people know what I was about.' (Meaning people at this end; this is part of my cover.)

'I see. I'll tell James. Anything else?' A pause. 'Are you still there?'

'I can't think of anything,' she said truthfully. She could think of no way to convey to him the information that Argent had not been travelling alone when he disappeared.

# Chapter 6

At the first bend on the return journey Miss Pink realised that it was going to be impossible to study the verges and watch for oncoming traffic at the same time. Moreover a driver could go over the edge anywhere: lighting a cigarette on a straight stretch for instance; someone had said that Argent was smoking heavily. That brought fire to mind. A falling vehicle would have exploded and the resulting fire would have been visible for miles – except on the high ground between the two escarpments. But how could he have fallen off the road up there, an experienced traveller like Argent? He might have been lost, could have mired the Jeep in a bog – but this man would then have walked out, using a compass. All the same, the possibility of anyone being lost on top deterred her from leaving the main trail herself. She compromised, driving slowly across the range, keeping a weather eye open for signs of a vehicle having left the road precipitately, watching for a pale gleam through trees, a pale blue gleam, but she felt that the chance of finding any trace of him on the high ground was increasingly remote. Grimly she began to look forward to Dogtown where information was surely available once she hit on the correct method of extracting it.

'You're wasting your time. You followed the Joplin Trail clear to the other side; Danger and Crazy Mule are just blind ends. You'll only get yourself lost.' Rose Baggott's coveralls were splotched with paint and, far from being in a welcoming mood, she was clearly resenting Miss Pink's reappearance.

'I'm sorry I interrupted you.'

'Well, look at me!' The tone was conciliatory. 'I'm decorating one of the bedrooms. Sorry if I sounded rude. You'd better register. The boys at the Queen tell me you write,' she went on as Miss Pink completed the form. 'I'm afraid I haven't read any of your books.' She was trying to make up for her lack of welcome.

'They'll be in the library.' Miss Pink signed her name and straightened her back. 'Who owns the big house in Danger Canyon?'

Rose blinked, taken by surprise. 'Granville Green. He's another Western buff: a member of the Western Trails Association. You went up Danger? So why go back there?'

'I went only as far as the locked gate. Did I meet the landowner: a young dark fellow, drives a pick-up?'

'That's Brett Vogel; he looks after the place.' Sharp eyes studied Miss Pink. 'What did he have to say?'

'Well of course, he was deeply suspicious of me . . . ' Miss Pink paused, waited, her eyes unfocused, but Rose was waiting too. She continued smoothly: 'Hostility towards strangers is to be expected, I suppose?'

'Why should he be hostile to you?'

'I didn't think it was personal; I assumed that was his manner towards everyone.'

'No –' Rose looked as if she would say more but thought better of it. Absently she turned the registration form towards her and regarded it blankly. 'How many nights are you staying?'

'I don't know yet. But he was even more hostile towards Timothy Argent.'

Rose gave a little snort of amusement. 'No wonder.'

'Certainly they didn't get on. Was it because of the locked gate?'

'The locked gate?' Miss Pink was attentive. Rose continued: 'You mean that gate at the start of the forest. But Timothy would –' She checked. 'I was going to say he would just have climbed over it – but they probably had a set-to about Timothy being on private land. He'd have spoken

59

his mind about blocked trails. Tim hadn't much time for Brett Vogel.'

'Local people can be extremely possessive about their own territory.'

'Vogel's not local. They – he's only been here a few months.'

'I didn't meet his wife.'

'Miss Pink! I shall start to think you have ulterior motives: all these questions.' Rose was arch but the tone was contrived. She said, more naturally: 'Vogel's on his own.'

'I have ulterior motives,' Miss Pink confessed. 'And I think I have to come clean. I called my agent from Credit and they want me to take over the book that Timothy was supposed to be writing.'

'Isn't that a bit unusual?'

'Timothy's been given the push.' Miss Pink looked embarrassed. 'I'm afraid he's by way of being an alcoholic and he appears to have taken to the bottle again. Tragic circumstances, but that's basically why I had to come back: to explore the canyons, take photographs and so on. I could write a romance based on a quick drive across Breakneck but for an in-depth travel book, that would be altogether too superficial. After all, Timothy was here – how long?'

'No one's quite sure. How can you take over a book in the middle? Half will be his, the other half yours. It will be disjointed.'

'I don't know what the publishers intend to do. There was a hint that, once I'd finished this California section, I might go back to the beginning and start where Timothy did, on the Missouri River, make the whole thing consistent, scrap Timothy's contribution.'

Rose looked past Miss Pink at the sunshine in the street. 'Poor Timothy,' she said, and sighed heavily.

Miss Pink sauntered out of the hotel, moving purposefully once she was out of sight. She entered the Red Queen and went straight to the door at the back that led to the kitchen, startling Verne Blair who was drinking coffee at a scrubbed table with a cookbook propped in front of him.

'You came back!'

'I've taken over from Timothy.'

He gaped at her. 'Taken over what?'

'Why, his book. I've been in touch with my agent . . . ' She repeated her story patiently. He showed no surprise but then he'd guessed that Argent was an alcoholic. He appeared to accept the explanation for her return, only asking how long she intended to stay: 'Earl's in Endeavor right now; I'd like to catch him, tell him we have you back.'

He went to a wall telephone and dialled a number. After ascertaining that Lovejoy wasn't in what was presumably a store, and hadn't been in, he left a message that Miss Pink was back and for the shopping list to be amended accordingly. He put down the receiver, and she returned to the subject of Timothy Argent as if there had been no interruption: 'His publisher is furious about the girl, maintains she has to be responsible for his falling off the wagon – which is what everyone assumes has happened.'

'I don't know.' Blair was morose, unthinking. 'She could take the liquor or leave it. It's unfair to blame her for *that*.' He did a double-take. 'Who told you about her?'

'Everyone knows.' She was dismissive. 'What *would* you blame her for?'

He slumped in his chair. 'Quite honestly, I'm not interested in other people's private lives.' He thought about this and added: 'If you want my opinion they got what they deserved; they're both adults, they knew what they were letting themselves in for. Oh, we liked Timothy but he had his weaknesses. I mean, it's one thing to be fond of the ladies, but Joanne!' He grinned wryly. 'But then he won't have gone into details to his publisher. Maybe he didn't know the truth about her himself; didn't care, is more like it. He was quite besotted.'

'Why do you refer to him in the past tense?'

'It's two months ago now. He's in the past.' He grinned again as he caught the implications of that. 'Nothing sinister about it, I promise you. Tell you the truth, they arranged a special dinner-party for Joanne's birthday and never turned up. Left us with the bill –'

The telephone started to ring. He excused himself and

lifted the receiver. As he listened, he threw a startled glance at Miss Pink, then turned slowly until his back was towards her. When he replaced the receiver she waited for him to return to the table, to say something, but he was silent and he didn't sit down.

'That was Rose Baggott,' she told him, 'telling you I was asking too many questions.'

He had a cornered look. 'You're certainly asking a lot of questions. Why's that?'

She improvised quickly. 'Because his publishers gave Timothy a huge advance and they're rather keen to know where he is. I'm afraid they'll have to sue.'

'I hadn't thought of that. What was the sum?'

'Fifty thousand pounds, around there. That would be getting on for a hundred thousand dollars.'

He was astonished. 'So much? No wonder they have to find him. And no wonder Joanne got her hooks in him – although I never thought of her as mercenary. She wasn't an ordinary gold-digger.'

'Hiram Wolf is even more partisan.'

He couldn't restrain a giggle. 'Hiram was another sucker.' His eyes glazed. 'She was flawless,' he said, adding quickly: 'except for the dirt. Went barefooted, her feet were always grubby. But the rest of her . . . Her skin was translucent.'

'Someone said she wasn't white.'

'She had some Indian blood. Timothy said that accounted for her beauty.'

'But she was English.'

'An illegal alien obviously. Keeping out of the way of the police.'

'In Dogtown.'

'She mostly kept out of Dogtown. She stayed up Danger Canyon, minding the store.'

'That's an expression I've not come across: "minding the store".'

'Looking after the place, answering the phone when Vogel was out. I guess, because they were both taken on for the job, when Vogel went away, she had to stay behind, look after the ranch, otherwise they weren't doing their job as caretakers.'

'In that case, going off with Timothy was somewhat irresponsible.'

He shook his head and sat down. 'Stupid guy. He's the same age as me, and here he's making a fool of himself over someone young enough to be his daughter, who'll stay with him just until they get to Hollywood or wherever. He'll buy her some proper clothes, take her to a few posh restaurants. Soon as she finds a director – and she'll find one quicker'n she found Tim – soon's she finds the right guy to get her into the movies, she'll dump poor Tim like he's caught something unmentionable.'

'I'm surprised Vogel wasn't glad to be rid of her.'

He regarded her thoughtfully. 'What makes you think he isn't?'

'Because he's so hostile towards Timothy.'

'Vogel's from Texas and all Texans are macho. His pride's been dinted, is all – and then there's no one to cook for him. Not that Joanne could cook, she hated it –' He stopped short. 'You do draw people out, don't you? Rosie Baggott said you were like an investigative journalist.' He smiled, wanting to keep on her good side, taking the sting out of his words. 'I don't think there's anything else to tell. All we know is that Timothy went off with Vogel's woman – you could hardly call her a lady – and that's it.'

'You didn't mention it when I was here before.'

'You were just someone passing through – and Timothy was our friend.'

'Doesn't that still apply?'

'Well no, because you've obviously found out where they came down on the other side and you've come back primed with information. I just filled in a gap. No good holding out on you once you got half the truth.'

The kitchen door opened and Julius Semple stepped over the sill. He gaped at sight of Miss Pink. She smiled broadly. 'Yes, it's me, Mr Semple. Unforeseen circumstances. Joanne –'

Her expression remained benign as he put out his hand, feeling for a counter top, his eyes going from her to Blair and back again. 'Joanne?' he breathed. 'You found her?'

'What was her last name?' she asked. No one answered. She nodded as if their silence confirmed something. 'I see; she wasn't married to Vogel?' She raised her eyebrows at Blair, who shrugged. Semple took a step towards the table, regarding Miss Pink as if she were a snake. Consternation sat oddly on his raddled good looks. 'Don't know as I ever heard a last name,' he muttered.

'What makes her so frightening?' she wondered aloud.

Semple passed a hand over his face. Blair threw him a glance. 'She was trouble,' he said: 'for everyone. We should be grateful to Timothy for taking her away.'

A muscle twitched in Semple's jaw. 'Yeah, she was big trouble.'

'The past tense with you too, Mr Semple?'

'What's that?'

'People refer to them both in the past tense.'

He hesitated. 'I told her,' Blair put in, 'that it all happened two months ago. It's ancient history. We'd forgotten about them until this moment.'

'That's right,' Semple agreed. 'They left, went over the other side –'

'She's traced them.'

'Traced 'em?' Semple's eyes swivelled to Miss Pink.

'Not really,' she confessed. 'I merely picked up some information here and there. Just gossip, you know: something about a girl – er – operating on the Pacific slope.'

'Not –' Semple stopped short.

'It can't be Joanne,' Blair said, and grinned. 'She'd stick with Timothy – all that money.' He turned to Semple. 'Miss Pink says he got a hundred thousand dollars for his book, in advance!' Semple looked blank. 'He wouldn't have it with him, of course,' Blair went on, addressing Miss Pink. 'Joanne would be persuading him to use his credit cards. A hundred thousand would be a fortune to her.

64

She was poor as a wetback, and she loved – loves pretty clothes.'

'I gotta get back,' Semple said. 'There's a faucet leaking –'

'What did you come over for, Julius?'

He blinked. 'A washer – for the faucet.'

'Another one? They're in the hog-house out back. I'll show you. You need new faucets, not washers – but then, don't we all?'

Miss Pink strolled across the street to the museum. She opened the screen door and a figure moved in the gloom of the barn. 'I thought you might be back,' came Charlotte Semple's voice, unsurprised. 'How far did you get?'

'Only to Credit. And I've not come back by choice so much; I've taken over Tim Argent's job. Odd things have been happening.'

'Such as?'

'How much did you know about Timothy?'

Charlotte looked bewildered. 'He was an author, an explorer – you asked me this before. And I told you we never got to know him properly.

'It's more important now. He's disappeared, which is why I'm going to complete the book about the Joplins.'

'What do you mean: "disappeared"?'

'His publishers have lost contact with him. They think he's indulging in a protracted drinking bout with the girl. He's an alcoholic.'

'The girl.' The tone was neutral.

'Joanne.'

'So you discovered that affair. It was none of our business, besides we weren't unsympathetic –' She smiled, no longer neutral. 'I thought it was rather romantic in fact; except he had a Jeep instead of a white charger, it could have been young Lochinvar stuff – well, middle-aged Lochinvar. Joanne was ready to leave Vogel anyway. You should have seen her, she was much too decorative to be stuck up there, in Danger Canyon. I don't blame Tim or her, good luck to 'em, I say, although she won't stay with him;

65

she's not exactly what you'd call constant. I don't mean to sound bitchy; it's just that she wasn't very mature, emotionally.'

'You're only confirming what the men say.'

'No doubt. Which men? Who did you talk to?'

'Anyone, everyone. People do talk, don't they? What would a girl with her looks be doing in Danger Canyon? And English at that.'

'We-ell –' she drew it out, '– people hide in the canyons. We don't ask questions.'

'Criminals?'

'Not all of them. There are other reasons for going into hiding: like getting away from a violent partner – or debts; being an illegal alien, that kind of thing, not really criminal. Live and let live is my motto, but not everyone else's apparently. Who told you about Joanne?'

Miss Pink was puzzled. 'I can't remember. I'm not sure that it wasn't Vogel.'

'You were up to Danger Creek! You asked him? How did you know she was with him in the first place?'

'How did I?' She was becoming flustered now. 'Dear me, *did* I know at that point? How could I unless someone else –' She regarded Charlotte earnestly. 'I think Vogel must have mentioned her.'

'Not voluntarily then. More likely he let something slip and you pounced on it. Is it important?'

'Not in the least. Except that this girl seems to have aroused intense emotions in everyone with whom she came in contact.'

'You're exaggerating, of course. In some of the men, yes: Timothy, Brett Vogel . . . Who else?'

'Hiram Wolf.'

'Oh. Hiram, yes. She made a play for him.' Charlotte paused. 'Verne and Earl wouldn't be interested – you realise why –'

'On the contrary, Verne says she's flawless.'

'What! Then he's referring to . . . to her complexion, must be. He's being technical – objective. I mean, she's what used to be called high-yaller, probably a quadroon. You were at the Red Queen?'

Miss Pink smiled. 'Your husband came across while I was there.'

'Oh dear.' Charlotte returned the smile. 'My old boy was terrified of her. When he saw her coming he'd climb up in the loft here, leave me to cope. Not that I minded; she was fun. We'd rap for ever, her telling me all about herself, not that I believed everything she said, but it was highly entertaining.'

'What did she tell you?'

'It varied. One time I remember she said her grandfather was an Indian rajah, another time he was the chief of an Afghan tribe; you could take your pick.'

'What reason did she give for coming to Dogtown?'

'You won't leave that alone, will you? Like I said: I didn't ask questions and you couldn't believe what she said anyway, not that kind of thing. In any case she retracted immediately. "I didn't say that," she said. Now that was unusual. Other times, like who her grandfather was, she'd hold eye contact and lie like a little kid. Not this time. I never saw her frightened except then.'

Charlotte started to fidget with a bridle. She didn't look happy herself.

'You haven't told me what reason she gave for coming to Dogtown. What was it she said that she tried to retract?'

'It was ridiculous. You English don't get mixed up in that kind of thing.' Miss Pink waited patiently. 'She said it was the Mafia!' Charlotte threw it out like an accusation.

'The Mafia are used to hide a multitude of sins,' Miss Pink said comfortably. 'They're a convenient scapegoat, even a glamour object – and Joanne appears to have been fascinated by glamour. I suspect that she's in Hollywood at this moment.'

'You do? And Timothy: where d'you think he is?'

Miss Pink picked up a geode sparkling with heliotrope crystals. 'Difficult,' she murmured. 'I'd hazard a guess that he's in Hollywood too, not necessarily with her. People are unpredictable once they start drinking heavily. I rather think she will have ditched him. Drunks are a liability.'

The screen door opened and Semple stepped inside. 'Why, there you are, sweetie,' exclaimed Charlotte. 'We've been discussing Timothy and Joanne, speculating what happened. Miss Pink reckons Joanne's in Hollywood and that she's ditched Timothy because he's a liability. She knows he's an alcoholic but she figures he fell off the wagon. His publishers have lost touch with him.'

'I know all that,' Semple said.

'Don't be a bear, sweetie. You're so transparent, isn't he, Miss Pink? She saw you were terrified of someone so I had to tell her it was poor Joanne – well, not so poor, just impoverished.' Semple seemed to have sagged inside his clothes. 'Don't look so beaten, honey,' Charlotte persisted, 'Joanne's got other fish to fry now. Movie directors, no less. You're safe.' She took his arm and turned to Miss Pink, laughing. 'This old boy's personality don't match his looks,' she confided. 'He's shy as a mule deer where the ladies are concerned; I have to drag him to parties even if the only women present are Lorraine Wolf and Rosie Baggott.' She gave him a playful push. 'A good job you've got me to look after you. Now you go and fix that faucet. I'm going to show Miss Pink our collection of geodes.'

# Chapter 7

'I can't believe any of this.' Rose Baggott reined in her grey at the fork and looked helplessly up the Crazy Mule trail. 'Timothy had to go over Breakneck, so what are we doing looking for him in Crazy Mule?'

Miss Pink shifted in her saddle. 'I haven't told you everything,' she confessed. 'Not what's in my mind. I told you what the deputy said, and that wasn't much: Joanne came down to Credit on her own, that is, she was alone when she met the logger above the town. There was blood on her, she called herself Fay. Prostitutes often give false names –'

'She wasn't a prostitute! I told you that already.'

'All right. Let's say there could be an innocuous reason for her giving the logger a false name, but the blood bothers me. Nothing about her story rings true; it's more like something invented on the spur of the moment because she hadn't realised that the blood had soaked through her outer clothing. And Timothy is an experienced explorer: he'd never have put a deer in the back of his vehicle, all the bother of skinning and butchering . . . rubbish! Nor would he leave a woman on top of a mountain range. All the same she had blood on her. I'm very disturbed about that. It's why I felt I had to enlist your help even though his publisher wants me to keep it confidential. I can't find him on my own.'

'I promised I wouldn't talk, and I mean that. What's on your mind then? You think she ditched him –' Rose's hand flew to her mouth and it was Miss Pink who looked away. 'No!' Rose exclaimed. 'That doesn't make sense. She'd have taken the Jeep – and she was on foot when she met the logger.'

'When she came to the wagon,' Miss Pink amended. 'She could have abandoned the Jeep close by.'

'If she – stole the Jeep, where would she have left Timothy?'

'I know only as much as you do. That's why I want to talk to Asa Fortune. According to the Semples he knows the area like his own backyard.'

'He'd talk only if he was innocent.'

'Innocent of what?'

'You know the story about the plane crash and the missing money, jewellery, stuff like that? If he found the Jeep and moved anything, removed it, he's not going to say so, is he?' She paused. 'Suppose Timothy was *in* the Jeep?'

'That possibility crossed my mind.'

'Is that the real reason for having me with you when you tackle Asa?' Miss Pink said nothing. Rose sighed. 'OK. I said I'd help – and you'll certainly get no help from the police. After two months, and no proof that Timothy's up there on the mountain, they wouldn't even send a chopper over.' She started along the Crazy Mule trail and Miss Pink's sorrel followed. 'There's no proof of anything,' Rose muttered when the horses were level again.

'It's his silence worries me, not contacting his publisher.'

The decision to take Rose into her confidence had not been easy until she reminded herself of the extent of the area involved, and remembered that, although Asa Fortune knew it intimately, he'd be most unlikely to talk to a stranger, and a foreigner at that. When she considered which of the Dogtown residents was best qualified to assist her, and to keep that assistance confidential, Rose was the obvious choice, and Rose owned horses, which could reach places that were inaccessible to vehicles. When the proposition was put to her she'd been intrigued and, although stressing that she was very busy, trying to get her hotel rooms fit for next season, she agreed that if anyone knew what had become of Timothy Argent, Fortune was the best bet. That was last night; this morning her confidence seemed to be on the ebb.

70

'Are you bothered about Asa?' Miss Pink asked, holding back her quick-stepping horse.

'He hasn't got much time for people – particularly now, in the fall.' Rose smiled thinly. 'Hunters don't come up Crazy Mule; word gets around.'

'What word is that?'

'That Asa's a homicidal maniac.' Miss Pink stared at her. 'Of course he's not,' Rose went on quickly. 'He's been known to shoot over people's heads though.'

'Why doesn't he like people coming here?'

'It's his territory. He figures he owns it. He was born in Dogtown: the bastard son of Nellie Fortune who managed the hotel around 1900. The place was winding down even then but a few miners hung on scratching a living, hoping to strike it rich, and Nellie boarded them at the Grand Imperial. She lived until she was ninety-three, died in the seventies. Asa used to visit her in the old folks' home at Endeavor; he'd hike out to the highway, thumb a lift with a local. No tourist would stop; he looks like an old Indian scout.'

'What made him take to the woods?'

'I guess nothing else suited. When we get close to his cabin I'll say the word, you keep quiet and watch.'

They rode on, each sunk in thought. Hoofs thudded softly in thick dust, leather creaked; the loudest sounds were those of the horses breathing and the chuckle of the creek among its boulders. The sudden drilling of a woodpecker was so explosive that even the horses threw up their heads.

A deer came out of the trees, observed them calmly, then walked across the trail. Miss Pink glanced at Rose who laid a finger on her lips.

The deer had gone down the path that led to the old cabin and the horses followed. The cabin door was open today and a man stood there, a rifle held casually in one hand. Two does grazed at the side of the clearing, a fawn slept under the cabin wall, and sitting upright and alert on the chopping block was a grey fox.

The horses stopped. No one spoke. Asa Fortune and Miss

Pink studied each other while the deer went on grazing and the fox watched the scene with interest.

Miss Pink saw a man from the past; small, old, hard, he was dressed in greys and browns although the brown of trousers and shirt had faded to a non-colour, like soil, like his face – that part of it not obscured by beard and whiskers. He wore a stained felt hat that shaded his eyes. Evidently reassured by the attitude or the smell of the stranger, he stood the rifle inside the door and turned to Rose. 'Good day for riding,' he observed.

'This is my friend, Miss Pink.'

At the sound of her voice a scrub jay erupted through the doorway waking the fawn which blundered towards a doe. The deer slipped away like mist and when Miss Pink looked over at the chopping block nothing was there except an axe.

'Sorry we drove them away,' Rose said.

'They'll be back. What can I do for you?'

They dismounted and tied the horses to trees. Rose explained that Miss Pink was writing a book about the Joplin Trail, that went over Breakneck, she added pointedly. A man had been here, she said, an Englishman, driving a pale blue Jeep. 'Does that mean anything?' she asked hopefully. 'You know everything goes on in this neck of the woods.'

He thought about this for so long that Miss Pink decided he wasn't going to answer, but Rose was waiting so she kept quiet too.

'He came by,' Fortune said.

'Did he go back down again?'

'Had to.' He looked at Miss Pink. 'No Jeep at the trail-head, is there?'

'Not at the trail-head,' she agreed, 'but could he have left the trail, taken the Jeep into the forest?'

'He didn't.' He contradicted himself immediately: 'He coulda done.'

'Do you know where the Jeep is?' Rose asked.

'It's not in this canyon.'

'Well, is it in Malachite or Danger?'

'I don't go there.'

'Oh, come on, Asa! You go everywhere!'

'I don't go up Danger.'

They studied him. Rose appeared uncertain how to proceed. Miss Pink observed pleasantly: 'Joanne liked the animals.'

'They was her friends too.'

In the same tone she went on: 'They left together.'

'They did?'

'But she came down to Credit alone, that is: not with him. She came down with a logger.'

He looked surprised. 'I didn't know that.'

Miss Pink said quietly, holding his gaze: 'So since they started out together and she reached Credit with a different man, people are wondering what happened to the Englishman.'

'What did happen?'

Rose broke the ensuing silence. 'How did you get along with her, Asa? You had to like her or she'd never have got near your pets.'

'They aren't pets.'

'You know what I mean.'

'We was friends.' He glared at them. 'So what?'

'You don't want her to get in trouble with the police, do you?'

'Are they holding her?'

Rose hesitated. Miss Pink said: 'There was blood on her when she met the logger.' He hadn't moved much before but now he was tense as the fox had been, and as silent. She went on: 'If they think she had a hand in the Englishman's disappearance they'll find her.'

'If she's got away they'll never find her.' He was harsh. 'She'll disappear in LA. I don't know what happened to the man. I thought he'd gone, I thought they went away together. It's what they're saying in town.'

'Did he come here?' Miss Pink asked.

'I never met him. He come up the trail but I slipped out the back.' He jerked his head at the cabin.

'He never spoke to you?'

'No.'

'But you were friendly with Joanne.'

'Of course.'

'Why "of course"?'

'You knew, so no need to ask was we friends.'

Miss Pink suppressed a sigh. 'Did she say anything that might throw a light on where and how Timothy Argent disappeared?'

'No, she only come once after he arrived, and that were to say goodbye. She was going away with him, she said. She *needed* him, so she never woulda hurt him. She'd have married him if he was American.'

'It had to be an American,' Miss Pink said, 'to get papers? She was illegal. So why didn't she marry Brett Vogel?'

He shrugged. 'He's probably married already.'

'What was her last name?'

'She never said.'

'What was she doing with Vogel?' There was a note of desperation in Miss Pink's question and, like an animal, he caught it. A smile couldn't show behind that beard but there was amusement in the answer, which was explicit relative to most of his answers.

'Vogel was her man. She was bored with him and the Englishman came along, asked her to go with him, so she went.'

'Just like that,' Rose said, with a touch of envy.

'Was that any help?' she asked as they continued up Crazy Mule.

'How much of it was the truth?' Miss Pink countered. 'Joanne was in the habit of going there; he wasn't lying when he said she was friendly with the animals (what a strange fellow he is; that beautiful fox: he must have known it from a cub), but the rest – that he never met Timothy, he thought they'd gone over the mountains? I don't know. If he were lying to protect someone, who could it be other than Joanne or himself?'

'You mean that if something happened to Tim, either Joanne or Asa must be responsible?'

'Unless Asa has other allegiances.'

'Only to his pets. What are you proposing to do now?'

'The obvious thing to do is to look for the Jeep, so we'll go to the trail-head, and perhaps we ought to look in the lake.'

'Weren't you here before?'

'The situation's changed. I didn't know about Joanne then.'

They came to the little lake and rode round it, seeing nothing on its muddy bed but a few cans. On the far shore Miss Pink stopped, her attention caught by a rocky skyline.

At the head of the canyon a subsidiary ridge ran out from the main divide to form the spur between Crazy Mule and Malachite Creek. The crest of the spur was of pale granite: a broken spine that cleared the timber by a hundred feet or so and was crowned by a neat square butte. To the left, westward, the spur rose in bare scree slopes to the divide.

'Now what are you thinking?' Rose asked.

'I'm trying to get my bearings. Does that butte have a name?'

'It's Sardine Butte. The trail to Trouble Pass goes up to that crest; you can see the switchbacks: those light patches on the slope.'

'There's something shining at the top of the scree.'

'That's the remains of the airplane, the one that crashed three years ago.'

'Sad. Only a couple of hundred feet higher and it would have got over the ridge. There'd be a fine view from that butte. Why Sardine?'

'A mule fell there in the old days. It was carrying boxes of sardines.'

'Not a way for horses then.'

'I've been over it a few times. The mule fell in an early snow, when the trail was drifted. Were you thinking of going up there?'

'Why not? Let's go.'

The trail ran level for a few hundred yards and then it started to climb out of the bottom in long zigzags, graded for pack trains. It may have been two air-miles from the trail-head to Sardine Butte but would be more than twice that distance by the meandering path. It was a southern slope and there was little shade despite the dense timber. Occasionally they stopped to give the horses a breather and at the third halt Miss Pink asked what kind of boots Fortune wore. Rose glanced at her, then at the dust of the trail. 'Climbing boots,' she said. 'Not riding boots. You saw a track?'

'I've seen the mark of cleated soles. Someone with small feet was here recently.'

'Asa has small hands and feet. Hold my horse, will you?' Rose got down and walked up the side of the trail. 'There was only one person,' she called. 'He went up and then came back.' She returned and took her reins. 'Of course, Asa will go all over the place. He has to eat.'

'What do you mean by that?'

'Why, he has to shoot deer, and he's not going to kill the animals near his cabin.'

'He has a long way to carry the carcass back, or does he cache some of the meat, like hanging it in a tree?'

'He uses a mule to pack it out. He didn't have a mule here though, so maybe he wasn't hunting this time.

'He shoots all the year round?'

'You met him. What makes you think he's a guy would bother about regulations? Open season is when Asa's hungry.'

The sun was high by the time the firs thinned enough for them to see something of the surrounding country. On this eastern slope of the Sierras the air was still but thin and clear. In the well of the canyon behind them a red-tail hawk called and then, from a scatter of rocks, a marmot chirped his alarm. They were the only sounds apart from those made by the horses.

The trail edged left and passed under the south wall

of Sardine Butte. Below, the ground dropped steeply to the timber. 'That's where the mule went down,' Rose said. 'Give your horse his head, let him see where he's going.'

They came to the far side of the butte where there was a depression scattered with the ivory trumpets of alpine gentians. They tied the horses to a juniper and, taking lunch from their saddlebags, moved to a stunted tree to eat in its shade. Rose produced cans of beer.

'Any other time,' Miss Pink remarked, 'this would be a perfect day: riding along the crest of the Sierras.'

'It's still a perfect day.'

'Objectively, yes. But I have a sense of urgency.'

'I don't see why. After two months, if Timothy did meet with an accident up here, he died a long time ago. As for Joanne – No, I won't say it.'

Miss Pink had no such inhibition. 'If Joanne had a hand in it, you would suggest it's a matter for the police?'

'Whoever had a hand in it, if there has been foul play it's a matter for the police. Nothing to do with us.'

'There's something unethical about inheriting a book from an author without knowing what's happened to him. As if he didn't matter: it's just a commercial enterprise.'

'You mean, you owe him. Like a family connection: you're not just taking over someone's house or an office; it's like adopting his child.'

'And rearing it, sending it out into the world, something like that. But I agree it's a gorgeous day.' Miss Pink was suddenly brisk. 'Nothing much we can do here. So, identify the features for me.'

Rose shot her a doubtful glance, then decided to go along with the change of mood. 'You know Breakneck; it's the lowest point *there*: the timbered saddle. Trouble Pass is hidden by this scree slope. And the spur the Breakneck road climbs is hiding Danger Canyon and Deadboy Pass. Dogtown's hidden too: outside the mouth of Malachite, sort of round the corner.'

Miss Pink looked up the slope to what she could now see was a jagged piece of metal, a part of a wing perhaps.

'That would be why people in Dogtown didn't see the air-craft crash. There was a fire? Why wasn't it seen from the highway?'

'It was bad weather; the cloud was down.'

'Of course. One never thinks of that in California.' She looked across the headwall of Malachite Canyon to the road that climbed to Breakneck Pass. 'If I hadn't been up and down that road already, the sight of it would terrify me. No wonder people warned me not to take it.'

'It's the same as everything else in the wilderness: riding, skiing, hunting; fine so long as nothing goes wrong, but it's coping with emergencies that weeds out the survivors. You wouldn't want your brakes to fail coming down that road; there'd need to be some quick gear-changes. And you have to take those bends carefully: up as well as down; you'll have discovered that for yourself. A number of people have gone over the edge.'

As these words penetrated her brain Miss Pink's casual regard started to sharpen. She turned and saw that Rose was watching her. She took a pair of binoculars from her saddle-bag. 'There's nothing obvious,' she said, focusing. 'Wherever it did come off, a vehicle would fall towards the creek, and I can see all of that except the bit below the bottom bend.' She started to move along the ridge, traversing below the north wall of Sardine Butte.

'That's a very dark chasm,' Rose called, squinting down-wards. 'If a truck was upside-down it wouldn't show any blue paint.'

Miss Pink had moved out of sight round a rock but-tress. Rose glanced back at the horses, then followed. Her companion was standing at the top of a shallow gully, a seasonal water-course, dry now, which ran down the slope like a funnel and pointed towards the lowest bend on the Breakneck road.

Below the point of the bend dark rock plunged for over a hundred feet to what must be a small level plat-form between waterfalls. And there, resembling something stranded, something that might have leapt upstream like a salmon but was more likely to have dropped, was a pale blue object the size of a Jeep.

The road was only two miles away but the slope was precipitous; they had to continue the line of their intended route by way of Trouble Pass to Breakneck and approach the Jeep from the divide. 'I wonder can we reach it ourselves,' Rose said. 'We might be able to traverse in from the side; we certainly can't climb up or down to it, because of the waterfalls.'

Miss Pink made no response; someone had to reach the Jeep even if it meant bringing in climbers with ropes.

They were shocked, of course, and it affected them differently. Rose couldn't stop talking, Miss Pink was thoughtful. As they plodded up the slope towards the aircraft wreck Rose said, following her own train of thought: 'But she didn't just walk away and leave him! If she was with him, if she'd been with him, she'd have been killed too. Are you certain it was Joanne came down to Credit?'

'Is it likely there are two beautiful English half-castes – or quadroons – in one corner of California at the same time?'

'Maybe she jumped clear.'

Miss Pink dropped back, and since it is difficult for riders to converse when they're in single file, they continued in silence until they reached the wreckage of the plane. It lay strewn about a stony knoll and all around was the evidence of fire: scorched and melted plastic, charred foam attached to contorted metal, blackened rocks.

'The bodies must have been flung clear,' Miss Pink observed. 'Otherwise currency bills would have been burned.' She stopped and looked back at Sardine Butte and beyond, to Crazy Mule Canyon.

Rose was walking on, approaching the brow of Trouble Pass. Miss Pink trotted after her and they crossed the saddle to find their trail contouring the slope of the divide, almost level and just above the timber. Westward the lateral ridges sloped majestically to the flat lands with here and there a glimpse of meadows like alps. In this dry season grass was tawny as a lion's skin. A great raptor banked on a thermal. 'That could be a condor,' Rose said. 'My first condor,' responded Miss Pink. Neither of them evinced any excitement.

They started to descend – Breakneck was lower than Trouble – and entered a stand of red firs. Soon they saw the flash of dirt through the trees and they stepped out on the road and turned for home.

The Jeep was invisible from any point on the road, which was why no one had seen it. They stopped at the lowest hairpin and looked at the ground. There were fresh scars on the lip of the chasm but new growth had erased all signs of where the Jeep had left the road.

'It didn't skid,' Miss Pink said. 'So wherever it went over, he wasn't braking.'

'So what? It had to fall from here, didn't it?'

Miss Pink looked up the slope. 'It may have gone over from higher up and tumbled down the bed of the creek, but then it would be more knocked about. From a distance it looked scarcely marked. The reason why I was looking for signs here was because I wondered whether it was going up or down when it left the road.'

They descended a short distance and saw the faint line of a game trail running in to the platform between the falls. Leaving the horses they continued on foot. In the lead, Miss Pink stopped suddenly.

'A bear's been here. There's a paw mark.'

'My God! If it's still there – '

They moved a few paces and the Jeep came into view, the passenger door hanging broken from one hinge, a litter of paper spewing from the interior. They stood still, holding their breath. The Jeep didn't move.

'Hi, bear!' Rose shouted. 'Bear! Go away!'

The echoes died and they watched like hawks.

'There's nothing inside,' Miss Pink said. 'No bear.' But their approach was still cautious; they didn't want to see what *was* inside the Jeep. There were flies; those were to be expected. There was a mess of trash in the passenger seat, and in the well in front of it: a welter of paper and plastic bags, and rags that had been clothing. The driver's seat was somewhat stained, but with mud rather than blood, and empty. They peered into the back and poked about gingerly, discovering cartons under the clutter produced by the bear in its search for food. The flies had been attracted by scraps in the smashed icebox. There was no body in the Jeep.

'He was thrown clear?' Rose asked doubtfully.

From points round the lip of the waterfall they peered at the pool below the drop. Sodden sheets of paper had accumulated at the outlet but there was nothing else.

'He survived and crawled away?' Rose ventured, and answered her own question: 'He couldn't have; look at that drop between the road and here: it's over a hundred feet! Even with the Jeep landing upright, the jolt would have detached most of his organs.'

Miss Pink turned back to the Jeep. 'It's in gear,' she said, 'bottom gear. Was he going up? What gear would he be in?' Her Cherokee was automatic.

'On that bend? Second, I would think.'

Miss Pink picked up a sheet of paper. 'This is a copy of Permelia's diary. I wonder?' She reached behind the passenger seat and moved some clothing scattered with cereal flakes to expose a squashed carton. She straightened its sides and they saw the spines of books: field guides to wildflowers, birds, mammals, a hardback on the California Trail, three paperback Chandlers, a tour guide to the western states. Rose crowded close then stepped back and reached down. 'Look what I was treading on.'

It was a thick spiral notebook. The ink on the pages had run but it had been open, face-down, and the cover had escaped the water. On the outside was the title: Joplin Trail. Inside was Argent's name, James Dorset's address and telephone number, and the legend: 'Substantial Reward to Finder'. Although the writing on the pages was indecipherable they could see that the book was nearly completed.

'It's his notes,' Rose breathed. 'I wonder could a laboratory bring up the writing somehow? You could use it.'

'Possibly.'

'Aren't you interested? This was the basis for his book!'

'Let's see what's missing.'

'Nothing will be missing. This is the most valuable item. It's priceless – to an author.' But Miss Pink was clearing the passenger seat, carefully transferring objects to the well.

They searched the Jeep methodically, seeing what was there and what was absent. They could tell; both knew what was needed in wilderness travel. The results were interesting. There was a large rucksack and a small tent but no sleeping bag. There appeared to be a full complement of clothing but no boots and no down jacket. There were maps, personal items such as shaving gear and towels but a sponge-bag was ripped and empty. They did find a cake of soap and a tube of toothpaste which had been punctured, almost certainly by large teeth. There were no cameras and no binoculars. In the glove compartment, along with a pair of designer sunglasses in a case, a tyre pressure gauge, Band-Aid, toothpicks and the driver's manual, was a black biro pushed to the back with an address stamped on it: 'Thunderbird Motel, 190 Main Street, Seeping Springs, Texas'. 'When was he in Texas?' Miss Pink murmured, and clipped it to her shirt pocket. 'And who took the cameras?'

'How do you know he had any?'

'The book was to be illustrated, and he always took his own photographs. He was something of a naturalist too so he'd have had binoculars. Why am I talking in the past tense? There's no body. And where's his sleeping bag?'

'The bear?'

'Never. A bear might pull it out and rip it but once it found there were only feathers inside, it would lose interest. Where are the feathers? No, someone else was here besides the bear.'

'Of course. Timothy was.'

'Why did he leave his notebook behind?'

# Chapter 8

'I'm too exhausted to cook,' Rose said, closing the corral gate. 'I guess I'll join you for supper at the Queen.'

Miss Pink, about to say she must go to her cabin first, changed her mind. Rose hadn't been out of her sight since they found the Jeep, had had no chance to use a telephone. 'A good idea,' she agreed, 'I'll wash my hands in your kitchen.' Rose blinked at such familiarity but evidently she was too tired to remind her guest that the cabins were only a few yards away.

It had been dark by the time they returned to Dogtown. The horses were stumbling with weariness and their riders were in little better shape, but by the time they'd unsaddled, Miss Pink had found her second wind. She staggered a little as they walked to the Red Queen but her brain was functioning smoothly. There was a light in a cabin at the back of the museum and she was considering the question of the Semples when Rose asked: 'What do we tell them?'

'Why,' Miss Pink stopped as if she were too tired to walk and talk at the same time, 'just tell people what we know.'

'We don't know anything.'

'So we'll tell them that.'

'We'll have to call the sheriff.'

'Leave that to Blair and Lovejoy. We've done our bit for today.'

'I can't hold out much longer.'

'What you need is a good stiff drink.'

The restaurant was empty of customers, the partners sitting at one of the tables drinking coffee and reading newspapers. Lovejoy smiled as he stood up. 'We were expecting you,' he said. 'We heard the horses –' his smile faded, '– What's wrong?'

Miss Pink and Rose subsided in the nearest chairs.

'Something happened?' Blair approached, full of solicitude. 'Are you all right?'

'We've had quite a day.' Miss Pink gave him an apologetic smile. 'We could revive with brandy.' Lovejoy rushed to the bar.

'We found the Jeep,' Rose said. 'Timothy's rig.'

'My God!' Lovejoy froze, a bottle in his hands.

'Were they –' Blair's eyes were horrified.

'No.' Rose's voice climbed. 'He's not *there*! No one's there. Only a bear was there.' She giggled.

Miss Pink said loudly: 'The bear had just pulled out the food, that's all. There's no sign of Timothy. Mr Blair, I wonder if you would call the sheriff and tell him the Jeep's been found – empty. Now I come to think of it the sheriff on this side won't even know that a Jeep was missing, unless the one at Credit told him. However, it has to be reported. Perhaps you should tell the Semples as well; they knew Timothy. We're too tired to go over. They might like to come here.'

Rose was quiet now, regarding her in a lacklustre fashion. Lovejoy came over with the brandy and she started to drink it.

'Here, go easy,' he chided. 'That's not water, Rosie.'

Blair went to the kitchen where he could be heard telephoning. Miss Pink sipped her brandy. Lovejoy turned to her. 'No horrors?' he asked meaningly.

'No. Just a crashed Jeep. He – it left the road at the first bend on the way to Breakneck and landed right way up in the creek.'

'What do you think happened?'

'We have no idea.'

'Could you get down to it? Oh, of course, you had to or you wouldn't have known –'

Disjointedly she told him what they had found. Blair returned and Lovejoy repeated it to him. He said the sheriff would be out in the morning, and that he had called the Semples. Rose had another brandy. Food was forgotten. Charlotte Semple came in, looking puzzled.

'I don't understand it,' she said. 'If the Jeep broke down why didn't they go back for it? Or was it a total wreck?'

The other women were silent. Alcohol had been the final straw for Rose whose eyelids were drooping, while Miss Pink regarded Charlotte with a bemused expression and took another pull at her brandy.

'It's in the creek,' Lovejoy supplied eagerly. 'He ran out of road on the first bend up to Breakneck.'

Charlotte stared at him with parted lips. 'How ghastly,' she whispered, and glanced at Miss Pink who nodded earnestly. 'You found them?' Charlotte went on, frowning as she took in their appearance and realised that they'd come straight to the restaurant without changing their clothes. Blair spoke for them: 'They've been riding all day. They're exhausted. I'm going to heat some minestrone.' He went to the kitchen and Lovejoy, after a glance at the wilting customers, took up the story. Charlotte listened with an air of increasing bewilderment, while Miss Pink exuded approval as if Lovejoy were a pupil repeating his lesson. When he said that the Jeep must have been empty when it left the road, Charlotte made the obvious comment: 'So they jumped before it went down.'

'Who's "they"?' Rose, who had been sprawled across a table, raised her head from her arms and made an effort to pull herself together. 'Someone said "they". I thought you were talking about the Jeep.'

Blair came back with steaming bowls of soup. 'We were,' Lovejoy said. 'But if they were both in the Jeep to start with, then they both had to jump clear, one out of each door.' He turned to Charlotte. 'Are you thinking the same as me: why didn't they come back to Dogtown? That's easy. They didn't want to run into Brett Vogel. So they walked past here – in the night? – hiked out to the highway and thumbed a lift to LA.' He beamed with satisfaction. Blair regarded him doubtfully, Charlotte looked confused. Miss Pink, who had turned her chair to the table, applied herself to her soup.

Rose picked up a spoon and tasted the minestrone. 'God, that's good! I'm *hungry*.'

'I can't see Timothy being worried about Brett Vogel,' Blair said. 'Even if he had gone off with Brett's lady.'

'He didn't.' Rose was reviving with every spoonful of soup. 'Joanne wasn't with him –'

'Now, wait a minute – ' Miss Pink began, but the two men were speaking together. Blair stopped. His partner was saying: ' – can't be another girl like her. It must have been Joanne. You thought it was her originally, didn't you?' He was addressing Miss Pink. 'You said a hooker was working the logging run on the Pacific slope.'

'Oh, come on!' Charlotte jeered.

'True! She heard it when she was over to Credit. The sheriff told her.'

Miss Pink finished her soup and asked Blair for a second helping. She seemed much more alert now. She repeated what she had learned from the deputy in Credit about the girl who called herself Fay, and that included the story of the deer. At this point Lovejoy interrupted: 'That's not true for a start. It's ridiculous. Anyway, Timothy didn't have the Jeep on top. It was sitting in Malachite Creek.'

'Exactly,' Miss Pink said. 'The story was just a cover for bloodstains on the girl's clothing.'

'She must have hurt herself falling out of the Jeep.' Charlotte was starting to work things out. 'What a tragedy. I suppose they've found a cabin on the west side of the divide and he's drinking, living on what Joanne can earn – But that's uncharitable!' She was suddenly defiant. 'What he's doing, he must be beavering away at his book – and – and what she does is no business of ours.' She avoided their eyes.

The others were plainly embarrassed, except for Rose. 'Miss Pink didn't finish,' she said coldly. 'Joanne was alone. She went to Bakersfield with the logger and then she split. The deputy didn't say anything about her coming back, did he?'

'No,' Miss Pink said.

'So where's Timothy?' Lovejoy asked.

'That's for the sheriff to find out,' Miss Pink said. She

was thinking that the discovery of the Jeep hadn't taken them much further forward. At one time there had been a connection between Timothy, Joanne and the truck but at some point they became separated. Did that separation occur when the truck left the road? Were Timothy and Joanne together at that point, or had they parted previously? She looked down at a fresh bowl of soup, veiling her eyes. That question might be answered in the morning, with the help of tracker dogs.

'No way, ma'am. After two months? There wouldn't be a trace of scent left.'

The county line followed the crest of the Sierras so Malachite Canyon came within the jurisdiction of the sheriff at Endeavor: a big, florid man with a thin mouth under a beak of a nose. He wouldn't have looked out of place in a Yorkshire dale and Miss Pink wasn't surprised to find that his name was Charlie Raistrick. He was accompanied by a young dark fellow, Leon Padilla, with honey-coloured skin and looks that were pure Spanish.

There had been no occasion to tell them that she had come to the United States specifically to find Timothy Argent. Raistrick had accepted that she was following the Joplin Trail and had seen the crashed vehicle yesterday when Rose Baggott was showing her the country. His immediate interest centred on the Jeep.

He had arrived in Dogtown after breakfast and she had led the way up Malachite Canyon in the Cherokee. When the men had traversed in to the platform, had duplicated the women's actions of the previous day: peering over the fall, studying the cliff above, searching the interior of the vehicle, finally she had asked the question about tracker dogs, and got the answer.

'You knew the driver,' Raistrick went on. 'What do you think happened?'

'I never met him, but I can't imagine any author would deliberately leave his notebook behind. His boots are missing, his sleeping bag, cameras and binoculars. He'd be wearing his boots, of course, but why take the other things, and no rucksack to carry them in?'

Raistrick smiled thinly. His deputy grinned. 'Valuables disappear from crashes in these mountains, ma'am. There's people in the woods is a little light-fingered when it comes to items like cameras, and an author would have something expensive, like a Nikon? As for binoculars and sleeping bags, he'd probably have the best of those too. Terrible temptation for a hunter. I'm not surprised at what's missing. After two months I'd be surprised if those items was still here.'

'You were thinking of the young fellow in Danger Canyon?' Miss Pink asked innocently. 'I met him. He didn't strike me as the criminal type.'

They had been wryly amused, now their smiles faded and they were more attentive. 'That's the caretaker at the Green place?' Raistrick asked. 'What's his name?'

'Brett Vogel,' she said.

'Ah, yes. Vogel.' The sheriff looked at Padilla whose dark eyes were giving nothing away.

Miss Pink said: 'There's gossip in Dogtown that Timothy Argent went off with Vogel's lady.' And she told him everything they were saying because he was going to find out shortly, and she needed help to find Timothy. She told him what she had learned in Credit, she kept nothing back except the fact that she had been commissioned to find the author. She did say that she had been asked to take over the book, because that justified her concern about Timothy's present whereabouts. 'It's his book,' she told them earnestly. 'If he's alive, he should complete it. I have to know what's happened to him.' Hers was the attitude of an elderly spinster determined to do the right thing by a colleague.

Raistrick nodded, approving her concern. 'Have you thought maybe he doesn't want to be found? He's had plenty of time to get in touch with his publisher – that's if he's still alive.'

'Oh, he has to be. He jumped clear. He wasn't in this vehicle, was he?'

Everyone stared at the passenger seat, unmarked by even

one drop of dried blood. 'No, no one was in it when it landed,' Raistrick agreed, and looked up at the cliff. 'And no one was thrown clear. With a fall of over a hundred feet, there'd have been too many bones broken for anyone to crawl away. This cliff is sheer too: no trees; nothing to catch hold of as he fell. The driver jumped clear before it went over.'

Miss Pink thought about the gears but she said nothing. She'd seen him nudge the gear lever and glance meaningly at Padilla.

They returned to the road. 'Are you going to start a search?' she asked, looking towards Breakneck Pass.

He hesitated. 'You mean, assuming he's in the mountains? No, ma'am. All the signs here point to him not being injured. He wasn't in this crash, so he could be anywhere. There's nothing to show he's dead, and if he's alive he's committed no crime. How do you know he didn't have another bag, a nice piece of luggage, and he took his camera and stuff before he pushed the vehicle over?' He saw her surprise. 'It was in bottom gear, ma'am. You don't go up or down this road in bottom. That's the gear people use when they get out of a vehicle and send it off the road.'

'Why on earth would he do that? And why didn't he take his notebook?'

'Ah, but he took the most valuable things, didn't he? And there could be any number of reasons for ditching the Jeep that we don't know about, but the one that comes to mind immediately is an insurance scam.'

'Not Timothy Argent.'

'Well, I guess you'll find out eventually if it is insurance. Someone will be claiming. But that Jeep was sent over, ma'am. And if you ask me, your man will surface somewhere, if he hasn't already, perhaps under another name, a new identity. There's a woman in the case too. A very lovely lady, so I've heard. This gentleman was at a dangerous age and the lady could have been the reason for his disappearance, or wanting to stay disappeared. Did you think of that?'

She looked down the canyon. 'Brett Vogel knows more than he's letting on.' She said it reluctantly, but someone had to question the caretaker.

'Did he say anything to you that might throw some light on this?' Raistrick gestured towards the creek.

'We exchanged only a few words. He was surly. I mentioned Argent and although he didn't say anything relevant he reacted – with hostility. But then you'd expect that; the relationship between Argent and Joanne wasn't a secret.'

'Not now maybe; he might not have known about it at the time.'

'Maybe no one did,' Padilla put in. 'They only know now because those two disappeared together.'

'Disappeared?' Raistrick repeated.

'Joanne reappeared,' she reminded them. 'Floyd Bailey at Credit might be able to help you get in touch with the logger involved.'

'I'll bear that in mind. Now we have to go and talk to Vogel.'

As they went downhill she allowed the police car to draw ahead and by the time she reached the place where the trail forked for Danger Canyon the only sign of them was some dissipating dust. She rolled on a few yards and turned up Crazy Mule.

The cabin door was closed and there wasn't an animal in sight when she pulled up at Fortune's place. She cut the engine and walked down the path and round the back of the cabin. A window was open in the back wall. 'I go out the back,' he'd said.

'Mr Fortune!' she called. 'I have to talk to you before the police come.' Water chuckled in the creek bed. Behind her a small twig snapped. 'There aren't any witnesses,' she added. 'I need to know where the driver of the Jeep is. I don't care about the sleeping bag and the cameras.'

There was no response. 'Look,' she said desperately, 'you can bury the stuff as you did everything else. If they can't find anything, they can't pin anything on you. You've always got away with it. At least tell me who pushed the Jeep off the road. Timothy's a friend of mine.'

Suddenly he was there, materialising like a phantom, the colouring of skin and clothing a perfect camouflage in the shadowed undergrowth.

'Where are the police?' he asked.

'With Brett Vogel.'

'They would be. Is there any news of her?'

'Not so far as I know. Did she send the Jeep over?'

'I been thinking about that. Why should she? She needed it to get away; they both needed it. I can't figure that truck in the bottom, whichever way I look at it.'

She studied his eyes. 'How did you discover it?'

'I saw it from Sardine Butte. I went down, thought they were inside, but they'd got out.'

'Before it left the road?'

'Of course.' He looked at her slyly. There was no point in scolding him for not having told them yesterday; he'd only shrug and wait for the next question.

'When you found the Jeep how long was that after Joanne's last visit to you, when she said goodbye? And when did she say she was going?'

'That's a lot of questions.'

'Only two. And it's not as if you were a stupid man.' She was tart, and regretted it immediately, but there was a gleam of something in his eyes: amusement? Appreciation?

'I found it a few days after she came here the last time. She said they were leaving shortly, when Vogel was away.'

'Where did he go?'

'She never said.' He hesitated. 'It wasn't the first time. He was away quite a bit, several days at a time.'

'What was he up to?'

'Joanne didn't know, or if she did, she wasn't telling. Drugs probably.' His casual tone indicated a wild guess. Miss Pink reverted to the question of the Jeep.

'Which way was it travelling when it left the road?'

'It was going up, towards the pass.'

'No skid marks?'

'No, it were *sent* over.'

She said carefully: 'I'm not asking any questions about the cameras and sleeping bag except this: were they in the Jeep when you reached it?'

He thought about that for a long time but finally admitted that they were.

'A bear's been there,' she told him.

'It'd be after food.'

'Was there any sign of what had happened to Argent? Did you look?'

'I didn't do nothing more than just look around casual like. That wasn't no accident. No one got hurt is what I'm saying.'

'What do you think happened?'

'Maybe someone stole it and ditched it because it ran out of gas.'

'It wouldn't be out of gas if they were just starting over the mountains.'

'You wouldn't think so.'

She drove down Crazy Mule and turned up Malachite. At the first bend she stopped and traversed in to the Jeep. The keys were still in the ignition but they wouldn't turn; they must have jammed under the impact. With some difficulty she worked her way under the rear end, grimacing at sharp stones and cold water, and rapped on the fuel tank with her knuckles. Fortune could be right; it did sound empty, and there was no sign of a leak, and no smell.

She returned to the Cherokee and switched on the ignition. She was facing uphill, contemplating Breakneck Pass, and automatically she looked at her fuel gauge to make sure that there was enough petrol for the climb. You always looked at your gauge when about to enter a wilderness area; it was a mark of the seasoned traveller. What was Timothy doing, starting over the Sierras with an empty tank? He wouldn't, she thought, not unless he was mad, or drunk.

She turned the key, put the Cherokee in Drive and started to climb.

# Chapter 9

The distance from the crashed Jeep to the place where timber was being felled on the western slope was more than twenty miles; too far for most people to walk in a night, and Sierra nights were cold. There had been no down clothing in the Jeep, but that didn't have to mean that the driver had taken it with him; to Asa Fortune a padded parka would be as tempting as a snug sleeping bag. With the thought of frosty nights in mind Miss Pink crossed Breakneck Pass and headed purposefully for the only shelter between Dogtown and Credit: the cabins at Palmer Meadows.

The small community looked no different from when she first saw it: the shuttered dwellings and closed barns, and a few cows grazing in the distance. At the first cabin she was surprised to find that the rear windows, although secured on the inside, were unshuttered. Peering through the panes she saw a table, chairs, bunk beds. Everything looked as it should do after the owners had cleaned and closed it for a long period. The door had an old-fashioned keyhole, it could be locked only from the outside and with a key.

The next cabin was larger, with the same kind of lock on the door and two windows at the front, one of which, to judge by the size of the frame, must be a picture window. The wooden shutters were not secured, only held in place by a long spar on brackets. Removing this she discovered that the shutters consisted of five panels that fitted into grooves. She detached two of them, revealing a big sheet of glass, a solid and unbroken fixture.

The interior of this cabin was more luxurious than the first. She could see a living room with upholstered sofas and

93

chairs, a solid table, books, a stone fireplace with German beer steins on a shelf, a corner with crockery stacked in a wall cupboard. A door in the wooden wall of the living room was ajar, leading to what must be the bedroom. In the far wall were two sash windows, their glass black.

She went to the rear of the cabin and removed the shutters from one of the living-room windows. The swivel that should have clamped the two halves together was broken. She raised the lower half, discovered there was no sash cord, propped it open with a couple of logs and climbed over the sill. She sniffed the air. It smelled faintly like a dustbin.

The living quarters and the corner kitchen were light enough for her to see that there was nothing obviously wrong here. The bedroom was another matter. She went outside again and removed the shutter from its window.

The bedroom was empty, that is, it wasn't occupied. She told herself that she hadn't really expected to find Timothy, merely some evidence that he had been here. Once she had recovered from her relief – it was just the kind of place you might expect to find a corpse – she looked first for the source of the smell.

It was easy to find. The last person to use the kitchen hadn't emptied the garbage. In a pedal bin there were empty cans which had contained a ham, peaches, pineapple chunks. There was a dirty plate and a used mug in the sink. She went to turn the taps and found them open. The water system had been drained, and someone had come along since that precaution was taken against frost, had used one mug and one plate.

There were two single beds in the bedroom, blankets and pillows neatly folded and stacked. Behind a curtain shabby clothes hung on wire hangers, the kind of clothes that are good for nothing other than wilderness living: camouflaged jackets and trousers, faded woollen shirts, slickers, drab anoraks, a pea jacket. They had belonged to big men. Nowhere was there any indication of the identity of the last person to use the cabin.

She replaced the shutters and took the road back to

Dogtown. She met no one. She didn't stop at the bottom bend nor at the junctions of the trails up the side canyons although at Danger Creek she slowed down, deep in thought. She came out of the mouth of Malachite Canyon and turned left. When Dogtown came in sight, tucked between the mountains and the Rattlesnake Hills, she was struck again by its peculiar air of abandonment. This could be attributed to the lack of fences and gardens, to the absence of people in the empty street. There were power poles and swagged cables, cars and the notice outside the Grand Imperial; for all that, the place still looked like a deserted mining camp. A pick-up stood outside the Red Queen.

Brett Vogel was at the bar in conversation with Lovejoy. She greeted them politely. Lovejoy looked flustered. 'Your dinner will be a little late tonight,' he told her. 'Verne went to the dentist and he's been held up in town.'

She nodded affably. 'That's fine. All I want at the moment is a long cold drink. I'll have a Budweiser.'

Vogel emptied his beer and straightened, making movements to go. She was all embarrassment: the elderly lady apologising for invading a masculine domain. 'Don't leave because I've come in, Mr Vogel. I was so thirsty! I've been up to Palmer Meadows.'

Lovejoy blinked. Vogel scowled at her. 'Have one yourself, Mr Lovejoy,' she added quickly, 'and I'm sure Mr Vogel won't refuse to join me in a drink. What was Joanne's last name?'

'Emmett,' he said. 'What's at Palmer Meadows?'

'Someone broke into one of the cabins.'

'How did you find that out?' Lovejoy was divided between consternation and amusement. 'Or did you get it from the police?'

'Were the police up there? I didn't see them.' She turned to Vogel. 'When did Joanne leave? Do you have a date?'

'The police asked me that.' He signalled Lovejoy to give him another beer, opened it and drank deeply. When he looked at her again he appeared concerned to get his facts right, his eyes suddenly earnest. He was an attractive fellow when his face wasn't set in hard lines. 'She wasn't interested in me once Argent came on the scene,' he said. 'She was about to split anyways. She spent most of her time with him, in the canyons. I don't know when she left. I thought she was just away longer'n usual and I come down here after a time and Earl tells me he hasn't seen Argent for a few days, so we figure they're gone for good.'

Lovejoy, who had been waiting impatiently to get a word in, asked eagerly: 'Who was it broke into a cabin? Timothy and Joanne? I thought they'd have come back this way after ditching the Jeep.'

'We know Joanne didn't,' she reminded him.

'Suppose they quarrelled, and Joanne went on, over the other side, and Timothy came back, thumbed a lift – Why are you looking at me like that, ma'am?'

She sighed. 'The Jeep was crashed deliberately. Why should Timothy do that?'

'Insurance?' Vogel suggested.

'What company's going to pay out on a crashed vehicle and no body inside?'

'No body anywhere.' Lovejoy looked smug, as if he had just solved a problem in detection.

'We don't know –' The screen door opened and Julius Semple came in. Miss Pink smiled and nodded, and went on: 'We don't know that there isn't a body somewhere.'

Semple gaped at her. 'Whose body?'

'Why, Timothy Argent's.'

'I thought he was with Joanne!'

'I expect so.' Before anyone could react to this volte-face, she added pleasantly: 'What did the police have to say to you, Mr Vogel?'

The atmosphere was electric; questions like that were not asked in small communities, and by strangers. Miss Pink said gently: 'The circumstances are not normal.'

Vogel swallowed. 'Like when I saw Joanne last.'

'You're in the clear,' Lovejoy said angrily. 'She was seen

long afterwards: way down to Credit and beyond, to Bakers-field.'

'No one's suggesting Joanne was a victim,' Miss Pink pointed out.

Semple's mouth opened and closed. Vogel's eyes narrowed. He smiled. 'There was nothing left to the relationship. She were free to go whenever she liked; I wasn't stopping her.'

'No one's accusing you, Brett,' Lovejoy said.

'No one's accusing anyone.' Miss Pink addressed Semple. 'But where's Timothy?'

'Oh come on!' Lovejoy spluttered. 'How would Julius know?'

'I don't think he does,' she said, surprised.

'You were looking at him.'

'I was *wondering* where Timothy is, not asking anyone in particular.'

'He's in Hollywood,' Lovejoy said wildly. 'Why're you smiling, Brett? Did I say something?'

'I think the Mafia got to him.'

Lovejoy started to laugh, then sobered. 'You shouldn't joke about it. Most likely thing is he's holed up, pretending to write and drinking himself to death. That's not funny.'

'Who was in Texas recently?' Miss Pink asked.

'*Texas*?' Lovejoy shrilled. 'Why?'

The other two had tensed, hanging on the answer. 'The police mentioned something,' she said vaguely. 'It couldn't relate to Timothy; he drove straight from Missouri to here. Joanne?' She was as ingenuous as a child. 'Did Joanne come from Texas?'

'Did she?' Lovejoy looked at Vogel.

'Could be. She'd been all over.'

'You're from Texas,' Semple said harshly.

''Course I am. I were raised in Fort Worth. What's that got to do with it?'

'Did you mean recently?' Semple asked Miss Pink. 'Someone came from Texas in the last few months.' He was excited. 'Do drugs figure in this?'

'Why drugs?' Miss Pink asked.

'That's how they come into the country: across the Rio Grande into Texas.' Semple stopped as if Texas was a cue.

Vogel accepted it as such. 'And these consignments come along the border, through New Mexico and Arizona, cross the Colorado, and they comes into Dogtown which is the main distribution point for California.' He was smiling.

'Ask a silly question,' Miss Pink said.

Semple's eyes wandered. He tried to sketch a grin but succeeded only in looking foolish. 'What are the police doing now?' he asked.

'They didn't take me into their confidence,' Vogel said.

'Did they search your place?'

'Now why would they do that?'

'Looking for Joanne.'

Miss Pink stared. Lovejoy said: 'But Joanne –' and stopped, looking scared. Vogel, who was shorter than Semple but young and hard, had gripped the man by the front of his shirt, pulling him close. 'Joanne,' he said tightly, 'went over the pass and down to Bakersfield. She were alive and well. Why would they search my place, man?'

Semple's head was high, exposing his craggy throat. His eyes were half-closed, his arms hanging loosely. Lovejoy and Miss Pink made no attempt to interfere. Vogel twisted his fist in the bunched shirt. 'Why would they want to search my place, Julius?'

'There's – only the logger's word – about Joanne. It coulda been another girl on the Pacific slope.'

The fist opened. Semple stepped back. He passed his tongue over his lips like an embarrassed cat.

'You're a fool, Julius,' Vogel said.

Semple turned and shambled out of the restaurant. They watched him go and then Miss Pink turned back to Vogel.

'What did she take with her?'

'Oh no! Not you too!'

'She was seen after she left your place. But no one knows why she left. If she didn't take her clothes she could have been forced to leave without warning – or she could have left Timothy's campsite in such a hurry that she didn't have time to come back to your place and pick up her possessions.'

'They're still at my place.' His eyes glazed. 'All her stuff –' He trailed off.

'Where did Timothy camp?'

'How would I know? In one of the canyons, I guess.'

'He packed up and left,' Lovejoy reminded Miss Pink. 'When you found the Jeep it was loaded, wasn't it?'

She nodded absently, her eyes on the screen door.

'Timothy was here for only eight days but during that time Joanne was ostensibly living with Vogel, and there was something going on between her and Hiram Wolf, and with Semple. How did she manage the logistics?'

Rose snorted. 'Logistics? How do they apply? Are you talking about arrangements, timing, stuff like that?'

'I'm after information.'

Still thirsty, Miss Pink was drinking beer in Rose's living room at the back of the hotel. The room faced east and through the open windows they could see the corral and the horses dozing in the balmy shade. The shadow of the Sierras reached almost to the top of the Rattlesnake Hills and the crests were glowing red-gold in the last of the light.

'Kind of time she liked – likes,' Rose observed dreamily. 'Me, too: warm and soft, and the dark coming. She wasn't a hooker, you know, whatever anyone says.'

'You're determined to convince me of that.'

Rose drained her beer and reached behind her to open the refrigerator. On the table in front of her were three empty cans; Miss Pink was drinking from a glass.

'You get women like her,' Rose said, popping a fresh can. 'She adores men, or should I say: adores having them around? And because she's so striking she can take her pick. Actually there was no one here good enough for Joanne.'

'Not Timothy?'

'He was all strung out: the drink problem, smoking. Joanne likes a drink, she hates smoking. They used to

99

fight over that; she'd move away when he lit up. Joanne's an extrovert: very young and out for a good time. Ask me, Timothy suited because he was good in the sack, and he was English, kinda familiar?'

'What was Vogel's attraction for her?'

'Basically security – until someone better came along. She met him on the road and shacked up with him because he was offered this job in a remote place, away from the authorities. She had no Permit to Stay, no green card – and no money. She wasn't bothered, except she didn't want to be deported. She loved the life here, said England was cold and drab. But she'd soon have found someone to marry her. She told me that.'

'Why didn't she get Vogel to marry her?'

'Hell, she could do better than that! Dogtown was just a staging post on the way to the coast. She wanted to be rich too; she's sick of roughing it – at least in winter-time – so she was going to try and get into the movies.'

'Had she come here from Texas?'

'*Texas*? She never mentioned it.'

'Someone said she met Vogel there.'

'I didn't know that. He's from Texas, of course; can't you tell by the twang?'

'I must have misheard something. Where do Semple and Wolf come into the picture, with Joanne?'

'They don't, not how you mean. Julius was terrified of her – and Hiram Wolf couldn't get anywhere. Hiram went to pieces when she was around and she treated him like she would a big dog. Exactly like one, I mean. She'd plant a kiss on his nose – she was tall enough – stroke his back . . . I was waiting for gas one time, Joanne in front of me at the pumps, and Hiram was talking to her and she looked up from filling the tank, saying something. He took a step towards her and I thought: Uh, uh, now what? and she said it: "Stay!" He stopped as if she'd hit him and she laughed and put the pump up and got behind the wheel and blew him a kiss. It was awful. I mean, it was deliberate, like a command to a dog. Lorraine in the office too. God, it was embarrassing. I didn't know how to face him, what to say. He knew I'd seen it all. Trivial you'd think, but it wasn't trivial. Fortunately he sloped off, back to the garage.'

'And Lorraine?'

'When I came to pay she was looking at a magazine; you'd never believe anything had happened.'

'Are you saying Joanne played with men?'

'I don't think she realised the effect she had on them. She'd be so used to it, never known any other reaction. Why, even the boys weren't immune: Earl and Verne – and I guess you've realised the relationship between them. Actually it's Earl liked her, but Verne was careful not to show any antagonism. I mean, with a girl like that, Earl could have gone off with her, it's not impossible is it? – what do they call it: ambidextrous? Anyway, Verne wouldn't care to upset Joanne, she could be very outspoken. But I never saw her tease either of the boys; she knew what's what.'

'In that case she did know what she was doing when she teased Hiram Wolf. And Julius – how did he react?'

'I said: scared stiff. Metaphorically he hid behind Charlotte, who's big enough, again metaphorically speaking.'

'What was it specifically that frightened Julius? You're not suggesting he thought she'd accost him in public, or come to the museum, make a scene perhaps?'

'Well, she visited . . . ' Rose gave the matter some thought. 'No, there's no way she'd attach herself, take the initiative; she didn't have to. But men are pretty stupid on the whole, aren't they? They misinterpret behaviour. I mean, to most guys, at least these out here in the sticks . . . If they weren't born in the sticks, they got that kind of mentality or they wouldn't gravitate to places like Dogtown: emotionally immature, unworldly, men like that, the way Joanne behaved was a kinda promise, an indication. For them she was flashing signals.' Miss Pink was silent. 'But she was – is very beautiful,' Rose insisted, as if that explained everything. 'You shoulda met her.'

'I may do yet.'

'You figure she'll be back? Never. She'll have learned a

lot from Timothy but she didn't need to learn much: just a bit of finesse is all. She's moved on.'

'What intrigues me is how everyone keeps dropping into the past tense when they talk about these two people.'

Rose shrugged and waved her beer, spilling some. 'Nine days' wonder. A bright spot in our lives. We'll never see them again 'cept on our television screens. Ships that pass in the night.'

'Why do you think the Jeep was sent over the edge?'

'Ah.' The exaggerated astonishment could be attributed to four beers. 'Now there you have me. The Jeep I can't explain. I'm aware that the inter – inference –' she was slurring her consonants, '– is that Joanne was – is responsible for Timothy's disappearance, and that she put the truck in the creek, but no one can tell me she would – what? Hit him over the head just because, fr'instance, she didn't like him smoking? She'd have packed her bags and left.'

'They could have quarrelled, come to blows and someone hit harder than he intended. An accident.'

'Come on! Over passive smoking?'

'No.'

'What then?'

'Over a man?'

# Chapter 10

'You been holding out on us. You never thought that was deer blood on Joanne.' Charlotte's hair, newly rinsed, flamed titian in the morning sun. Miss Pink had found her on the back stoop of the museum, scrubbing rust off an old pick with a wire brush. From her cabin across the yard came the sound of television voices. 'You're not interested in the Joplins,' she added calmly, busy with the brush.

'They're connected. Timothy was following their trail, Joanne left with Timothy.'

'I doubt he was bothered with the Joplins after he met Joanne; she was much more exciting than a bunch of old ghosts. Julius tells me you said they broke into a cabin up at Palmer Meadows.'

'Someone broke in, but it looks as if it was only one person: just one dirty plate and mug. And Joanne was on her own when she met the logger.'

'Did you think of it this way: they could have separated on top, in the forest, and Timothy got lost, but Joanne found her way to the cabin?'

'*Timothy* got lost?'

'Yes, it sounds unlikely. Sprained his ankle perhaps?'

'Then why didn't Joanne go back to look for him instead of abandoning him, never mentioning him?'

'But she did! She told the logger she was with a man who threw her out of a truck, told her to walk –'

'That was the story about the deer, which can't be true, given Timothy's good manners.'

'That's so, she had to say something to account for the blood. Maybe she took up with someone else, after Timothy, and that guy threw her out of a truck, wouldn't pay her price, hit her, gave her a bloody nose?' Miss Pink was frowning. Charlotte stood up. 'Why are we talking about a slut on a lovely morning like this? Come and have a coffee.'

Miss Pink followed her across the yard to the cabin where all the doors and windows were open to the air. The interior smelled of lemons. In the living room people in gaudy evening clothes chattered on the television screen. Charlotte switched off the sound. Miss Pink sat on a sofa and surveyed her surroundings. There were a few books but the walls were virtually covered with pictures, Remington and Russell prints of the Old West: bucking broncos, taut-roped steers, arroyos, buttes, sunsets, tanned cowhands sprawled round camp-fires. The stuffed furniture sported flouncy chintz, and there were lace curtains at the windows, tastefully draped, secured by bows. Everything was as clean as it could be in this country where dust rose in clouds behind every vehicle.

Charlotte brought coffee and brownies on a plastic tray. 'Timothy's alive and well –' she began comfortably, but checked herself. 'He's alive; he may not be well. How can anyone figure what an alcoholic will do? A man who's just plain drunk is unpredictable, but one like Timothy, comes off the wagon – there's no reason, no logic behind his actions at all. You can't say: he'd have done this, he wouldn't have done that; he wouldn't have got lost, they should have come down together. He could do something quite wild, the sort of thing would never occur to normal people. And when he surfaces he could be stupefied, then full of guilt, wallowing – he'd be capable of anything. And then Joanne's reaction to him would appear irrational.'

Miss Pink was astonished. 'I never thought of it that way, not following through to that extent.' She regarded her hostess intently. '*Did* he confide in you? You said he didn't, but were you keeping something from me? Was he drinking while he was here?'

'Not that I know of, and I didn't keep any facts from you, just, you know, feelings. He was pretty tense: one of the reasons I thought Joanne'd be good for him. Man of his age, falling heavily for a girl, particularly one as uninhibited as Joanne, he might relax some. She'd be therapy for him.'

'You'd hardly have a feeling about that,' Miss Pink observed, smiling. 'You make it sound more like fact. By feeling, did you mean something – ominous?'

'Before he met Joanne he was all screwed up: bothered about where he was going – literally too. Which canyon did the Joplins go up? Rose Baggott says it's Breakneck, Fortune says it's Danger to keep him out of Crazy Mule; Vogel says it was anywhere else but Danger because he don't want anyone round that ranch –'

'Why not?'

'Guys like Brett Vogel always have something to hide. Now what did I say?'

'What do you know about his employer?'

'Granville Green? He traces old pioneer trails. It's his hobby. You'll meet him, you stay around. They'll be here in a few days, following the Joplins. Granville's retired from the Marines. He's got loads of money, lives in St Joseph, Missouri, but he's moving out here, probably next spring. He built the ranch house for retirement, it's not a hunting cabin. Why are you interested in Granville?'

'I'd like to meet him. If I'm to take over Timothy's book, I'm interested in anyone who can tell me more about the Joplins.'

'I doubt he can tell you anything we don't know.' Charlotte was affronted.

'It's another angle. Tell me, was Joanne in Texas before she came here?'

Charlotte thought about this. 'She didn't say. She could have been. What makes it important?'

'I wondered where she met Vogel – and incidentally, why she teamed up with him in the first place.' Miss Pink looked worried. 'I'm not altogether happy about those two. As you say, people hide in the canyons. Asa Fortune is a likely recluse; he has a hermit's attitude towards authority, and blatant hostility towards invaders of his territory, to people who may not be well-disposed towards wild animals. Asa is a type. But Vogel? He's not a wilderness man.'

'Don't ask questions.'

'Is that a warning?'

Charlotte nodded solemnly. 'It's all right here –' She pondered that. 'Yes, Dogtown's safe, but don't ask questions of Brett Vogel. You saw how he was with Julius yesterday. That man's violent.'

'What does he do when he goes away? Where does he go?'

'Look –' Charlotte lowered her voice, '– the road out to the highway doesn't come through here. In fact, if you're not looking that way you can't see headlights at night. We don't look, know what I mean?'

Miss Pink raised an eyebrow. 'But if he's into something illegal, Joanne had to be in it too. And where does that put Timothy?'

'Timothy,' Charlotte repeated heavily, 'Timothy was asking questions.'


'For God's sake, Melinda, James is climbing up the wall! Where are you phoning from? Can you – er –' Martin Jenks trailed off in embarrassment.

Miss Pink was soothing. 'I'm calling from the airfield at Endeavor. I expressed a letter to you today with the details, but this is just for my benefit. Has James heard anything from Timothy?'

'No, nothing. And you?'

'The same. Consensus is that he's on the binge, with a lady.'

'What do you think?'

'It's the obvious explanation.' There was a pause. 'I'll track him down,' she said airily. 'As I said: the details are in my letter. I'll be in touch. 'Bye.'

In London her agent replaced the receiver and stared at it. She was still bothered about open lines so why had she rung? Who had given whom information? She had initiated the conversation and she'd had only one question . . . she'd wanted to know if Timothy had communicated with Dorset.

That meant she hadn't found him, was probably no further forward. Did an airfield have any significance, he wondered. Morosely he started to dial Dorset's number.

Back in Endeavor Miss Pink followed a grizzled man in jeans and a ball cap to a battered Cessna. He helped her aboard and they took off to trundle over the desert at a speed that had her reflecting that at this rate it would take her most of the day to cross four states. But in the event it was the familiar problem of a few miles at either end of a journey, whether you did it by road or in an air taxi. On the long hop she flew so high that all colour was lost in space and the deserts were merely a pale floor smudged intermittently by crops in the irrigated areas. Rivers, the Colorado and the Rio Grande, didn't show at all where they weren't lined with trees.

Her jet landed at El Paso and she took another little aeroplane and chugged on across Texas to come down in a bumpy field among strange and spiky yucca. Beyond a fence were humped bulls in shades of roan, pink and blue. There was no sign of a town. A man in a shack telephoned for a car which arrived half an hour later: a dusty old Cadillac. The driver was a Mexican boy whose English was so poor that beyond giving him her destination she made no attempt to converse.

The town of Seeping Springs was hidden in a dip in the ground. As they approached she saw one wide street running to a single set of traffic lights then rising, narrowing to an arrow's point that was lost in the distant hills. She felt a twinge of compassion for this tiny outpost of civilisation. What did people *do* here?

There was a library, a courthouse with white palings, a post office. There was the usual sprawl of fast food joints, gas stations, stores, a laundromat, while side-streets gave glimpses of adobe houses under shade trees. The driver stopped. 'Thunderbird,' he said.

The motel could have done with a coat of paint. On a motheaten patch of astro-turf a large metal and plastic bird was outlined in broken neon. There was an open courtyard: the familiar caravanserai with cell-like rooms on three sides, and in the centre a small pool where three heads, seemingly disembodied under hats, were motionless on the surface of the water. Three pairs of eyes in leathery faces observed Miss Pink dismiss her taxi and enter the office.

The receptionist was fat, middle-aged and vivacious, with a ruffle perm designed for a teenager. Miss Pink registered, using the office pen that was stamped 'Thunderbird Motel, 190 Main Street, Seeping Springs, Texas'. She gave the address of her New York agent and when the woman remarked on this in conjunction with an English accent, explained that she was a writer.

'You got company. Mrs Harshberg's a writer. Her in the pool.' Miss Pink smiled and made her way to her room, wishing the bathers good afternoon as she passed. Smiles flickered under hat brims; someone called out that she should join them.

She showered and emerged from her room wearing a black regulation swimsuit. As she lowered herself into the water, her face lit up with pleasure. Seeping Springs was hot but the pool was only warm. She gave them her name, said she came from London and left the rest to them. The inquisition commenced.

No, she was not on holiday, she told them; she was by way of being a writer. The questioning was checked there while Dulcie and Jan informed her that Mrs Harshberg – Ingrid – was a published author, and Ingrid explained that she was a historian and had written the history of her home-town: Bluewater, Minnesota. She was now engaged on a history of her late husband's family. Miss Pink listened, fascinated, and confessed that she hadn't the mental capacity for research; she wrote light romances. Everyone assured her that they read little else and, after a small pause, Dulcie asked politely where she set her stories.

'That's why I'm here!' Miss Pink beamed. 'A new departure: America. It was my agent's suggestion, but I'm loving every minute. In fact, I can't decide where to locate the next book; it's all so exciting, isn't it?' They nodded acquiescence, waiting to see what made America exciting. 'One feels born again,' Miss Pink enthused, 'as an author, I mean.' Her voice dropped. 'I've even had the thought, the urge to turn to crime.'

Water swirled. There were shaky smiles. Miss Pink added quickly: 'Like Agatha Christie?'

'Oh, Agatha Christie!' Relief: she wasn't mad, they'd misunderstood.

'I always thought I should try my hand at a mystery,' Ingrid said.

Miss Pink turned to her, a kindred spirit. 'There's so much material!' She shuddered. 'Too much. The rising crime rate –'

They burst into speech. 'Mugging seniors!'

'Your home isn't safe, leave it for a few hours –'

'– rape –'

'I'm terrified every time someone overtakes me on the interstate. I never look 'case I'm looking down the barrel of a gun. I expect it all the time.'

'Not in Texas,' Miss Pink said indulgently. They stared. 'Is it as bad here as elsewhere?' The innocent question of the English tourist. 'You're not suggesting it would be unsafe to walk through Seeping Springs after dark?'

'Oh, no!'

'That's why we winter here –'

'This is Slumberville –'

'Well –' Ingrid had a treacly voice, portentous. It stopped them in their tracks. 'We're not far from the border,' she said meaningly.

Miss Pink became chatty. 'I was quite sure my driver was under age to be driving a taxi, and he was very dark and his English was poor. I put him down as a Mexican.'

'Wetback,' Ingrid said. 'Illegal alien. It'd be a relative's cab and they'd risk letting him go out to the airport just, probably knew the police were someplace else. They all listen to the police waveband. It was safe for the kid to pick you up.'

'Well, no harm done.' Miss Pink was cheerful. 'Nothing sinister about the boy. I'd have no qualms about riding with him, even at night.' This was met by silence, the words hanging in the air.

'I wouldn't do that,' Jan said at length, and looked at her companions. Dulcie pursed her lips, Ingrid gave a reptilean grin. 'No one goes anywhere at night this close to the border,' she said. 'Even driving your own vehicle. It's like a voluntary curfew.'

'No one except the Rangers,' Dulcie amended.

'And the DEA,' put in Jan. 'Not forgetting the Border Patrol.'

'And the rest,' Ingrid said darkly.

'I'm not with you.' Miss Pink looked from one to the other.

'Texas Rangers,' Ingrid explained. 'They're the ones concerned with serious crime hereabouts. And officers of the Drug Enforcement Administration.'

'Ah, drugs. Of course. We're that near the border. You mean people bring them across in vehicles at night? I thought boats and planes were used for that kind of traffic.'

'They use every way they can,' Ingrid said. 'There was a good thing going across the Rio Grande, people bringing it over on mules. There's no proper border along the river, you know, and on the other side it's third-world stuff. You wouldn't believe it 'less you've been there. The river's the actual border but it's so shallow you can wade it at the fords. You could drive a truck across: four-wheel drive, but they don't do that because then you got to cross the mountains and deserts. They use mules. Come over at night, lay up in the hills, go on next day to rendezvous with trucks: old pick-ups, campers, cars, you name it.'

'It sounds almost too easy. Why aren't they caught?'

'They are, occasionally, but it's only the couriers get caught, the little men, bottom of the heap. The men at the top are never at risk; they just start up again someplace else. Losing the occasional courier goes with the territory. Like you said, there are boats and planes, and it's one hell of a long border. California and Arizona they got wire but there are gaps in the wire all the way across Arizona – and hell! what are wire-cutters for? But here there's not even wire. The drugs barons have the border parcelled up, like you rent a stretch on a trout stream.'

'Fascinating,' breathed Miss Pink. 'When the couriers are caught, do they talk?'

'Not often. Their families are looked after while they're inside and they're well-paid anyways. They save their money. The big men don't employ guys who drink, splash money around. It pays a courier to stay loyal.'

'So how do they get caught?'

'Why, on the road: spot checks. There are patrols all through the night. Stop a car, search it: kilos of cocaine in the trunk.'

'Cocaine?'

'Well, heroin, marijuana, you name it. Drugs are part of life down here.' And with that Ingrid reverted to her historical works. After a discreet interval Miss Pink steered the conversation back to herself: 'I've been given the name of an author in this region who writes light fiction: Emily Smallwood. Does the name mean anything to you?' They shook their heads, baffled. 'Married to a man who writes Westerns: Brett Vogel?'

They were annoyed that there should be local celebrities of whom they hadn't heard. They had been wintering here for years; three widows, they had a possessive feeling for Seeping Springs but the name Brett Vogel meant nothing to them, nor that of Joanne Emmett which Miss Pink dropped delicately as another person she might look up while in the area. Nor did those names mean anything to the receptionist when Miss Pink wandered into the office in a search for postcards. She did elicit the information that she was the only English person to have stayed at the Thunderbird this year and she retired to her room well pleased with the way things were going. She now knew whom she had to find in the morning, and she had her guidelines for the interview.

★

'The idea is to collect enough material for my producer to form a judgement. You could say I'm a kind of scout, looking to see if it's worth bringing in a camera team.'

'So what exactly brings you to Seeping Springs?' asked the Texas Ranger.

She had run him to earth in a kind of prefabricated office on the edge of town. Rod Larsen was a portly, grizzled fellow edging towards retirement and predictably curious at the idea of an elderly spinster researching for a television documentary on cross-border crime in West Texas.

'I was available,' she said, wilfully misunderstanding him, 'and it means only a couple of days away from my travel book.' She had told him she was following the California Trail.

'I meant why Seeping Springs? Why not Presidio or Brownsville?'

She blinked. 'I didn't ask them. It would have been a tip no doubt, a telephone call from a stringer? No, not from Seeping Springs. I expect some BBC journalist in Dallas or Houston saw a clipping. About yourself perhaps? You must make the headlines often enough.'

'More than that.' He looked smug, leaning back in his chair, relaxing. 'So how're you going to go about this?'

'If you have no objection I'll take notes – just facts, you know, and statistics. They're always impressive. In travel writing, for instance, one doesn't say it's cold – that's a value judgement; you say it's fifty below, and everyone knows what you mean.'

'I like it. We don't deal in value judgements here neither. What kind of facts?'

'At the Thunderbird they gave me masses of information – gossip, I should say –'

'Who were you talking to?' ·

'Some widowed ladies – snowbirds, is that the term? Mrs Harshberg is a historian from Minnesota, spends the winter in Texas. They told me cocaine and marijuana comes across the river on pack trains that meet up with trucks on this side.'

'Old ladies' gossip.'

'That's what I thought.' She looked rueful. 'It made an exciting story though, from my point of view.'

'They got it wrong about cocaine. It's mostly marijuana here, some heroin, no coke. But it's exciting enough.' He was grim. 'The Drug Enforcement people lost one of their officers a while back when a load was coming across the river at night. They don't use that run no longer, but they'll be back, soon as they figure the crossing's safe again.'

'You can't patrol the whole border.'

'If we could, how do we reach the planes? There are landing strips in the Mexican mountains and those little planes can land on a sixpence, Vietnam vets piloting them, and they can fly! On this side of the river the spreads are so big a plane can touch down, drop his load and be away before anyone on the ranch is the wiser. The guys on the ground, they use pie pans and charcoal fuel for landing lights. Or they hack out their own landing-strips back in the hills, cut down the brush so the wings don't touch. The strip's invisible 'cept from the air. They drive goats across to cover the wheel marks. We can still find 'em though.' He grinned. 'Narcotics was waiting one time when a plane come down, moved in while the prop was still turning. The pilot, normally he stays inside ready to goose it if there's an emergency. But this guy didn't, he was snorting cocaine and when the agents moved in he went for his gun but the seats had been pushed forward, make room for the load, they had so much. Couldn't find his pistol so he ran: straight into the prop. He was decapitated.' Miss Pink swallowed. 'Sorta thing your producer might go for?' he asked.

'You know it's more than they could use.' She was reproving. 'Can you give me some statistics?'

'Why not? It's estimated that twenty-five per cent of air traffic through here is carrying illegal cargo. A Cessna can carry six to eight hundred pounds of drugs. The Cessna 210 has a range of around nine hundred miles. They'll pay fifty thousand dollars for rent of an airstrip. Narcotics reckon to catch one in ten runners.'

'Why don't they catch more?'

'Someone has to talk, and mostly they don't. Terror keeps them quiet but sometimes, for one reason or another – greed, revenge, just for the hell of it – a guy will inform. We depend on informants in this business.'

'And I suppose you might suggest immunity if they turned to informing.' She was guileless.

'They can be turned round.'

'They continue to work for the organisation?'

'You got it. Nearly all our arrests are based on information received.'

'It must be hideously dangerous for the men concerned.'

'It's all of that. If an informant's caught, the penalty is hanging by barbed wire.' If he was trying to shock her he'd succeeded. 'They're tortured first,' he went on. 'Not too much, or they wouldn't appreciate the points of the hanging.' And he laughed at what was no doubt an old joke.

She closed her eyes. 'How?' she asked.

'Burning's the method of choice. No equipment needed, just cigarettes.'

'My God!'

'It's effective. As a deterrent. Other informants go to ground after a wire-hanging. Some disappear, vanish into thin air. There was a hanging back in the spring on this side of the river. Usually they're on the other side. This was a warning to an Anglo operating on the American bank and the young fellow I was after just faded away two or three days after the body was found. Some snowbirds discovered it. They use some hot springs down on the river-bank, soak in 'em, do their arthritis a power of good. They saw this body hanging from a cottonwood soon as they come down one morning.'

'Are you telling me that a white man was tortured and hanged in barbed wire, in Texas?' She considered this. 'That could have been what my producer saw in a newspaper, or heard about.'

'It didn't make the media, not the wire bit, or the torture, and the snowbirds wouldn't talk, not if they wanted to keep coming down here for the winter: "Hear all, see all . . . " You know how it goes. It was in the local paper but just as an Hispanic found hanged. He wasn't white. I was interested in the Anglo, the one who disappeared. He used to stay at the Thunderbird when he came by.'

'Brett Vogel,' Miss Pink murmured.

'What was that, ma'am?'

'Is there a local Narcotics agent called Brett Vogel?'

'Not in my time. I never heard the name.'

'My mistake. He must be in California. No matter. About this informant of yours, the one who disappeared –'

'He wasn't an informant yet. I was working on him, on the quiet: slip away, have a few beers with him after dark, blinds drawn, feeling him out. It's a delicate business, trying to turn them around.'

'Evidently he was about to "come over" – is that the term? – or he wouldn't have run. Perhaps he thought he'd been seen with you. Would a man like that set up in business elsewhere?'

'You mean, try to set up his own operation? He couldn't do it nowhere along the border. Word would have gone out all the way from the Gulf to the coast. No one would employ him, no one would allow him to operate; he wouldn't *dare*. If he's still operating it's in another country, like Burma, and even there he's going under a different name. For my money he's working some other kinda scam where he's never likely to meet someone who knew him when he was running drugs.'

'That's a good point.' Her pen poised, Miss Pink approved the change of direction. 'What else goes on here besides the drugs traffic?'

'Illegal aliens: "wetbacks" we call 'em. Then there's artefacts, old Indian stuff comes across, artwork, jewellery, that kinda thing. There's wildlife.'

'I mean smuggling.'

'Yes, wildlife. Rarities like tarantulas, Gila monsters, some

115

kinds of snakes, tropical birds – not them so much, they take up a lot of room – you name it, if the traffic's illegal and valuable, someone's going to smuggle it.'

As her jet levelled out above the Sonora Desert Miss Pink wondered if she should have abandoned the disguise of television researcher, should have taken Rod Larsen into her confidence and asked him for a description of the drugs runner who had stayed at the Thunderbird. Or for that matter have asked the question of the ruffle-permed receptionist, even the widows, who might have been there last April. But there was no way she could have obtained this information without implying that she knew the man, and even if she could withstand the consequent barrage of questions, could lie effectively, Larsen might trace her back to Dogtown. And whatever scam Vogel was engaged in now, if he *were* the runner who had vanished from the Thunderbird, even if his present scam involved heroin, she had to think again before she would expose him to the fate that had overtaken the Mexican informant. If the authorities got on his trail, in no time the criminals would follow. No way, she thought, regarding the pen that she had found in the glove compartment of the Jeep. Only three of the people involved in this business could be associated with that pen and two of them were English, and no English people had stayed at the Thunderbird this year before her own arrival.

# Chapter 11

Not a light showed on the scarp of the Sierras when Miss Pink turned off the highway and .ook the road through the Rattlesnake Hills. As she approached Dogtown her sense of frustration, increasing as she flew westward, became overwhelming. She knew the cause; so far as Timothy was concerned she felt that Vogel could at least point her in the right direction, but at worst she didn't want him to. The same fate might overtake her as had overtaken Timothy, and who knew what had happened to him? To tackle Vogel on her own was out of the question, and if she were to ask someone from Dogtown to accompany her when she did so, what right did she have to put other people at risk? Nevertheless she was playing with the idea of a suitable candidate when the lights of Dogtown appeared through the trees.

There was something odd about the ghost town tonight, something about the lights. She peered through the windscreen; how could lights be different? And then she realised that there were more of them, and the increased illumination came from lights on tall poles at the back of the Red Queen where there was a car park, or rather, a stretch of desert, hitherto unlit because no one used it. Now, like new houses erected overnight, white walls gleamed where two RVs – recreational vehicles the size of coaches – were drawn up side by side. She glimpsed Jeeps, and a strange Toyota was parked in front of the restaurant.

The Grand Imperial's foyer was dimly lit and there was no sign of Rose. She left the Cherokee outside her cabin and walked to the Red Queen. She was extraordinarily tired and her mind was still involved with the problem of forcing

Vogel to reveal what he knew of Timothy's movements. Because of her preoccupation she was momentarily bewildered at the transformation of the restaurant. There were so many people inside and they were so lively that no one noticed her entrance. It wasn't until Lovejoy saw her and shouted a welcome that the other occupants were aware of her arrival.

The bar was crowded. There was Rose asking if she'd had a good time, and Lovejoy, wielding a cocktail shaker and calling: 'You look as if you could do with one of these, ma'am!'

Full of *joie de vivre* Rose performed the introductions. There were three strange couples. Miss Pink had an impression of tall beaming men and wives with smooth skins and immaculate coiffures. The names passed her by, except one, Granville Green: a broad-shouldered, well-proportioned fellow whose frame had become comfortably padded in middle age, and small wonder. Lovejoy was filling glasses and to judge by their gaiety it was by no means for the first time. Miss Pink found one in her hand and tasted it warily. It was delicious.

'We've gone all sophisticated,' Rose said, eyeing her. 'The circus has come to town. Didn't you have a sidecar before?'

'Is that what it is? I haven't. Is it Cointreau?'

'Cointreau, brandy, lemon,' Green informed her. 'So you're the lady is writing a book about the Joplins.'

'That's the idea. Did you meet my predecessor, Timothy Argent?'

'No, we just arrived. Rose has been telling us all about it. So you figure he's holed up with that gorgeous lady somewhere on the coast?'

She hesitated, and a man with keen eyes behind aviator spectacles asked: 'What's the position now? Will the publishers take him to court to recover their advance?'

'My husband writes,' explained a blonde in a slubbed-cotton pants suit. '*Graves Along the Oregon Trail* by Gene Bader?'

'Really? Fascinating. In practice I never heard of publishers suing in such circumstances.' Miss Pink smiled, feeling the sidecar start to soften muscles that had been stiff with strain. 'I always meet my deadlines,' she went on, 'so it's something I'm not familiar with. The publisher covered his options: getting me to take over the Joplin book.' A thought struck her, the kind of enlightened flash that occurs when the first drink stimulates the brain and before a second overwhelms it. 'Which canyon are you going up?' she asked Green.

'Someone will be in each one, but me, I'm concentrating on Breakneck. That's the crucial one.'

'Danger Canyon,' intoned the third man, the only person there who wasn't overweight. He was bald, with an egg-shaped skull and a stubbly white beard that did little more than follow the line of his jaw and chin.

'I'm not arguing, Marsh,' Green said, as if this was an old bone of contention. 'We got plenty of time; we'll try 'em all, even Crazy Mule.'

'We'll have to watch out for Asa,' someone said.

'Asa's all right. Wait till he sees what we brought him. We bring him a few delicacies and some clothes always,' he told Miss Pink.

'How do you travel in the mountains?' she asked. 'Those are your RVs out there? Don't you own the ranch house in Danger Canyon?'

'The RVs belong to these.' Green indicated the other couples. 'Lucy and me, we came in a Land Cruiser: the Toyota that's outside. We enjoyed their hospitality all the way from the Missouri, now they can use my place. On the trail, like here in the mountains, we use four-wheel drives. These guys towed Jeeps behind their RVs. Rose says you been everywhere, ma'am, on horseback too.'

'Well, not up to Deadboy.' She was diffident. 'There's a locked gate.'

'You can go up that trail any time you want. Brett Vogel would have given you the key if you'd asked.'

'I'll take you up to Deadboy Pass,' said the bald man, Marsh – Beck? 'Rose'll rent us a coupla horses.'

'Did you figure out how the Joplins went from Breakneck?' Green asked Miss Pink, treating her as an equal.

'No. When you're alone, you're concerned not to get lost, so although I've been all the way to Credit, I was paying more attention to my own safety than to the Joplins' route. In this kind of country I prefer company. There's not much you can do on your own.'

'You must join us.' Green was expansive. 'It's not right, a lady travelling alone. Of course, that's if you have no objection.' It was plain he didn't expect any.

'Oh, not at all. How kind. I'd be delighted.'

'That's settled then. How about another round of drinks, Earl?'

Miss Pink's eyes widened, only fractionally, but Lucy Green caught the look and said quietly: 'It's all right, we're not going up the canyon tonight. We're staying with Gene and Carol. The Baders,' she added kindly. 'You won't have caught all our names.'

Miss Pink saw that she was going to be treated like a fragile old soul but she'd asked for it. She made an attempt to capitalise on it before Lucy should recall that she'd been in the Sierras alone, and on horseback. She said wistfully: 'If I had a house in one of these canyons, particularly one like yours, I couldn't wait to get to it.'

'It's difficult to heat. It's a big place inside and it's not properly insulated, not how we insulate homes in the Midwest. We called Brett from Denver but he's not there – either that or he's not answering the phone. The beds will be cold and damp. I wanted him to turn the heating up, make sure the water's running. Granville's hopping mad. We don't expect them both to be there all the time, but the reason we employed two people was there'd always be one of them around, particularly this time of year, hunting season coming up. But no way am I walking into that cold house tonight; we'll go up tomorrow, get the place properly aired out and the heating going, have a nice cosy evening by a wood fire.'

'I suppose in the usual way Joanne would be there if Vogel was away,' Miss Pink observed.

'I told you, didn't I?' Carol Bader broke in, addressing Lucy. 'Didn't I tell you when you said you'd employed a young couple not even married: you got no security there, I said; one of them's going to split eventually if they don't go off together – and what are they going to take with them? You've got some nice things in that house, Lucy; there's two Navajo blankets for a start.'

'Not things I'm fond of – and don't tell me, tell Granville; he picked them up, he engaged them. I never knew anything till he came back from El Paso that time, said he'd sent them to the ranch as caretakers. I said then, didn't they have references, but you know Granville, said the guy was all right.' She turned to Miss Pink. 'Just because he was an officer in the Marines, he thinks he knows men.'

'Vogel might have been all right in the normal way,' Miss Pink mused, 'but losing his girlfriend in that fashion could have knocked him sideways. How did your husband run into them?'

'He was in El Paso in April and he came home through New Mexico, stayed a night at Carlsbad. That's where he met Brett and Joanne. He took a shine to them.' Her tone sharpened. 'I never saw her, but he said Joanne was a very striking lady, didn't you, hon?'

'What's that, sweetie?'

'Joanne Emmett. Beautiful, you said.'

'Very beautiful. Very young. Too young for an old man.' He grinned and moved towards them.

'Tell Miss Pink how you met them.'

'How? Nothing to it. Met them when I was having a drink after dinner in Carlsbad someplace – the Ramada, was it? Holiday Inn, whatever. We got talking and they were looking for work and I wanted someone to look after the ranch until we move in next year; too much of a temptation for vandals, poachers, people like that.'

Miss Pink looked shocked. 'I can't imagine anyone in England engaging a couple to caretake a nice house without asking to see their references first.'

'I had a long talk with the guy. He's a Vietnam vet, had a bad war, couldn't settle since he came home, you know how it is, your soldiers have problems too, I hear, like in Ireland? I felt I'd like to give him a chance and –' he looked at the women with a kind of helplessness, '– she, well, you'd have had to see her. You couldn't say no to Joanne.'

'Really.' Lucy's eyebrows rose in a travesty of astonishment. She turned to Miss Pink. 'Did you meet this paragon?'

'No. I'm hoping to. She sounds too good to be true.'

'Don't you believe it.' Rose approached nursing a full cocktail glass. '*Femme fatale*, that's what Joanne is. Do you notice how men who associate with her disappear?'

'Not my man,' Lucy said firmly, slipping her arm through her husband's. 'In any case, she's disappeared too.'

'And Brett hasn't disappeared,' Green said. 'He's just not there at the moment.'

The kitchen door opened to admit Verne Blair who seemed to take real pleasure at seeing Miss Pink again. 'You were away,' he said, as if he'd forgotten.

'Problems, problems,' she murmured. 'I had to stay overnight. Timothy left a troubled wake behind him. Taking over someone else's book isn't easy. However, I've got my business done –' she was talking fast to forestall questions and was glad to see no one was interested in where she was last night. 'What do you propose to do tomorrow?' she asked Green brightly.

'I'll leave Lucy to open the house and I'm going up Breakneck. I need to work out how the trail went from the pass to Credit.'

'Are you working solely from Permelia's diary or has something new come to light?'

Several people started to talk at once and the conversation became heated. She listened with apparent interest but increasing fatigue and after a while, pleading the need for an early night, she slipped away to her cabin.

★

122

She slept for nine hours and, judging by the golden silence enveloping Dogtown when she crossed the road for breakfast next morning, she and Lovejoy were the only people out of their beds. 'What time did the party break up?' she asked as he served her waffles.

'We didn't get to bed till late. Charlotte and Julius came over after you left. They were asking after you, wanting to know where you were night before last.'

'I warned Rose I'd probably spend the night at Endeavor.'

'Charlotte was worried you could have met with an accident when you didn't show. You can't blame her with what's been happening here, and the places you go alone. I'm glad you've decided to go with Granville and the rest of them. They'll take care of you.'

She was on her third cup of coffee when Green came in, looking raddled in the morning light but sounding hearty enough. The men were going up to the house, he told her; was she ready? She collected a packed lunch from the kitchen and, driving her own vehicle, followed the big Toyota out of Dogtown.

It was another glorious day, with a nip in the air where the sun had not yet penetrated. Fallen leaves were outlined with frost and some of the cottonwoods were starting to turn yellow. It was an exciting morning with a hint of danger: the night had been cold and winter was on the way. Miss Pink, not troubling to keep up with the Toyota, was aware of an odd resistance in herself, as if she were refusing to become involved with natural forces. Could this be because it was essential that her mind be blank in preparation for the confrontation ahead, a confrontation that might resolve the problems that had occupied her last evening? For the basic problem – of how to approach Brett Vogel – had been solved. Even if he were away from the ranch he would be back within a day or two; he always was. She could wait, exploring with the trail buffs, and the hiatus could be of benefit, or so she rationalised. She needed time to explain, to take Green into her confidence. He should know what she was about when she questioned

Vogel, for question him she would; she had slept on it and now there was no doubt in her mind that he'd had a hand in Timothy's disappearance.

She crossed the cattle-grid and the meadow opened before her, the huge chestnut-coloured house commanding the approach. The Toyota was at the back of the building, beside a pick-up which she regarded without expression; Vogel was back.

Bader and Beck were standing by the Toyota. She climbed down as Green emerged from the cabin. 'He doesn't mean to be away long,' he said. 'There's food in the fridge.'

'He's not away.' Miss Pink was bewildered. 'He wouldn't go away on foot.' She indicated the pick-up.

'That's not his truck.'

'It's the one he's been driving.'

'OK, so he's re-licensed it; he had Texas plates when I met him.' Green looked more closely. 'Not the same truck either. He had a Chevvy at Carlsbad too, but it was in better shape than this heap. Funny thing, exchange for something not so good.'

'Perhaps he didn't have a lot of choice, and maybe he needed California plates in a hurry.'

He looked at her sharply. Bader said: 'He has to be somewhere close if this is his vehicle.'

Green walked away a few steps and bawled: 'Vogel!'

'He'd have heard us arrive,' Beck pointed out, but he leaned in the pick-up and sounded the horn.

'May I go inside his cabin?' Miss Pink asked.

'Do,' Green told her. 'But there's no clue as to – What's on your mind?'

'Nothing. My mind is blank, except –' as he followed her through the door, '– except to wonder which is more likely: that he left on foot, or someone called for him?' Or that he's still around? was a third question, unvoiced.

She surveyed the cabin which at first sight held nothing remarkable. There was no sign of a woman's presence but there were signs of recent occupation. A chair was pushed back from the table, on the surface of which was a mug half full of a greyish liquid, and a copy of the magazine *Guns and Ammo* – open as if someone had been reading an article, had pushed his chair back and walked away. Beside the magazine was a cheap table lamp and a telephone.

The kitchen alcove was in a corner, with plates, mugs, cutlery and saucepans, all clean, drained dry, on a plastic tray. The refrigerator contained two quarts of milk, one part-used, butter, eggs, bacon, bread, ground coffee in a tin and a parcel of ground beef. There were two television dinners in the freezer compartment.

'The bed's not been slept in,' Bader said, emerging from the bedroom.

Beck said, licking his finger warily: 'That's coffee in the mug. Know what this reminds me of? That ship they found floating in the middle of the ocean someplace, the *Marie Celeste*.'

'*Mary*,' Green said. 'It was the *Mary Celeste*. People always get it wrong.'

Miss Pink moved past him and entered the bedroom. There was a double bed with pillows side by side. She peeled back the tufted blue quilt to reveal fleecy blankets and sheets that, if not freshly laundered, were no worse than one might expect to find in bachelor quarters.

'Hell!' Green exclaimed behind her. 'This must be Joanne's stuff.' He'd pulled back a curtain to expose jeans on hangers, and a number of blouses that looked limp and tawdry without a body to fill them out, more like abandoned rags than adornment for what everyone agreed was a lovely girl. There was an Afghan coat of the type that was in fashion in the seventies, and two shabby pairs of running shoes.

'No wonder she didn't take this lot with her,' Green said, with mild contempt. 'Brett's a bit better off. Two new chamois shirts here – er – do you think you should –?' Miss Pink had pulled out the top drawer in a chest of drawers.

Inside there was clean underwear: bras and silk camisoles; there was make-up – and a two-ounce flaçon, almost full, of Chanel No 19.

'She left in a hurry,' Beck said at her elbow.

'I don't think we should be looking at her personal possessions.' Green was uneasy, edging towards the door.

'I do.' Miss Pink went back to the living room. 'I don't like this.' She was terse. 'I don't like any of it.' She was looking at the windows, one in the back wall, two in the front. They were sash windows, draped with layers of nylon net. Those in front were screened but not the one in the rear wall. 'He didn't have a dog?' she asked, adding *sotto voce*: 'No, he wouldn't have a dog. We have to look for him.'

'We'll shout –'

'You've done that. If he's near, he can't hear you.'

'Oh, I see!' Bader seemed relieved. 'You mean you figure he's had an accident, like a stroke?'

'An accident of some kind.'

Outside the cabin the men hovered uncertainly and she experienced a return of that peculiar resistance to the bright morning, but to them she merely looked stern, determined. This was Green's property and Vogel was his employee but he seemed not to know what to do next. 'What was that about a dog?' he asked.

'A dog might help us find him.'

'He didn't have one. Of course he might have acquired one since.'

They searched the outbuildings: a barn with a loft for hay, stabling and a tack-room below. There were two smaller buildings but all were new and as yet uncluttered with the kind of junk that, over the decades, finds its way into such places, and they were soon searched. There was no dog, not even a cat, and nothing untoward except a faint smell. Miss Pink remarked on it.

'That'll be the timber.' Green was casual, preoccupied. 'Planks drying out, probably not seasoned as well as they should have been.'

'That's not wood,' Bader said. 'It's more like something in a zoo, an animal smell. It's sour.'

'Dead rat,' Beck put in. 'Vogel's laid down poison.'

'It's nothing important.' Green turned and walked out

into the sunshine. He caught Miss Pink's eye. 'Vogel isn't here, is what I mean. You suggested this, ma'am, looking for him. Where would you start?' Under the facetiousness he was at a loss.

She looked down the gentle incline of the meadow. 'Let's assume he walked into the forest. How many trails lead out of this meadow apart from the access from Malachite Canyon, and the route to Deadboy?'

'I don't know of any more, only game trails. Perhaps we should look at the Deadboy route; it seems the obvious answer. I'll get the key to the gate.'

He went into the cabin and reappeared almost immediately. 'I think we got it,' he said grimly. 'The key's gone. There's a board —' But Miss Pink had stepped inside and was studying a pegboard on the wall. There were a number of keys, all labelled.

'Is anything else missing?'

He looked carefully, turning the labels: 'House: front door, back; cabin, big barn . . . Not so far's I can recall. Just the one to the forest gate.'

He walked out to the Toyota. 'Don't take it!' Miss Pink was sharp. 'We'll walk.'

'Why on earth —'

'We may have to track him. If you take a vehicle, the tyres could cover prints.'

Bader said in amazement: 'That's going over the top, surely?'

'Not at all. Looking for someone in wilderness areas, often all there is to help you is tracks.'

'Not much good if you don't know what he had on his feet,' Beck said slyly.

She ignored him. With Green she started down the knoll on which the house stood, walking on the verge. After one puzzled glance, Green took the opposite verge. The others followed Miss Pink. Everyone studied the dust as they walked.

There were no footprints, only tyre tracks, those of the Cherokee being the most recent. Under those, particularly where they swerved in from the meadow heading for the house, were the marks of another vehicle – the Toyota – and, turning leftwards *up* the meadow, the tracks of a third vehicle.

'I drove up to the gate about a week ago,' she said, 'but these aren't my tracks.'

'It'll be the Chevvy.' There was an edge to Green's voice.

The tracks led them to the gate. They didn't stop there but continued on the other side, into the forest. The chain hung loose from the gatepost, a key in the padlock.

'So maybe this isn't the Chevvy,' said Green, opening the gate. The others filed through silently.

Here at the fringe of the forest there were a few canyon oaks under which was an accumulation of leaf mould. No tracks showed in this but a spring was draining down the path and in the mud between washed stones they could discern the marks of tyres.

'Is he draining this section?' Bader asked.

'Could be if he felt like it,' Green said. 'I didn't employ him as a ranch hand.' There was no indication that anyone had been draining.

A squirrel erupted with raucous shrieks above their heads, making them start; a pair of doves took off with a batter of wings. The tyre tracks ended at a creek where old railway ties leaned against the eroded bank. There was no sign of a vehicle other than its tracks. Casting about, they discovered where it had backed into brambles and turned. 'So what we were following originally,' Bader said, 'was the Chevvy coming *back* to the house.'

'Has to be,' Green said. 'Unless it's another truck and that's still in here somewhere. We better backtrack, two to each side. With four-wheel drive, there are plenty of places he could have pulled off into the trees.'

About a hundred feet from the creek there was a place where the vegetation had been disturbed. Because they now knew what to look for, they could see that the growth of wild currant and gooseberry had been flattened by wheels that had headed straight for a clump of firs, the branches of which swept low to the ground. There was some granite by the trees, gently convex *roches moutonnées*. From a distance they could see the striations made by an ancient glacier, and there were tracks running over the first low lump of rock. Not right over, they saw, advancing, staring fascinated at those dark smudges on the pale surface.

The marks stopped before a magnificent white fir, as if the vehicle had run into the trunk, but there was nothing in the dim cave below the tree.

Not quite nothing. The searchers held the branches aside, like stagehands making space for an actor to take his curtain call, his last curtain call, for an inner branch came low, but not low enough to conceal a pair of boots, suspended.

'Jesus!' someone breathed.

After a moment Green lunged forward as if with speed he might be in time to save life. The others followed warily, Miss Pink last.

'Is it him?' Bader asked, but Beck was saying: 'It can't be him.' Then, on a rising note: 'Suicide?'

They stared. The man's head wasn't far above them; they would have preferred it much further away.

'Hanged himself – with barbed wire?' Green was scathing. He added tonelessly: 'Should you be here, ma'am?'

Miss Pink ignored him. She was studying the method that had been used in the hanging. A noose of wire had been attached to the end of a length of rope and this was passed over a limb, the end coming down to a branch near the ground and secured.

'Don't bandits carry out executions like this?' Bader asked.

'Mafia?' Green hazarded. 'No, there are no Mafia here.' He looked at Miss Pink helplessly. 'I don't understand it –' then, accusingly, the shock coming out: 'You seem to be quite at home. So what happened? Who is he?'

'It's Vogel,' she said. 'There's the tattoo on his forearm; I remember that. We'll know for sure when they cut him down –'

'Should we do that?'

'No, leave it to the police.'

'It can't be murder,' Bader said.

'Of course it's murder.' She looked at him sharply. Behind the aviator spectacles his eyes were strained wide. 'Let's go back to the ranch,' she said. 'There's plenty of coffee and milk in the cabin. We can take it to your house, Granville.'

'What's that? Coffee. Yes, of course. We'll go back, nothing we can do here.' They moved away with relief.

'Who took the pick-up away?' Bader asked, studying the ground with exaggerated interest. 'He seems to have turned here –' He pointed. They were some yards from the gallows tree now and marks in the vegetation showed plainly where the truck had come round in a three-point turn. 'What happened?' he asked querulously.

'He backed up to the fir,' Miss Pink said, 'and used the pick-up as horses were used. The victim's hands were tied and the rope thrown over a bough, then the horse was led out from under him. Vogel was on the back of the pick-up.'

'How in hell did you work that out?' Green asked.

'There's no other explanation.'

'His hands weren't tied,' Beck said.

'No. Could that be significant?' The question wasn't rhetorical but no one answered her.

They walked back to the meadow quietly, only at one point Green said: 'There was hardly any blood,' and Miss Pink murmured: 'I noticed that too.'

At the ranch Green opened his house while the other men removed coffee and milk from the refrigerator in the cabin. No one paid any attention to Miss Pink who moved about the cabin with apparent aimlessness, but fetching up outside one of the front windows where a neat hole had been punched in the screen, the ragged edges on the inside. She returned to the living room and smoothed a swagged net curtain. The material was new but there was a hole in it, another in the second thin layer of net. Both were in alignment with the hole in the wire screen.

She lowered the top half of the window. It ran smoothly, on new sashes, as if it were often open: at night, for instance, when it was too cold to do without a fire, but the fire might make the cabin too warm.

She lifted the cover of the stove and peered inside, then she went to the Cherokee and returned with a torch. Having shone it down the black maw of the stove she lifted the cleaning trap at the bottom and reached inside. When she straightened she was holding a man's wallet in her hand, but she was holding it by the edges. She took it to the table, brought a knife and fork from the kitchen and opened it without using her fingers.

There were no currency bills inside but otherwise everything was present that might be expected: driving licence, credit cards, a membership card of The Society of Authors and an Organ Donor card, the contact there listed as James Dorset. All the cards were in the name of Timothy Argent.

# Chapter 12

'I'm not surprised,' Raistrick said. 'This is California.' His listeners regarded him in amazement. 'We been keeping an eye on him,' he added easily.

Miss Pink looked round to see how Padilla had reacted to this but the younger man had slipped out, probably back to the cabin where the fingerprint people were at work – or rather, the sheriff's men with their fingerprint equipment. Everyone was in uniform.

The police had arrived at the ranch to find the occupants somnolent in the south-facing sitting room of the big house, drinking coffee and running out of new angles on Vogel's death, all except Miss Pink who had contributed nothing except the facts of the bullet hole and the wallet. She said she had no idea what these could mean.

She had accompanied them when Green led the police to the scene of the hanging, had been an intent observer as photographs and measurements were taken, as the body was lowered and the cut rope placed in a plastic bag.

When the body was on the rock, face upwards – a face that was unmarked and undisturbed (Vogel's face could never have appeared tranquil) – she expected comments, but there was none from the police. It was Green who said: 'Hanged men don't usually look like this, do they?'

A man with a camera, squatting and squinting in order to get a picture of the back of the head while another held it raised, grunted something inaudible.

Raistrick stooped and touched the skull where the hair was clotted with dried blood. He pressed gently, looked at Padilla and stood up. The younger man squatted and felt the skull and nodded.

Green and Miss Pink drifted back to the house. After a while they were joined by Raistrick who accepted a coffee and made his casual but, at least to the men, surprising statement.

'You were expecting it?' Green asked incredulously. 'I thought he was straight or I'd never have employed him. You're saying it was a Mafia killing, an execution?'

'Not Mafia, not here. But it's an execution. This is how they do it across the border. Your caretaker was probably an informant.'

'You knew that! Why didn't you call me?'

'I didn't know. I do now.'

'What was he running?' Beck's eyes were snapping above the crew-cut beard. As he emerged from his shock he was assuming a macho role. Miss Pink watched him lazily.

'We'll find out,' Raistrick said. 'I'll take his truck, get Forensics to work on it. It *is* his?'

'So she – Miss Pink says.'

The sheriff said thoughtfully: 'You found the Jeep too, ma'am.'

'That must have been a coincidence, despite the connection.' She didn't miss the flicker of interest in his eyes.

'A connection between your author and a drugs – the murdered informant?'

'The wallet confirms some kind of connection. Vogel was part of an organisation bringing drugs across the border into Texas. A Texas Ranger called Rod Larsen had been trying to induce him to turn informant, but in April a man who had talked – presumably – was hanged on the Rio Grande. After that Vogel disappeared.' She looked at Green. 'You must have met him in New Mexico shortly afterwards.'

'And how did you find all that out?' Raistrick asked silkily.

'There was a pen in Argent's Jeep; it was from a motel in a place called Seeping Springs in Texas.'

'We didn't see it.'

'It was pushed to the back of the glove compartment.'

'And you went down to Texas – without informing me.'

She was astonished. 'I was looking for Timothy Argent!

It was his Jeep. How would I know that Vogel was involved?'

'So how did you figure he was?'

'It's more a matter of when, not how.' She told him how she'd been led to Rod Larsen. The others listened avidly. Raistrick was bewildered. 'You lost me,' he protested. 'How can you tie this guy, disappeared in Texas, with one turns up here, in California?'

'First I thought Argent must have been in Texas, but when I talked to the Ranger I saw how the man who disappeared from there could well be the one who turned up here. The pen was the connection: it goes from Vogel to Joanne, to Argent's Jeep.'

'You're stretching it. Links as weak as that, you can tie everyone in Dogtown to that Jeep. The driver could have ate at the Queen, got his gas from Hiram Wolf, visited with Rose Baggott and the museum folks.'

Miss Pink started to tell him to contact Rod Larsen, then thought better of it. 'And the wallet in the cabin?' she asked.

'Vogel stole it.'

'When? Before or after the Jeep crashed? If it was before, then they must have met: Vogel and Argent. If it was after the crash –' She trailed off.

'The girl could have stole it.'

'There could have been a lot of traveller's cheques inside,' Bader put in. 'They're gone.'

'The wallet does suggest a connection between the two men,' Raistrick conceded. 'But you'll never find out what it was, now Vogel's dead.'

'No.' Miss Pink's mind was elsewhere. 'Not from Vogel.' She had been staring through him, now her eyes focused. 'Did you contact the logger who picked up Joanne Emmett on the other side?'

'The logger? No.' His tone implied he had far more important things to do than chasing wild geese in Alaska. 'I told you,' he said tightly, 'that's an insurance scam.' His eyes sharpened. An ambulance was coming across the meadow. 'If you'll excuse me –'

134

He left the room and the others immediately tackled Miss Pink about her trip to Seeping Springs. Green drew his own conclusions: 'You're thinking this guy, Argent, saw something he shouldn't, something dangerous – to him, and Brett got rid of him?'

'It crossed my mind.'

'So when you came up with us this morning you were going to ask him?'

'Well, not as baldly as that. I was hoping he'd give something away, some indication of what had happened. But it's obvious the sheriff thinks Timothy staged his own disappearance, that someone – Joanne? – would try to claim insurance eventually.'

Beck shook his head. 'A moron wouldn't follow through on that. There's no body.'

Green said: 'What Raistrick may be thinking, privately, is that there was some kind of scam going forward and it went wrong. After all, there was the blood on the girl – on Joanne. Raistrick might think they quarrelled violently and Argent came off worst. Either Joanne killed him, or left him for dead and his body's up there between Malachite Canyon and Credit. How would you find it? How would you even start to find it?'

'Dogs,' Miss Pink said.

'After two months?'

'Yes. A body that's been out for two months at the end of summer is going to be easy for a dog to find.' She looked round the circle. 'Who has a hound dog? I can't think of anyone.'

'Hiram Wolf's got a Shepherd,' Green said. 'But Raistrick's not going to look for your author, not now he's got a real body.'

'I don't think he's much concerned with that one either,' she said, and saw no reason to change her opinion when they went outside and found the police getting ready to leave. The cabin door was open and Raistrick emerged. 'It's all yours,' he told Green.

'You mean we can use it?'

'Sure, go ahead. We printed everything.'

Miss Pink was attentive, waiting for elaboration. It didn't come. 'No comparisons?' she prompted. 'We all handled stuff in there.'

'But you didn't string him up, ma'am.' He smiled indulgently.

'Have you taken the wallet?'

'Yes, for the time being. Padilla will give you a receipt.'

'Then you do think there's a connection with Argent?'

'So far as it's stolen property and it's in the dead guy's cabin, that's all. The connection was probably the girl.'

'Are you going to try to locate her?'

'No, ma'am. She's not my concern and nor is your author. Like I said, we got nothing to show he's not alive and well, just missing his wallet, is all.'

'So what do you do about Vogel?' Green asked.

Raistrick nodded as if the victim's former employer had a point there, which was more than Miss Pink had with her insistence on a significant connection with Timothy Argent. 'I think we got a drugs runner here,' he said. 'And there's not going to be no nationwide alert for his killers. It's a case of dog eat dog and we got enough to do trying to keep up with the muggers and rapists and weirdos setting the forest afire, decimating millions of acres, without wasting manpower looking for a gang killed one of themselves.'

'Why did they shoot him before they hanged him?' Miss Pink asked.

'Ah, you saw the hole in the screen.' He looked uncomfortable. 'I guess they missed.' He avoided her eye. 'We'll know more after the autopsy.'

As the police climbed into their vehicles she turned to Green. 'You can ask for the results of the autopsy,' she told him. 'You were his employer.'

'You mean you want to know. You're sure there's a connection, aren't you? I have to say, I'm intrigued about this guy, Timothy. And finding that wallet in the stove, that's weird.'

Beck said, scrubbing his beard: 'What puzzled you about the fingerprints?'

She blinked at him. 'What's the sense in lifting prints from the cabin without getting ours for elimination? He's just going through the motions.'

'Ask me,' Green said, 'he hasn't got the manpower to search the forest, or do much else for that matter. And why should he, with nothing to indicate Argent's up there?'

'Except his continued silence,' she said.

To explore the trails after the discovery of Vogel's body would have been an anticlimax; moreover the men wanted to get back to their wives, to close ranks. They were so eager that they would have left the ranch house and the cabin unsecured had not Miss Pink pointed out that the press would surely come to view the scene of the crime. Grumbling about ghouls, Green closed all the windows and locked the doors, and they left as they had come, the Toyota going first.

At Dogtown they parked in front of the Queen where the wives could be seen inside, drinking coffee. Miss Pink glanced down the street and saw Charlotte Semple emerge from the museum to shake a mat. They waved to each other. She murmured an excuse and turned back from the restaurant.

'I thought you were going into the canyons,' Charlotte said as she approached.

'Didn't you see the police cars?'

'Police? Where? What happened?'

'I forgot; you can't see cars on the canyon road from here, except at night. We found Brett Vogel.'

Charlotte gaped. 'So?'

'He was dead, hanged.'

'He killed himself?'

'He'd been hanged with barbed wire.'

'Oh, my *God*! Who'd do that?' After a pause she added bitterly: 'As if I didn't know.'

'I hadn't come across this method before.'

'How could you? It's not something gets in the papers, even on the other side of the border. Frighten the tourists, bad for the image of the country; even the Mexicans keep it quiet – more or less. But you live along the border, even here, a hundred miles away, you know about it. We don't talk neither.' Charlotte's mouth stretched in a travesty of a smile. 'We depend on the tourists for our living. Why can't they keep their quarrels on the other side of the border?'

'Did you suspect Vogel was a criminal?'

'Me? No. Not a criminal – not *serious* crime. Hiding out possibly, probably, but not mixed up in anything nasty. I suppose it was smuggling: illegals or drugs.'

'They'll find out. He used to go away for days at a time.'

'Joanne was in it too?'

'I understand she stayed behind to mind the store.'

'So that's why she ran. Timothy offered her an easy way out – security as well –'

'The timing's wrong. Joanne went two months ago but Vogel was killed in the last two days.'

'Why are we talking in the street? Come inside, have a coffee.'

Miss Pink started to walk through the museum and paused, horrified. There was a body on a trestle-table and Semple was doing something to its feet with a knife. 'Got this lot yesterday in Fresno,' Charlotte was saying happily. 'Beautiful condition, that dress is pure silk. There are two more in that chest, stinking of camphor –'

Miss Pink swallowed and moved closer. Semple straightened and picked up a small white boot. 'No way,' he told his wife. 'It's tiny! I'm having to pare the feet down.'

'You do that, hon; dummies are cheap but those boots are something else, and they gotta be displayed with that dress.' She appealed to Miss Pink. 'Aren't they a perfect match? And we got an ivory fan to go in her hand, buy a blonde wig. Now we have to find hats. We plan to have a whole section of effigies: ladies like this, farm women, teamsters, even children, we can find kids' clothes. It's Julius's idea, isn't my old boy creative?' She regarded him proudly and stroked his arm. 'Hon,' her voice dropped, 'Miss Pink brought bad news about Brett Vogel. Seems he was into something illegal, like drugs? And he's been murdered.' Semple's lips moved but he said nothing. 'Strung up with wire,' Charlotte said meaningly.

'I don't believe it! That's – that's –'

Charlotte nodded. 'An execution. The Westerners found him. Miss Pink was along. I don't expect the police are much bothered,' she said to Miss Pink.

'The sheriff's view is that dog eats dog. Meaning he's not interested in a drugs runner being murdered by one of his own kind. One assumes that it would be extremely difficult to trace them anyway; they're probably back across the border by now.'

'He was definitely a trafficker?' Semple asked.

'The execution implies that, and that he was an informant. The wire was barbed.'

He looked sick. 'It's obscene!'

'Mexicans!' Charlotte exclaimed. 'They're third world down there, you know? Extortion, torture, you name it. Things like this make you feel like pulling up stakes, moving to Montana, Minnesota, someplace you never see anyone except Anglos. Hell, let's go find some coffee.'

They left Semple staring at the little boot. 'He'll forget it soon enough,' Charlotte said fondly. 'The murder, I mean. Men are so squeamish, aren't they?' In the cabin's kitchen she went on talking as she prepared a tray: 'You think out here you'd be safe, not like in New York or LA, but it's worse when it does happen. These border gangs are like animals; thank God Joanne wasn't there. I can't believe she could have been in it with him, and I don't recall she ever acted as if she was on drugs herself.'

'She was living with Vogel,' Miss Pink pointed out. 'She had to know – unless –'

'Unless what?'

'If his job was to distribute the stuff: pick it up after it was brought across the border, take it into LA or San Francisco and return home empty, she needn't have known. He could have lied about the reason for his absence.'

'She wasn't stupid. More like she knew and turned a blind eye. Like I said, she wanted to run and Timothy came along, provided her with means and opportunity. She already had the motivation.' The kettle boiled and she made the coffee.

'That's normally used of murder,' Miss Pink said, accepting a mug: 'means, motive, opportunity.'

Charlotte sat down. 'Help yourself to cookies. They're homemade.'

'Timothy's wallet was inside the stove in Vogel's cabin.'

Charlotte sipped her coffee, her face blank. 'I don't understand you.'

'What would your reaction be if someone had been missing for two months, you're looking for him, and you find his wallet – minus currency but with credit cards – in a stove?'

'Someone needed to burn it? A cold stove? So he'd burn it next time he lit the fire – but he was murdered before he could do that. You're telling me Vogel stole the wallet . . . No, you're suggesting he was responsible for Timothy's disappearance? You think he's dead too – Timothy.' It wasn't a question.

Miss Pink drove to the garage ostensibly for petrol but in reality looking for Hiram Wolf. Lorraine said he'd gone to Bakersfield for tyres and wouldn't be back until evening. She asked for the lavatory then and was directed round the back of the garage. From there she could see the rear yard of the Wolf bungalow, and a slim German Shepherd watching her intently from the other side of a chain-link fence.

She drove back through the Rattlesnake Hills and took the road to Malachite and then the fork for Crazy Mule. The road was – so far – empty.

There were no animals outside Fortune's cabin and the door was closed. 'I can smell woodsmoke,' she said pleasantly, raising her voice, 'so I guess you're around. I came to tell you what's happening because I think you need to know.'

He came pushing through the branches carrying a shovel and two dead ground squirrels. 'You talking to yourself?' he asked, pretending he hadn't been hiding. She thought that was a good sign.

'Who are the squirrels for?'

'Snake.'

'It has to be a diamondback to swallow something as big as that. I thought snakes were in hibernation.'

'This one isn't. And he's not a diamondback.'

He dropped the squirrels on the chopping block and went into the cabin, emerging with a large plywood box. He put it down, reached inside and straightened up holding a sleepy claret-coloured snake. Miss Pink stared. Fortune raised troubled eyes. 'What is it?' he asked.

'I was about to ask you. I've never seen anything like it.'

It would have been a rather dull snake but for three broad and diffused stripes that gave it the claret tinge, and ran down a body that was surprisingly heavy for its length which was only three feet or so.

'It should be hibernating,' he said. 'It won't eat but it won't sleep neither. I'm afraid it's going to die. Here, you hold it while I cut up these squirrels. Maybe the smell of blood'll make him hungry.'

'These stripes are like a garter's,' she observed, taking the animal gently. It moved sluggishly until its head rested on her wrist. 'But he's far too thick for a garter.'

'You like snakes,' he observed, deftly skinning the first squirrel.

'Most of them. Not the venomous ones. I don't think I could form a relationship with a rattler. Where did you find this fellow?'

He came and held a squirrel's head in front of the snake which could have been dead, for all the response it made. 'He's not even tasting the air!' Fortune's tone was that of an anxious child. He touched the scaly snout with the bloody little head. The snake turned and tried to rearrange itself. Miss Pink sat on a log in order to provide a lap.

'When did it eat last?' she asked.

'I don't know. I've only had it a coupla days. It's took nothing from me.'

'You must have picked it up just as it was about to hibernate. If we took it back –'

'Not that one, not where it was.'

'A pity.' She looked down at the broad dorsal stripe. 'It's quite plump; it might survive if we could discover its own territory.'

'How you going to do that?' He was suddenly, fiercely angry. 'He were in Vogel's barn! That shit!'

After a pause she said: 'So Vogel keeps pets,' adding quickly: 'You couldn't say he has animals as friends.'

*'Pets!'* He spat. 'Merchandise! Snakes is so many dollars a foot! Filth, shittin' filth!'

Suddenly she knew what this was about, but she had to be careful; he could lie like the devil.

'We have to identify this snake,' she said firmly, 'and then we can find out what kind of country it belongs in and take it there. I think it's a desert snake, don't you?'

'It's not from around here. How you going to find out what it is? You going to take it away?'

'That won't be necessary. I can't believe there's anything else like this. I have a friend on the coast. I'll go and call her. I'll be right back.'

'Melinda!' crowed Grace Dodge, the naturalist. 'How nice to hear your voice. We got your card. Did you find any trace of Timothy yet . . . Well, I'm sure you will; you're tenacious enough . . . What? A *snake*? What kind of snake? . . . My dear, you've got a rosy boa, how exciting, how did you – But how did it come to be at that altitude in the first place? . . . Look, I suggest you get it back to the desert just as soon as you can. If necessary steal it from its so-called owner . . . Escaped? Great, so what are you waiting for? . . . I see. Let me think. There are rosy boas in Joshua but that's a long way south. There are colonies in Death Valley. You're looking for a rocky canyon with a spring in it. Why don't you take this specimen into Butcher Knife Canyon; you can get a Jeep all the way to the spring. Release it there; it's the best you can do. You go over Towne's Pass . . . I forgot, you know Death Valley . . . '

Asa Fortune didn't speak until they were on the paved highway and then it was only to protest when she told him to fasten his seat belt.

'If I have to stop suddenly,' she said, 'the snake will fall off your lap and get hurt.'

'You don't have to stop sudden.'

'What happens if a jackrabbit or a tarantula is on the road? Do I go over it? Have you never seen a squashed animal on the pavement?'

He fastened his seatbelt. He was amenable enough when people took the trouble to explain. They were silent again until he asked: 'What was it I needed to know? When you come to the cabin you said you come to tell me what was happening?'

'The boa put it right out of my mind,' she lied. 'Live snakes are more important than dead criminals. Vogel was hanged.'

'Hanged?'

'Hung: strung up with barbed wire.' He was quiet. She looked across the cab and met his intent gaze.

'When did this happen?'

She shrugged. 'Recently. In the last few days.'

'Where was he found?'

'In the forest.'

He turned back to the road. 'Joanne said he could be into drugs. He were away about three days usually.' She thought about the snake, coiled on a sack on his lap, but she didn't look at it. As if he had divined the thought, he went on: 'It weren't drugs here. This is what he were smuggling.' He glanced at the plump coils and smiled. 'He got his deserts.'

143

'How right you are. What's that raptor? A falcon. Must be a prairie falcon. What do you think?'

'If you say so.' After a while he said, almost meekly: 'I know the bird, I don't know what folk calls it. I only know the names of animals if someone tells me. And I don't meet many people.'

'I wouldn't say that. You know everyone in Dogtown; Joanne was your friend, you knew Brett Vogel –'

'He don't count.'

'Who killed him, d'you think?'

'Drugs traffickers caught up with him. When Joanne met him in New Mexico he were on the run, back in the spring. He told her he'd been part of a scam stealing new pick-ups from this side of the border, drive 'em across, Mexicans pay a fortune for them. He kept the purchase money from some trucks, and then he run. Joanne reckoned it wasn't cars but drugs; all the time she said it was drugs. I didn't find out the truth till I come across this guy in the tack-room.'

'If he kept smuggled animals at the ranch Joanne must have known –'

'He didn't, not before she left. She'd never have gone along with that kind of trade; more'n half dies on the road: no food, no water, terrible, drying heat. Joanne didn't know. I knew soon's I walked in that barn: the smell, sour-like, the smell of fear.' He touched the boa's back with a touch like a feather. 'This one must have escaped. I found him in a corner, curled up to die.'

'What would you have done if Vogel had come back? Were you armed?'

'I would have looked for a way to kill him, not then, later. I wasn't armed. I had warning; there are windows round that barn, in the tack-room too. I knew I'd see the headlights if he came back while I was there. That's what happened. I saw the lights and I slipped out and away.'

'That was the night before last?' He didn't reply. She went on smoothly: 'Because if it was, you were lucky, lucky they didn't have a dog either. If that pick-up came down the meadow from the Deadboy trail, it wasn't Vogel driving but the people who murdered him.'

'You could be right.'

'Was there another vehicle at the ranch? There had to be. I mean, if it wasn't Vogel in the pick-up.'

'I didn't see one. They could have left it somewheres. Wouldn't want to drive up and warn him, would they?'

'Did you go in the cabin?'

'No.'

'A pity. It could have been useful to know if it was in the same condition then as when we saw it this morning.'

'How was that?'

'With a chair pushed back from the table, a gun magazine open to a picture of some kind of automatic rifle, a mug half-full of coffee, the bed made –'

'I wouldn't know about any of that.'

'The police fingerprinted everything in the cabin.'

Silence. 'I opened the door,' he said at length. 'Looked in just. It was like you said. My prints will be on the door, but it don't matter, I never been printed.'

'You didn't look in the stove?'

'Why should I? I never went beyond the door.'

'What made you go there in the first place? Did you know he'd be away?'

'Granville Green likes me to keep an eye on the ranch.'

'When he's got a caretaker there?'

'More so then. To my mind anyways. Mr Green's too trusting. I never trusted Vogel so I still keeps an eye on the place. ''Sides, if he's using the ranch for running drugs from, why should Mr Green take the rap?' His tone hardened. 'I knew there were something going on, and I were right. Smuggling wild beasts! That's worse'n heroin.'

He lapsed into silence and she dropped the subject; they had to consider the comfort of the rosy boa anyway. The trees might be changing colour in the Sierras but out in the deserts the September sun was fierce. They opened the front windows and the sunroof (Fortune wouldn't hear of switching on the air conditioning) and put the boa on its sack behind them where the smoked glass of the rear windows afforded some protection. Salt flats glared in the heat and the mountains were in shades of brown; it was a land that froze in the winter and baked in the summer, and there was no neutral ground. They crossed a plateau where even the trees looked alien; Joshuas presenting sheaves of daggers to a sky that was drained of colour.

Three hours after they left Dogtown they were ploughing through the sand of Death Valley. Ahead of them was a mountain wall that showed no breach until they rounded a spur and the ruts they were following dived into a stony canyon.

They drove along the bed of a watercourse until they came to big old cottonwoods above a spring where they continued on foot, Fortune carrying the sack. They found a place where there were rocks and grass and rodents' holes. He put the boa in the shade of an undercut boulder and they sat down to watch.

The snake was still for a moment, lying awkwardly as it had been placed, then the muscles started to stretch and contract under the claret-coloured scales, and the tongue flickered, testing the air. It turned and looked into the depths of the undercut – and Miss Pink knew exactly what concerned it: was there a rattler in the gloom? 'Should we – ?' she began.

'Wait,' Fortune said. 'It will smell it if there is one.'

The rosy boa travelled the length of the overhang and back, its tongue never still. It turned again and, without hesitation but without haste, it slid from view in a silence so profound they could hear its scales displace the grains of sand. Miss Pink exhaled on a long sigh. Fortune folded the sack and they walked back to the Cherokee without speaking.

They sat by the spring and drank warm beer. There were no mosquitoes this late in the year and it was pleasant in the shade of the cottonwoods. A covey of quail worked their way along a slope among the pinyons; a little way upstream ducks rose with startled cries. Fortune sniffed. 'Coyote,' he said. 'Thinks we'll leave some food.'

146

'You're like an animal!'

'You get like one, live with 'em long enough. You don't do so bad yourself. You treat 'em right.'

She let that go, preoccupied with the problem of extracting information from him.

'Are you still looking for Timothy?' he asked.

'Yes.' He was clairvoyant too? She felt a little uneasy. When he didn't respond, she added: 'I think he must be dead.'

'So do I. Joanne wouldn't have left him.'

'She wouldn't?'

'I mean, if he was hurt she wouldn't have; not *abandoned* him.'

'So you're thinking that, because she crossed the mountains on her own, she had left Timothy behind, but that he was already dead, is that it?'

He frowned. 'He wouldn't have gone ahead of her and leave the Jeep behind.'

'You saw the Jeep in the stream after Joanne told you she was leaving with Timothy. When did you see Timothy last and what did he say?'

'I saw him the day after she were at my place. He were packing up to go and he said goodbye.' She waited, not daring to look at him. 'He camped halfway between my place and the trail-head,' he went on. 'Day after that I see his tent is gone, place as neat as a pin. I went to see if there was anything he might have left behind. A day or two later I was up to Sardine Butte and I see the Jeep in the bottom. I went down, took the valuable stuff out, keep it safe for him, 'case the Jeep had been stolen.'

'Didn't you go to the ranch to see if he was there?'

''Course I did. Vogel was there, no one else.'

'What did he have to say?'

'I didn't *speak* to him. I watched from a place in the forest. There was no sign of anyone 'cept Vogel.' He spoke hesitantly, his mind a long way off.

'Joanne would know what happened,' she murmured.

His eyes came back to her. 'What do the police think?'

147

'The sheriff was thinking that Timothy managed some kind of disappearing act for his own ends. Now his wallet's been found in Vogel's stove, he's saying either Vogel or Joanne stole it.'

'You found a wallet today? How long had it been there?'

'How would I know? The money had been taken out.'

'A good thing I didn't go no further than the door. So that's why you asked did I go inside.'

'If you didn't, then you're in the clear. That was one of the things I had to tell you, about the wallet.'

'You thought I could have stole it.'

'You could have, but you didn't kill Timothy or Vogel.'

'How do you know that?'

'You wouldn't have killed Vogel that way.'

'What about Timothy?'

'You had nothing to do with that. He liked animals.' It was an inspired guess but it worked.

'You want to find him, you look round the ranch. Just inside the trees, where you can get a pick-up to. Hiram Wolf's got a dog with a good enough nose.'

# Chapter 13

'I don't use her for nothing,' Hiram Wolf said. 'I thought she'd make a guard dog but she don't bark at strangers. She don't bark, period. I'm going to breed from her.'

He stood outside his yard and stared morosely at the German Shepherd. On the other side of the fence the dog stared back, wary but intelligent.

'She's alert enough,' Miss Pink said. 'I'd like her services for a few hours, to find something in the woods.'

'What kind of thing?'

'A body.' He stared at her but said nothing. She elaborated: 'Vogel probably killed Timothy Argent, and I have to find the body. I represent his publishers.'

'Do you now?' This excited his interest more than the request to use his dog to find a body. 'What happens to his belongings?'

'You mean the things in the Jeep? I removed those and I'm taking care of them until we know what's happened.'

'I didn't mean his possessions; I meant the Jeep.'

'The Jeep?' She said slowly: 'I hadn't considered that. I assume it will stay there, in the creek. It's not worth the trouble of recovery, surely? Do you want to get it out?'

'He promised it me, said I could have it cheap when he finished the trip. It's no good to me now as a vehicle, after that crash, but I could go in there, salvage parts of it didn't get damaged. Could I do that?'

She thought about it and reached a decision. 'The Jeep will belong to his estate but I'll ask his executors for permission. Then you could retrieve what's valuable before the snow comes. No doubt they'd accept a nominal sum.'

'I'm beholden to you, ma'am. 'Course, I don't know

149

but what there's nothing I can use. That truck has fell a hundred feet.'

'Quite. You'll have to go and see for yourself, but you can't remove anything until we have proof of Timothy's death. That needn't take more than an hour or so. Suppose I give you a hundred dollars, cash, for your time and the dog's services? You'll still have the afternoon free.' To go and cannibalise the Jeep, was the unspoken corollary. He fell for it. 'We'd better make a start,' he said.

At the ranch Granville Green put up only token resistance: 'You can't be serious: buried on my land!' When Miss Pink pointed out that another man had been brutally murdered on that land, he conceded the argument and agreed to their searching, but only in his presence. All the Westerners were at the ranch that morning and, seeing them crowding close at this juncture, Miss Pink said firmly that the bitch wouldn't work with a lot of people around. Green came with them; the others stayed behind, reluctantly.

They approached the forest on foot, the bitch leashed, Hiram Wolf carrying a coil of light rope. The Shepherd, untrained and straining ahead, was choking with excitement and Miss Pink wondered gloomily if the animal was so over-whelmed by new scents that she wouldn't be interested in the one that was most significant.

As he opened the gate into the forest Green said: 'Why this way? If you're right, there were two killers, or sets of killers. Would they both choose the same place for the bodies? It's too much of a coincidence.'

'Not if trucks were used,' she said. 'The alternative is to go down the meadow, towards Dogtown. Psychologically, someone who committed murder at the ranch – anyone – would feel under pressure to dispose of the body away from civilisation, not towards it.'

He looked unconvinced, as well he might. 'I don't see that a mile or so makes much difference. Anyway, why the ranch?'

'We have to start somewhere.'

Once in the trees Wolf fastened the cord to the bitch's collar and paid it out. Immediately she went wild, tangling herself among trunks and bushes. When he had brought her under control again they conferred. Wolf couldn't trust her if she were unleashed; he admitted he had never brought her into the forest before. Privately Miss Pink suspected that the animal hadn't been outside his yard since he bought her. Aloud she suggested that they return to the meadow where the bitch might be allowed to have her fill of smells, to work off some of her excess energy at the end of a long rope. In the event the three of them took it in turns to hold the rope while the Shepherd, nose to ground, padded back and forth, seemingly at random. When they saw she was starting to flag they returned to the forest, the bitch panting heavily, less alert now, using her eyes rather than her nose.

'I figure she's past it.' Wolf was resentful. 'You kept her too long in the meadow.'

Green said to Miss Pink: 'If a pick-up was used, they could carry the – it – a long way back from the trail.'

'Scent travels a long way.'

'She's wore out!' Wolf protested

They came to the creek and the dog drank thirstily. 'Do we go on?' Green asked, eyeing the trace of a path that climbed the far bank. Miss Pink said that first they should concentrate on places that were accessible to vehicles. They turned back, the dog in the lead again. She led them to the clearing where they had found Vogel and she made an indecent fuss about the rock below the hanging tree.

'That's it!' pronounced Green as Wolf hauled her backwards through the clearing. 'This scent here has ruled out anything else as far as she's concerned.'

'Not necessarily,' Miss Pink muttered. 'The other one would be different.'

'How's that?'

'It's been here two months.'

'What makes you so sure it's here at all?'

Wolf pushed past, dragging the dog. 'Asa Fortune told me to look here,' she said.

Comprehension dawned in Green's eyes. 'He knows something?'

'He said nothing other than that: to look round the ranch – with a dog.'

'Yeah, Asa's a man drops hints, leaves you to fill in the gaps. I'm surprised he told you that much. You must have –'

But Miss Pink was staring ahead to where the bitch had again tangled the cord in undergrowth as she tried to plunge away. Wolf sorted them out and shortened the cord but he had to exert himself; the bitch's hackles were up and bristling, her lips stretched in a terrible snarl, but for all that she made no sound and she wasn't looking towards the clearing. Her interest had shifted away from the rock below the hanging tree.

Miss Pink signalled to Wolf who slackened the cord a little. As she felt the tension ease, the bitch's attitude changed. She was no longer avid to reach the source of the attraction; on the contrary she was wary, but fascinated. She stalked forward, ears flicking at the sound of twigs snapping in the rear, but her eyes fixed on something none of them could see at first. Her head was high and suddenly they knew the reason. The scent wasn't on the ground. Now they could smell it themselves. They came on small white feathers, and down stuck on branches and tree-trunks, littering the dead pine needles. 'My God, you were right!' Green breathed. No one responded.

Scavengers had been there: bears, coyotes, animals that live on carrion. Miss Pink thought how poignant it was that one who wrote so delicately, who rejoiced in beauty of line and the human form, should have ended so – and reminded herself that this was only a shell, the essence remained in the books.

'Can it be him?' Green asked, a handkerchief held to his mouth.

'No one could tell,' Wolf said.

The smell wasn't too bad because most of the flesh was gone. There were rags of clothing, rent and filthy, and the

152

depression out of which the remains had been dragged was full of down – 'Goosedown,' Miss Pink observed. 'His parka wasn't in the Jeep.'

'Would you recognise this?' Green was holding a boot. It was an Austrian walking boot.

'It's a Dachstein,' she said. 'But I never met Timothy so I don't know what he wore. Joanne might be able to identify it.' Her eyes followed Wolf who had moved away with the bitch, which was suddenly docile, even cowed.

'Was he murdered?' Green asked.

She thought that this second shock in twenty-four hours must have knocked him off-balance. 'It's unusual for a suicide to dig his own grave,' she said, but without sarcasm.

'I guess so. What's that pale stuff?'

'It's goosedown, Granville: from one of those padded parkas –'

'No. That long thing.'

It was inextricably tangled with what was left of the torso: stained and torn, but seemingly complete. There was a semblance of coils . . . They stared in amazement as they identified it: familiar yet unexpected, apparently swathing the ribcage.

Green turned, bewildered. 'A bandage,' he told Wolf.

'He were in the Jeep then, and he cracked his ribs? He crawled out of the creek –' There were broken shafts of ribs poking through the bandage.

'It's a question for the pathologist,' Miss Pink said, and turned away. 'Dozens of questions. This time he has to come to the scene. Not like Vogel. That one was straightforward.' She considered her own remark. 'Well, compared with this,' she added.

When they returned to the ranch she wanted the dog put in the cabin.

'Should we?' Green was doubtful.

'The sheriff said you could use it. "It's all yours", he said. Remember? Take the dog inside, Mr Wolf.'

He stared blankly but she opened the door and he stepped over the threshold. She followed and went to close the door but Green shouldered his way inside. 'You're up to something,' he said.

'Unleash the dog, Mr Wolf.'

He did so. The bitch glanced at him then put her nose down and padded about the cabin. The focal point of interest was a rug between the table and the window. She scratched at it. Miss Pink folded it back to reveal planks that were just planks: dusty, unstained – but the bitch was inhaling deeply, even snorting at the cracks between the boards.

'There's something under the *floor*?' Green wondered. 'Not another –'

'These planks ain't been taken up.' Wolf was studying the nails.

'She's interested in the cracks,' Miss Pink pointed out. 'This could be the place where Timothy was killed.'

'There's no blood,' Green said.

'Of course not, the floor's been scrubbed; the blood will be in the cracks.'

'You suspected this? That's why you said to bring the dog in the cabin!'

'More than a suspicion. There's the bullet hole in the screen.'

He looked from her to the window. 'So he didn't miss,' he said.

The ranch became a kind of clearing house. As each newcomer drove up the meadow: the sheriff and his deputies, plainclothes men, people from Forensics and the pathologist (flown in by helicopter), they came to the house to find out where they should go. Green and his friends acted as guides. Miss Pink stayed at the house and Lucy Green, having despatched the other wives in a search for extra provisions, concentrated on looking after the police and her elderly guest. Most people were devoutly grateful for Lucy's coffee after a session in the forest and they talked without restraint, losing sight of the old lady virtually asleep in a corner, carefully shielded from the sun by a lowered blind.

'The ribs would have been broken by a bear,' the pathologist said in response to a query from Green. 'The bandage was put on before they were fractured. The ribs were marked by teeth anyway.'

'So how was he killed?'

'I can't tell you that until after the autopsy – but that's one hell of a lot of bandage, probably two or three of 'em, we haven't unwound it – and there was a big dressing under the body. You got a first-aid kit here?'

'My God! You think –'

'Did you look to see if anything's missing?'

Green went to the kitchen and returned with a box with a red cross on the lid. He opened it and extracted a sheet of paper. 'This is the checklist.'

The pathologist was sifting through the contents. 'How many bandages should there be?'

'There should be four one-inch, two two-inch, two three-inch and six triangular.'

'There are no wide bandages. How many dressings? There are only two here.'

'There should be four. Lucy! Come here.' She came bustling from the kitchen. 'When did you fill this box last?'

'Last fall when we arrived. I always keep it complete, you know that, Granville. Soon's we use anything I replace it next time I go to town.'

'She does too. She's meticulous about the first-aid box.'

'Why?' Lucy approached, staring at the contents of the box.

'Bandages and dressings are missing, that's why.'

'Who had the keys to this house besides Vogel?' the pathologist asked.

'No one. Rosie Baggott in Dogtown used to have a key but when I sent Vogel here as caretaker I phoned her, told her to give him the key when he arrived. There were two more. I had 'em both.'

'Well, well. It would look bad for Vogel if he was still alive. There's that bullet hole in the screen, and Vogel wasn't the guy got shot. He –'

Lucy interrupted excitedly: 'But if Vogel was the guy who put the bandage on this Timothy –' she glanced at Miss Pink whose eyes were half-closed, '– or whoever that is out there, he couldn't have murdered him. It doesn't make sense.'

'I'm just the pathologist, ma'am.'

'Hell!' Green exclaimed. 'You can't tell anything about the guy in the grave, the state he's in. How can you tell the difference between bone was broken by a bullet and broken by . . . like a bear's jaws? OK, I guess you can nowadays – or the lab can.'

As if on cue the sheriff entered. 'Did Vogel own a rifle?' he asked Green.

'I don't know. There's no gun in the cabin, I mean there wasn't when we went in there first. Did you go back in there yet?' The sheriff shook his head. 'Because we put the dog in there,' Green went on, 'and she got interested in the floor under the window, sniffing at the cracks.'

The pathologist and the sheriff exchanged glances. The sheriff went out again.

'You left the dog there?' the pathologist asked.

'No. We thought it could be blood, like he scrubbed the floor but couldn't get into the cracks. How come a guy is shot, then bandaged?'

'An accident?'

'So why bury him?'

'Guilty conscience? Doesn't want the police coming around, he's got a scam going and a guy dying in his cabin is going to complicate matters.'

'How did *he* die – Vogel?'

'He was hit on the back of the head with a shovel. It was in the pick-up the sheriff took in for examination, got blood and tissue on the blade, and there's matching stuff on the bed of the pick-up, no attempt made to clean that off. He was strung up after he died.'

'After he was dead! Why?'

The other man shrugged. 'To show other people who was responsible is my guess. These gangs are medieval.'

'Was he tortured?'

They squinted into the corner where Miss Pink was a dim shape. 'I thought you were asleep,' Green said accusingly.

'I was. Were there signs of torture on Brett Vogel?'

'Not physical marks, no burns; is that what you mean, ma'am?' The pathologist was intrigued.

'Perhaps they were in a hurry,' she observed vaguely.

She went outside for a breath of air. The shadows were long in the yard and it was cool at the back of the house. Men were emerging from the cabin carrying floor boards swathed in plastic, loading them on a truck. Hiram Wolf came up the slope to the yard.

'I'll be in touch with Mr Argent's people tonight,' she told him. 'I'll ask them if you can have the parts you want from the Jeep.'

'I been thinking about that. It's not worth it. There's nothing there I need anyways.' He'd got cold feet.

'As you wish. Tell me, how were you going to get hold of the Jeep when Mr Argent finished his trip? Was he going to bring it back?'

'No, I were going over there to fetch it.'

'Of course. To the place he'd rented for the winter.'

'I don't know about that. He said the Jeep would be with his – his agent, I thought he said. I were going to fetch it when he didn't need it no longer, get the wife to drive me over.'

'I have to tell his agent what happened. Do you happen to have his number on you?'

'It's back in the office someplace. I'm going down now, you like to follow me.'

There was no one in the foyer of the Grand Imperial and no response from the living quarters when Miss Pink called Rose's name. The telephone was on the counter. There were two numbers on the card Wolf had given her. She dialled the residential one. It was five o'clock; late, she thought, and prayed the man wouldn't yet have

157

reached home. The name on the card was Oscar Sloat, the address: Portola Canyon. No occupation was given. None of it meant anything to her.

The telephone rang a long time and then the rhythm was broken. She braced herself. 'Hello,' a woman said.

'Hi. Good evening,' said Miss Pink throatily and in a fair imitation of an eastern accent but one which would hardly have deceived an American. 'Do you carry insurance on your pets? Of course you do, but are they covered for every contingency, like toxic chem –'

'Look –' it was incisive, '– I don't have pets; if I had pets I wouldn't insure with someone running a hard-sell scam on the phone, and so stupid you don't realise the approach switches people off. Do you read me?'

The receiver was slammed down. Miss Pink replaced hers gently. She was smiling. The accent had been girlish, classless and unmistakably English.

Rose Baggot came in from the street. 'I owe you for that call,' Miss Pink said, placing a bill on the counter. 'I have to go to LA tomorrow. Do you mind keeping my room for me? I'll be back.'

# Chapter 14

The scent of sun-warmed citrus fruit was languid and sensuous. Not far from the city limits of Los Angeles Miss Pink was reminded of childhood holidays in Spain, which wasn't surprising, she thought, as the dark rows of trees wheeled past, the fruit like golden lamps in the foliage: California was colonised by Spaniards.

Down here on the flat lands the heat and humidity were oppressive. The humidity arose from irrigation, but that made no difference to the dust. She had come south on the interstate, had left that for a state highway, and now she was on a dirt road and heading for the hills. There was no way she could reconcile this country: half fruit farms, half timbered wilderness, with an American literary agent whose office was in Los Angeles. The only houses visible were at long intervals and set back from the road: a glimpse of roof and a gleam of glass under tall palm trees. There was no traffic on the roads, no one in the citrus groves. She would have turned round but for the fact that three miles back she had stopped and asked directions from a man working on an irrigation channel. He assured her that this road led to Portola Canyon, had indicated a break in the distant hills. There were no turnings, he said; she couldn't miss it.

Lunch had been a packet of sweet cookies and now she was thirsty. The roof of the Cherokee was a focal point for the heat, and the wind wafting through the interior was hot. Everything was hot. A roadrunner walked out in front of her, turned round and walked back. Even the dust was hot.

The citrus groves ended at the foot of slopes covered with manzanita. Higher, above oak trees, big conifers were a frieze on the skyline. The gradient was steep up there with rock showing through; down here, at the mouth of a canyon, the road deteriorated to a narrow track above a creek.

She came to a mailbox at the foot of an unpaved drive, the legend, '1 Portola', on its side. She drove on, noticing power lines all but hidden in the riot of foliage. She passed two more mailboxes and came to one marked 'Sloat'. She turned up the drive and entered a kind of tunnel under huge oak trees. After a hundred yards she emerged into a flood of sunshine so brilliant that she was momentarily blinded.

She stopped on level ground in front of a cavern. Squinting below her hat brim she saw that the cavern was in fact the interior of a garage. She put her hand on the door but she didn't open it. A harlequin Great Dane had appeared. It stalked to the passenger side and put its head through the window space. After one stupefied moment she realised that its front feet must be on the running board. The dog looked at her with interest but without hostility. A Siamese cat walked round the corner of the garage followed by a brown girl dressed all in white. She came up to the dog and put her hand on its neck.

Her eyes were as they'd said: the colour of asters, and her hair was black, drawn back from a face that held the eye like a fine painting. Miss Pink smiled, not at Joanne, but in appreciation. She wore no make-up and her only attempt at artifice was the way she had caught her hair back, fashionably, in a long, plump plait. Her blouse was a cheap imitation of *broderie anglaise*, and not particularly clean. Her slacks belonged to someone considerably larger. She was barefooted.

'I'm Melinda Pink.' Someone had to say something. 'Is the dog as friendly as it appears?'

Joanne stiffened at the accent and glanced towards the drive. 'Are you on your own?'

'Quite alone.' She risked it and opened the door. The dog walked round and sniffed at her shoes. 'Well, this is very nice –' Miss Pink was beaming fatuously, '– I'm from the Dorset Press. You'll have been expecting me.' Joanne

160

gave her a cool stare. 'You were expecting someone,' Miss Pink gabbled, 'not necessarily me. Can we sit down? I've had a hard morning.' She glanced at the corner of the garage and moved away from the Cherokee. Joanne moved with her.

There was a broad terrace on the hillside, part natural, part excavated. The garage stood at one end and beyond was the house: an asymmetrical timbered construction that blended so well with the vegetation that its boundaries were indistinct. Vertical and horizontal lines were interrupted by creepers, shrubs, saplings, trees. There was a collage of light and textures, of wooden balconies and glass, shade and sun and glowing blossoms. Terra-cotta pots trailed fuchsias, hummingbirds flashed through the hanging plants, a golden mobile twirled lazily. Behind the glass were signs of the lifestyle she had expected to find, but on the coast, not here on the unfashionable side of Los Angeles. There was a chair covered with a Liberty print, the corner of a carpet that hinted at Bokhara, a pale floor of smooth and slender planks.

They came to the far end of the house and an irregularly-shaped pool at the foot of shallow steps. A pair of amphorae stood in iron frames and there were cushion plants between stone slabs. The water reflected the sky and had none of that acidic blue normally seen in swimming pools. Shade was provided by slatted ramadas more usually found in Arizona deserts. Under the nearest were two long chairs and an iron table on which was an empty glass and what looked like a script.

'Sit down,' Joanne said. 'What would you like to drink?'

'Not for a moment.' She was dying of thirst but she wouldn't let the girl get to a telephone if she could help it. She seated herself with a deep sigh of satisfaction. 'So you're Joanne. No one has done you justice.'

The lovely eyes were thoughtful. 'You're from the Dorset Press, you said?'

'From James Dorset, yes.' Miss Pink waited. 'My job was to find Timothy Argent,' she added.

The girl licked her lips. 'So how far did you get?'

The dog and cat walked along the far edge of the pool to collapse, one by one, in the shade. Miss Pink, observing them idly, came to a decision. She turned to Joanne. 'Brett Vogel is dead.'

The girl looked away and swallowed. 'How did it happen?'

'He was murdered. The skull was fractured – by a shovel from his own pick-up.' Joanne looked shocked but not surprised. 'And they found Timothy's body,' Miss Pink added conversationally.

That did evoke surprise. 'They found Vogel, *then* they found Timothy?'

'That's right. You'd expect it to be the other way round.' It was not a question, and Joanne did not accept it as such. 'Are the police looking for me?' she asked.

'Why should they? The sheriff is of the opinion that Vogel killed Timothy, and that the drugs traffickers caught up with Vogel. *That* had the mark of an execution.'

'What? Hitting him over the head?'

'He was strung up afterwards: hanged. With barbed wire.' Joanne blinked. 'He was dead already,' Miss Pink said quickly, at the same time registering that the girl wasn't as horrified as might be expected.

'All right.' It was belligerent. 'So he didn't suffer. But the people who did it are disgusting.'

'You don't ask if *they* are after you.'

'Why, how would you know? You couldn't. They're not bothered about me. I met Vogel afterwards.'

'But you were involved at Dogtown, even if your job was only to answer the telephone when he was on a run.'

'Was it drugs?'

'You're asking me?' Joanne was silent.

'No,' Miss Pink said, watching her.

'You said the drugs traffickers caught up with him.'

'That was some time ago; he was involved in bringing drugs into the country from Texas. An informant was hanged and evidently Vogel, who'd been approached by the authorities to turn informer himself, thought the gang was on to him so he ran. That was in April, as you say: before

162

you met him. He told you he'd been involved with a gang stealing pick-ups.'

'How did you know that?' She didn't wait for an answer but went on: 'I always suspected it was drugs; he had too much money on him for it to have come from pick-ups. That was another thing made him run: he kept the proceeds from a sale.'

'How did you meet him?'

'On the road. He picked me up and we stayed together.'

'And then you met Granville Green in Carlsbad.' Joanne was surprised again. 'How did Vogel persuade Green to employ him?'

'We pretended we were married and he said he was a Vietnam veteran. He thought it would be a good place to lie low: Danger Canyon, until it was safe, or safer. I went with him because Dogtown was on the way to LA and I'd decided to come here. I'd been bumming around the States for nearly a year, I wanted a proper job, make some bread.'

'But Vogel didn't lie low, did he? Wasn't he bothered about starting a new racket so soon after the informant was murdered in Texas?'

'Well, that was Texas: a long way away. And it wasn't soon; it must have been June, the end of May before he went away the first time. The pass wasn't clear of snow until then.'

'Which pass?'

'Breakneck. He used to come back that way.'

'Then he had to come through Credit. What about people seeing him?'

'What's one more beat-up old truck? The roads are swarming with them in summertime: fishermen, loggers, ranchers. And he'd changed his truck so he had one with California plates. And even if he had been stopped, he wasn't carrying anything on the way back.'

'Did he go out that way too?'

'No, he went down the canyon, past Dogtown.'

'Where did he pick up the – merchandise?'

'I never knew and he'd probably have lied if I'd asked him. I only know he was away for three or four days and I was to tell anyone who called – anyone local, who we knew, like people in Dogtown – that he was cutting wood in the forest, or fishing, stall 'em somehow. If it was strangers calling I was an English tourist: snooty, not hostile, just very English, and I didn't know anything, they'd got a wrong number. No one like that ever called. I wonder how they got on to him.'

'How long was he away for?'

'I said: three or four days. I reckoned that gave him a day to reach the border, wherever the rendezvous was, a day to get to San Francisco which would be the distribution centre, a day there maybe, and another to come home, over Breakneck.'

'He never brought anything to the ranch?'

'Not that I know of, and I drove the truck sometimes. I could have found it, or traces of it.'

'He did bring one consignment, or part of one, but that would be after you left. Asa Fortune found a rosy boa in the tack-room at the ranch.'

'A rosy *what*?'

'Boa. As in constrictor. It's a comparatively rare snake, very gentle, makes a good pet.'

'I'm not with you.'

'Vogel wasn't smuggling heroin or marijuana. It was wildlife: rare snakes, Gila monsters, armadillos, that kind of thing.'

'No.' It was an indication of bewilderment rather than denial. 'I'd have known.'

'Didn't you notice a smell in the pick-up?'

'Why should I? It was open. He wouldn't carry anything like that in the cab!' Her voice was rising.

'They'd be very small cages, boxes really, with a few airholes. All under a tarpaulin.'

'I don't believe it. I can't believe it! The sod.' Her eyes were fierce. 'Asa would have killed him' – she gasped – 'but he didn't. He couldn't have. Strung up with barbed wire? Not that. Asa would have hit him, fracture his skull and leave him where he fell. That business with the wire: that's not Asa.'

'That's what I thought. He reckons it was the drugs gang.'

'Those who live by the sword . . . Vogel told me about those wire hangings, he had to impress on me to be discreet around Dogtown, to be careful on the phone.' She stared at the still surface of the pool. 'He'd left that morning,' she said dreamily, 'I didn't expect him back for two or three days and by then I'd be gone – with Timothy. Poor guy. Vogel shot him through the window.'

'I saw the bullet hole.'

'I would have killed him if I'd had a gun at that moment. I've never understood it. Why should he kill Timothy? It was all over between Vogel and me. I mean, he *knew*; I wasn't making a secret of it. Pretending to go away, sneaking back to kill Timothy like a jealous husband – it's so corny!'

'Perhaps he was more possessive than you gave him credit for. Maybe he looked on you as a valuable possession which he didn't want to lose. Or he could have had some kind of operation lined up in which you were to play an essential part. On the other hand, he might have meant to kill *you*; did you think of that?'

'Instead of Timothy? I never thought that. Both of us, yes, although at the time I didn't think at all, except that someone was outside and shooting into the cabin and I had to get out of there. When Timothy was shot he fell against me and we knocked the table over, so the lamp fell too and broke, and we were in the dark. I got out from under him and through the back window, which was open, thank God, and not screened, so Vogel didn't hear me go. And he'd missed seeing the Jeep. Timothy was having starter trouble so he'd parked it above the cabin to get a good run when he left. The keys were in the ignition. I'd driven it a bit so I knew where the lights were. I rolled down the hill and the engine caught and I roared out of the yard. I'd have run Vogel down if he'd got in the way.'

'Where was he?'

'I don't know. I didn't see him.'

165

'Was the cabin door open when you passed?'

'I think so. I saw something gleam – whether it was a gun-barrel or a flashlight I couldn't tell. I was expecting him to shoot and I was going like the clappers and I kept my foot down all the way to the cattle-grid, but there weren't any more shots –'

'Where was Vogel's pick-up?'

Joanne stared at her. 'His truck? I can't think. I don't remember seeing it; it must have been behind a barn somewhere.'

'Why did you turn up Malachite Canyon? Dogtown was much nearer. The other way you were a sitting duck.'

'Dogtown didn't seem a particularly friendly spot at that moment and all I wanted to do was get out of there fast. And I would have if only the Jeep had had a full tank. It was faster than the pick-up and I'm a good driver. But I got to the start of the climb out of Malachite, looked at the gauge.and the needle was on Empty! And then as I started up the gradient I saw headlights in the canyon behind me. I knew I could never hope to reach the top, let alone Credit, I had to abandon the Jeep . . . Did you find the Jeep? Yes, so you know what I did. I thought it would catch fire and he'd assume I was still in it. I couldn't believe it when it didn't explode. Of course, I didn't stop to watch; I scrambled up through the woods, keeping away from the road, and I only stopped when I ran out of breath.

'I saw the lights come up the track and stop at the first bend. The Jeep's lights were still burning. I couldn't see what he did but he didn't go down to the Jeep – probably afraid it would explode – I saw his lights sweep across the opposite slope as he turned round and went down Malachite. I suppose he went back to the ranch and disposed of poor Timothy. What did he do with the body?'

'What makes you so certain Timothy was dead when you left the cabin?'

'Wasn't he dead? He had to be.'

'He died later. After he was shot someone dressed the wound. There were bandages on the body.'

'You mean, I could have saved him if I'd stayed?'

'No, you'd have been shot as well. It had occurred to me that you could be the person who dressed the wound. Now it seems it was Vogel.'

Joanne laughed in disbelief. 'He shot him, then regretted it and bandaged him?'

'Perhaps you were the intended target all along.'

'So we're back to that. He certainly followed me up the canyon, and he knew the Jeep was in the gorge and I should be in it, but he never made any attempt to go down there and pull me out. You're right, it had to be me he was after.' She shuddered. 'I'm glad you told me he's dead. I'd never feel safe again if he was alive.' She shook her head. 'I still can't see Vogel being so attached to me he'd want to kill me. You live with a guy three months and you still don't know where he's coming from.'

Miss Pink gave a long sigh. 'Tea!' exclaimed Joanne, getting to her feet like a cat. 'A pot of China, how does that sound?'

'I take it Oscar was Timothy's new agent,' Miss Pink observed politely, squeezing lemon with silver tongs.

Joanne bit her lip, then laughed wryly. 'It doesn't matter now. Timothy wanted to stay here and Oscar was going to be his American agent, yes. He didn't tell James Dorset, something to do with changing publishers, business ethics, stuff like that. None of it matters any longer.' She looked sad. 'He knew exactly where he was going to build his house: on a cliff at Big Sur, overlooking the Pacific.' She sighed, shook herself and went on brightly: 'Try this cake, it's made with sherry. Oscar's away at a conference in Tucson, so I'm cat-and-dog sitting. Did you want to see him? I can call him and tell him you're here.'

'There's no urgency. How much did you tell him?'

'Everything. I had to, turning up here looking like something the cat brought in. There wasn't time to pull any clothes out of the Jeep before I sent it off the road. Even if I'd thought about it and had time there was only Timothy's stuff. I was leaving with Timothy, but you know that. I hadn't started packing though, and all my gear must still be in the cabin.'

'Including a bottle of Chanel.'

'So you saw that. I suppose everywhere was searched after the bodies were discovered. Where were they found? You didn't say.'

'A short distance inside the forest, a few yards off the Deadboy trail.'

'How did you know where to look?'

'When Granville Green arrived to open his house Vogel wasn't there but his pick-up was. We followed its tracks back into the forest. Evidently they'd carried his body in his own truck and then driven it back to leave it at the ranch.'

'And Timothy was in the same place?'

Miss Pink froze in the act of raising her cup to her lips. 'Not – quite. But the bodies weren't far apart.'

'How did you find – the second body?'

Miss Pink told her about Wolf's German Shepherd. 'Oh, Hiram.' Joanne smiled. 'He's like a Shepherd himself: doggy, you know? Have some more cake. Isn't it delicious?' She cut large wedges for each of them and lay back again, swinging her legs up on the chair. Her feet were brown and slender, and rather grubby.

Miss Pink said: 'Were you barefooted when you escaped from the cabin?'

'No – fortunately. I'd have torn my feet to pieces in the forest. But I had no warm clothes, and do you know what it's like up there, on the Sierras at night, even in summer? But you have to know what I did; you know everything else.'

Miss Pink nodded. 'You spent the first night at Palmer Meadows and you stole some clothing – and a wire coat hanger – which you used to open the door of a timber lorry. You spent the second night in that. In the morning the driver brought you down to the valley and you left him in Bakersfield.'

'That's about how it was.'

'Oscar Sloat must have been surprised when you turned

up on his doorstep. Or was he expecting you to arrive with Timothy?'

'He wasn't expecting anyone for another month and he didn't know about me anyway. He was a bit startled when I showed, but Oscar's a sweet guy, and he has charming manners. In fact he's like Timothy – was. I guess that's why we get on so well.'

'You say you told him everything?'

'Everything I knew at the time. Of course, I didn't know that Vogel was dead –'

'He was alive until four days ago.'

'I'd assumed he was alive until this afternoon. I had to, I remembered that gunfire and me roaring out of the yard and the headlights coming up the canyon. Takes a long time to get over: the feeling a killer's after you. But Oscar said Vogel wouldn't try to trace me because he'd be working on the assumption that I'd report Timothy's death to the police, so he'd have cleared out as soon as it was discovered my body wasn't in the Jeep. He said Vogel would have been gone next day. But he didn't go, did he?'

'We didn't find the Jeep until a week ago.' Miss Pink gave Joanne no chance to assimilate this but went on smoothly: 'Why didn't you report the shooting?'

Joanne was astonished. 'I'm illegal! I don't have a work permit. They'd deport me soon as look at me –'

'I doubt that,' Miss Pink interposed drily.

'But Oscar's going to see I get a work permit. He knows everyone in LA. I've had an audition –' she gestured to the script on the table, '– and he says I've got the part, so I'm learning my lines. It's only a TV soap but so what, it's a start. Oscar wants us to get married but if I can stay in the States without having to get married, I think it's better to remain single. I'll live here in the canyon for a while. Oscar's a very comfortable guy to have around.'

'If you'd reported the shooting you'd have had to stay here as a potential witness. That is, if the killer came to trial.'

'Maybe, but I'd have been under surveillance, and they'd

go back over my time in the States and make a meal of it. Individual policemen are all right – thick usually but human – but Authority as an institution, with a capital A, that would come down on me like a ton of bricks. Besides, what good would it do Timothy to report his murder? His body would be found soon enough, I reckoned, and it was, wasn't it?'

'Rationalisation,' Miss Pink murmured. 'Weren't you concerned about justice?'

Joanne's eyes widened. 'I was concerned not to become Vogel's next victim. Mind you –' she shifted on her chair, '– Oscar put that argument forward too – justice – but he dropped it when I pointed out the first thing they'd do would be deport me. Oscar's easily influenced. You look doubtful. You haven't met him.'

'I'll take your word for it.' The conversation lapsed and in the silence the Great Dane walked round the pool, sat, and placed a large foot on Miss Pink's thigh.

'He can have a small piece,' Joanne said, maternal but firm.

Miss Pink gave him a piece of cake and asked: 'Who looked after the animals before you arrived?'

'A lady called Isabella: Spanish type, with a trace of Negro blood. Oscar likes exotic women. I never thought of myself as exotic but I suppose he just means having some coloured blood.'

'What happened to Isabella?'

'She left a few days after I arrived. We didn't get on.'

'You told the logger you had an Algerian father.'

'Did I?'

'But Charlotte Semple says your father was an Indian rajah when he wasn't the chief of an Afghan tribe.'

'That's coming closer, but I'm a quadroon, not a half-caste – not that being a quarter-Indian – or Afghan – would make me superior; it's just to set the record straight. Remember the war?'

'What? World War Two? Of course I remember it.'

'My grandmother was Welsh, the wife of a quarry manager in Blaenau Ffestiniog.' She smiled and dropped into the lilt of rural Caernarfonshire: 'Very proper, we were:

chapel on Sundays, Granpa Parry in his black suit and Nan in her best hat. She's dead now but I remember a big woman, rather plain and very firm-looking: the pillar of the Mothers' Union.' She resumed her English accent, her face sparkling with delight: 'And a regiment came over from India, a mountain regiment with mules, can you imagine! They were stationed in Nantmor. My real Grandad was a muletier from the Northwest Frontier!'

Miss Pink was smiling too. 'Did your grandmother leave her husband?'

'Not a bit of it.' Joanne sobered. She looked bewildered, as if there were something here she'd never really understood. 'Curious, isn't it? In that closed community: claustrophobic, hellfire-and-brimstone religion, they brought my mother up just like one of themselves. Of course, by the time the nine months were up, the Indians had moved on, and my mother says Nan never kept in touch with this guy – my real Grandad. Evidently no one else knew what happened until my mother was born – in hospital. And the story goes that Nan told Granpa Parry that he could have her back with the new baby or neither of 'em, and in that case she'd take the other kids with her too. There were two children besides my mother. Granpa Parry chose to take Nan and the new baby. I always reckoned Nan must have had something going for her that wasn't obvious to us kids, I mean something that gave her some kind of power over men?'

They exchanged questioning looks, Miss Pink realising with amazement that this seductive creature had no idea that the power had been inherited. 'What happened to your mother?' she asked.

'She went in for nursing, married a doctor and they live terribly dull lives in Liverpool. My father's white; that's why I'm not particularly dark. My mother's very beautiful – but you got to watch it with this Indian blood. We all run to fat in middle-age. Mum has to fight like hell to keep the flab down.'

'Is your father handsome?'

'I guess. Men lose their looks with age, don't they?

He's a *type* –' she pronounced it in the French fashion, '– like Gary Cooper. Julius Semple has the same sort of blurry good looks, a kind of ghostly presence behind the wrinkles.'

'And what is Oscar like?'

'He's just an ordinary guy to look at, a bit fat, but then he's old, he's thirty-nine, although that's not nearly as old as Timothy. You mean, personality? He's sophisticated. I like that, it was what attracted me to Timothy. Basically men are all the same – well, with a few exceptions – but superficially there's this distinction: knowing what's what, knowing the right places to eat and where to go to buy good clothes and not just the expensive flashy gear. Like guys who can tell you the difference between a Mozart concerto and one of Beethoven's. At home my folks go in for opera and *Lieder* and they never get any further. I've had *Lieder* up to here for as long as I can remember. With Oscar I feel I'm evolving.'

'I'm surprised you didn't stay in a city, like New York. Concerti must have been somewhat thin on the ground as you came across America.'

'Oh, this is all new! I was asleep from the neck up. Timothy brought me to life. He taught me to listen, to read, to look properly: see the essence of things. If I'd stayed with him, I mean if he'd lived . . . but he didn't. As it is, Oscar fills the gap, sort of.'

'If you prefer sophisticated men, where did Asa Fortune fit?'

'I'd forgotten Asa. He's a sweet guy too. Totally asexual, of course, but we were good friends.'

'Why didn't you go to him the night Timothy was shot?'

'I never thought of him. Perhaps I was so orientated to approaching Asa's cabin quietly so as not to frighten the animals, that the prospect of exploding up Crazy Mule with a homicidal maniac chasing me, firing shots, was a kind of subconscious taboo. I can't think of any other explanation.'

'Asa stole gear from the Jeep.'

'He would. He scavenged round the crashed plane too. So what? Timothy would have given him anything he could use. What did he take?'

'A sleeping bag, binoculars, a camera.'

'There you are: just essentials. The camera he'd sell for food.'

'You're fond of Asa.'

'Anyone would be who knows him. There's no nonsense about him. I like men who are honest. Timothy was too. With most guys it's "Hi, babe, your place or mine?" Not Timothy – nor Oscar, come to that. As for Asa: he was one of those exceptions: treated me no different from how he treats his animals. The others are just a load of dogs on heat.'

'How do you handle them?'

'I don't bother – unless I want something.' She grinned. 'Like that logger above Credit. My feet were so bloody sore – all that walking, and I was filthy; I needed a bath. No skin off my nose if we go to a motel in Bakersfield. I needed food, drink, lashings of hot water – and money to get to the coast. What's a few hours with a healthy guy? Cheap at the price. Prostitutes do it all the time.'

'You inspire remarkable loyalty. All the men in Dogtown assure me you are not a tart.'

'Really? How sweet. But the women won't say that.'

'In fact the women regard you as a kind of crusader.'

'Now that *is* surprising. Rose I can believe it of, but Lorraine and Charlotte – never. Lorraine hasn't an idea in her head beyond clothes and make-up, and Charlotte, that old dike! She may admire me but not because I'm picky about my men.'

'Are you telling me Charlotte is a lesbian?'

'Well, maybe that's going too far –' she squirmed on her chair, '– but she gives me the willies. Gushing, you know? Effusive. Poor old Julius dragged along in her wake, having to agree with her comments on a person's appearance. I'd run a mile, I mean, I did when I saw her coming.'

'She says you suggested that the Mafia were after Vogel.'

173

'I did? Maybe. I prefer my men to be honest but me, I like to play games with some people. Stupid git.'

Miss Pink frowned. 'Charlotte's stupid?'

'Not really. I just can't stand the woman. Look –' she was suddenly incisive, '– I've been doing all the talking, but you haven't told me much about what happened back there, in Dogtown, how you found out things. I can see how you could trace Timothy, and everyone would tell you about me, but how on earth did you find out Vogel was smuggling wildlife, had been into drugs? Even I didn't know, and I was shacked up with the guy.'

Miss Pink gave this her careful attention. 'Obviously something was wrong because Timothy had dropped out of circulation without a word, so I started looking for clues as soon as I reached his last fixed point. Vogel's behaviour was suspicious from the beginning but he was even more touchy after the Jeep was found. Then, in the Jeep, there was a pen with the address of a Texas motel on it.'

'Seeping Springs. Lovely name. It was Vogel's. But there's nothing sinister about that. I must have put it in the Jeep, not Vogel. I picked up anything that was lying around. You don't *steal* a pen.'

'That's not important. What I found curious was that I knew Timothy hadn't been in Texas, and there was no indication that you'd been that far south, so I acted on the assumption, a hunch if you like, that Vogel was the connection. After all, he was a Texan. So I went to Seeping Springs and found the Texas Ranger who'd been trying to recruit the runner who disappeared in April. I returned to Dogtown convinced Vogel was involved in Timothy's disappearance, only to find Vogel had been murdered.'

'You must have thought I was involved.'

'You have to admit that your behaviour was suspicious. You gave a false name to the logger, there was blood on you, you spun a fantastic story about hitting a deer –'

'I got the blood on me when Timothy was shot! I couldn't tell the logger it was human blood.'

'Hardly, if that was the way you were going to play

it: going to earth, keeping quiet about the shooting –
but I wasn't to know that. And then Hiram Wolf and
Julius Semple reacted very strangely when your name was
mentioned.'

'That has to be subjective; they're all mixed up, fantasising,
you know – like the guy, the count in *Rigoletto* –' And she
burst into a spirited rendering of '*La donna e mobile*'.

'A good voice too,' Miss Pink said drily, trying to wriggle
out from under the spell.

'Thank you.' There was a long pause. 'So what are
you going to tell the police about me?'

'Do I have to tell them anything?' Again there was a loaded
silence. 'I would advise you to marry Oscar quickly.'

'So you are going to the police.'

'I don't intend to. And there's no reason why they should
come to me. The official attitude is that the case is closed,
or I think it's moving that way: Vogel shot Timothy and
was murdered in his turn by a drugs gang; the killings
aren't connected. Even if some effort were made to find
Vogel's murderers, you're not involved. Why should anyone
ask me where you are? I never met you until this afternoon.
All the same, I think you should move on, and keep a very
low profile.'

'What about the animals? They're my responsibility. How
do you keep a low profile hitching with a harlequin Great
Dane and a Siamese in tow?'

'Put them in kennels or engage someone to live here
and look after them. Phone Oscar and ask him to come
back from Arizona and take you to – say – Mexico. Get
married and stay away.'

'You're joking! The drugs people come from Mexico.'

Miss Pink said firmly: 'I'm not thinking of the people
who killed Vogel, but the one who shot Timothy.'

'That was Vogel! You said the police closed the case.'

'I said that was the official attitude. Do you really think
he hated you enough to kill you?'

'He didn't hate me at all, or if he did he never showed it.'

'And he had a very nasty temper. The more you tell

175

me, the more difficult it is to see him as the man who fired at Timothy. Whether the gunman meant to shoot both of you, he certainly meant to get you, otherwise he'd have gone down into the gorge to pull you out of the Jeep. He'd think you were in it. Now if that gunman was Vogel, he might not have approached the Jeep over the next two months, but when it was found with no body in it, meaning you were free, and free to talk, he'd have run then.'

'He could think that if I hadn't talked for two months I wasn't going to. He knew I was an illegal alien.'

'Too big a gamble. He had everything to lose; the worst that could happen to you was deportation.'

'How did he react when he heard I wasn't in the Jeep?'

A blue jay was scolding the Siamese on the other side of the pool. Miss Pink regarded the bird absently. 'I don't know how he reacted because he already knew when I met him one night in the Red Queen. He acted naturally then. I thought at the time that he wasn't worried about your absence. He said you used to go to Timothy's camp and when you didn't come back he thought you were merely staying away longer than usual. Eventually he went along with the Dogtown people and assumed you'd gone for good.'

'And leave all my gear behind? That's a lie for a start.'

'It wasn't worth much – except the Chanel, and he might not appreciate the significance of that.' Miss Pink's thoughts were elsewhere. 'Besides, Timothy had money . . . That was the night Vogel attacked Julius.'

'Why would he do that?'

'I have to think.' She massaged her temples. 'It was a highly charged discussion right from the beginning; we were speculating on Timothy's disappearance, on his whereabouts. Vogel mentioned the Mafia, but as a joke. Lovejoy told him it wasn't a joking matter; Timothy was probably holed up, drinking himself to death, he said. Then Julius brought up the question of drugs, of Texas . . . no, I mentioned Texas. Vogel didn't like that; he wouldn't, it was getting too close to what he wanted to hide, but it wasn't mention of Texas that precipitated the scene . . . I remember! It was Julius insinuating that Vogel had killed *you*. He asked if the police had searched Vogel's cabin; the implication being that they should be looking for your body, or traces of it. Then Vogel went for Julius – but he didn't hit him. He merely grabbed his shirt and reminded him forcefully that you'd been seen alive as far away as Bakersfield. Julius was terrified but he did manage to get out that the girl on the Sierras could have been someone else, that the one the logger met wasn't you at all. At that point all the aggression went out of Vogel and he let Julius go, called him a fool. His attitude was one of contempt, not anger. But then –' her eyes brightened, '– then I asked Vogel what you'd taken with you and he said you'd left everything behind. He looked really puzzled. It confused me because I'd accepted it was you at Bakersfield. There can't be two people like you. Obviously Vogel hadn't murdered you, no one had – but why leave in such a hurry that you took nothing with you?'

'Now you know why, and you still look confused.'

'I'm thinking. I'm going back to the premise that Vogel didn't shoot Timothy, that he didn't come back early from his run, but came back a couple of days later, found Timothy still alive, bandaged him – that's another odd feature: someone bandaged Timothy – but it was too late. He died and Vogel buried the body. It's possible that he thought you shot Timothy.'

'Why on earth?'

'An accident? A quarrel, a struggle. The first suspect in a murder is always the spouse or lover. By burying Timothy and keeping quiet, Vogel could have thought he was protecting you.'

'Timothy would have told him it wasn't me.'

'If he was conscious. He could have been delirious. Alternatively he could have told Vogel who it was. No, that won't work because if he'd been conscious when – if – the gunman came in the cabin, he'd have been shot again in order to silence him. Maybe. This scenario: of Vogel coming home to find Timothy alive and bandaging him, never realising that the Jeep was in the gorge, works better than the assumption that he was the killer.'

'So who did kill Timothy? Who killed Vogel?'

'That's why I'm suggesting you find another place to hide.'

*'Who was it?'*

Miss Pink sighed. 'You don't make it easy, but you have to face facts. If Timothy was shot in mistake for you, who hated you?'

'No one. Why should they?'

'That's what I mean. You treated Hiram Wolf like a dog. Not my words; even you say he was "doggy".'

Joanne was incredulous. 'So he'd hate me for that? Oh, come on!'

'How do you know what he felt, how anyone felt regarding you? Was he your lover?'

'Of course not.'

'Did he want to be?'

'I guess. Are you being polite? I can't see Hiram as my lover, but he'd probably want to go to bed with me, you could say that.'

'You said he had fantasies regarding you.'

'I think Timothy said that originally.'

'Hiram could be the killer: drunk perhaps, out poaching. Coming to call on you, seeing the Jeep outside, overcome by jealousy, not caring which one of you he shot.'

'So it could have been Hiram, or Julius, or Asa; it could have been Earl Lovejoy, he had a crush on me. And Verne didn't like that. You're surprised? It happens. What are you going to do about it, about any of it?'

'There's one thing you can do. Tell me the date of the shooting.'

'That's easy. It was July the twentieth, the day before my birthday.'

# Chapter 15

'Where were you?' Granville Green asked, ushering Miss Pink into his dining room. 'You missed all the excitement. We had the press here. And now we have the report on the autopsy on Timothy Argent.'

'Nice to see you back.' Lucy Green stood up with the Beck and Bader wives. 'If you will excuse us, we have to prepare dinner,' she said, leading the way to the kitchen.

'They're squeamish,' Green explained apologetically. 'What can I get you? We're drinking margaritas.'

'We been wondering what happened to you.' Beck's beard fairly bristled with curiosity.

'I was visiting friends. Tell me about the autopsy.' She sat down and accepted a margarita although she would have preferred tea. She had spent a comfortable night at Oscar Sloat's house but the drive back to Dogtown had been hot and dry.

'There was a bullet close to the body.' Green was going round with the cocktail shaker, freshening drinks. 'It must have fallen out of the remains; there were traces of tissue on it. The track's gone, of course, but it must have missed a vital organ because he was alive after the shot – well, he lived long enough for someone to bandage him up. And then he died. And was buried.' He looked at Miss Pink as if for approval.

'He could have died of anything,' Bader put in. 'Infection of the wound, pneumonia, whatever. He had no medical attention.'

'They're sure of that?'

'He couldn't have. The shooting wasn't reported.'

'Couldn't afford to report it.' Green was sharp. 'Vogel comes home, finds a dead man in his cabin –'

'Wait a minute,' Miss Pink interrupted. 'Vogel finds him dead? Then who put the bandage on?'

'That would be Joanne,' Bader said. 'Who else? She was there, with Argent. She bandaged him but he was mortally wounded and he died so she cleared out, took the Jeep, couldn't drive it, and crashed at the first bend.'

'And Vogel comes home and finds a body, and doesn't report it.' She sounded doubtful.

'With his background no way was he going to bring police into this canyon.' Green's grin was not amused.

'They uncovered his background?'

'The sheriff did. You told him about Seeping Springs. Vogel had a snake tattooed on his left arm. So did a guy at Seeping Springs called Ed Fisher who the Texas Ranger down there says was smuggling heroin. That's not all: the prints taken from Vogel's body correspond with a guy's called Hudson who's got a record: for possession. I employed a drugs runner as a caretaker!'

'And the girl got away,' Bader said slyly.

'Oh, I don't know.' Green didn't like the insinuation. 'She could have been under some kind of duress.'

Miss Pink suppressed a smile and said: 'Joanne joined him shortly before you met them in Carlsbad. She had nothing to do with the drugs. She was just a hitch-hiker.'

'How do you know that?'

'Vogel told me.' She was bland. She went on: 'Do the police think the people who murdered Vogel are still around?'

Green shook his head vehemently. 'No way. They'd be far too obvious. It was one quick strike: in and out, more like an operation. A terrible thing though, Argent being shot by mistake –'

'By mistake?'

'There had to be a mistake. The sheriff – no one can go along with two murderers, or two sets of 'em, and they're drugs-related crimes anyway, not crimes of passion.'

'Theories change with the evidence,' Beck told her gravely. 'The killers were after Vogel, they saw a man behind the screen in the cabin and shot him. When they realised they'd got the wrong guy, they came back and that time they got the one they wanted.'

Miss Pink shrugged. 'I'll go along with that,' she said neutrally.

Her tone touched a chord in Green. He said persuasively: 'Why don't you get away from all of it, come out with us tomorrow? We're going up to the country west of Palmer Meadows. Make a nice change for all of us, get on the trail of the Joplins again.'

'Actually I must write a letter to Timothy's publisher. I've spoken to him but one forgets the details on the phone. The following day perhaps.' She stood up.

'You're not leaving? Stay and eat with us.'

'I promised Rose I'd see her in the Red Queen.'

She drove away, wondering what they'd make of her visit. If they came to the conclusion that she'd gone to the ranch to find out if there were any news that might not be public property in Dogtown, and having obtained it, had left satisfied, did that matter? On reflection she didn't think so; it was most unlikely that any of them – Green, Bader or Beck – had been in the locality on July 20th. A strange vehicle would have attracted attention immediately.


'July twentieth,' Lovejoy repeated. 'That was the day before Joanne's birthday, the night it all happened, if it happened at night. Is that why you're asking?'

Miss Pink had gone over the salient points carefully while soaking in a bath in her cabin. She had come across to the restaurant with Rose and noted the dawning awareness on his face when she asked Lovejoy if he remembered the night of July 20th. Now she said: 'I'm trying to make sense of things for a letter, a report I have to write for Timothy's publisher. I spoke to him this morning and he asked me when Timothy was shot. I thought no one could tell – except Joanne and Vogel, and I suppose none of us will see Joanne again. But Rose says it must have been July the twentieth.'

'It had to be,' Rose broke in eagerly. 'Joanne was down

the afternoon before her birthday and she was excited about the party next day. The shooting had to be that night, Earl; Joanne and Timothy would never have stood you up, and then not called to apologise. It was special –' she assured Miss Pink, '– lobsters flown in to Endeavor – Timothy was paying; I mean, he left owing all that – but of course he didn't leave . . . ' Her face was stricken.

'Why did it have to be the twentieth?' Lovejoy asked. 'Why not next day?'

'It almost certainly happened in the dark,' Miss Pink said, knowing it had, and going on quickly before they called it into question: 'No one could have sneaked up on Timothy in the daylight.'

Lovejoy frowned. Verne Blair came in and took a bottle of brandy from under the bar. 'Miss Pink figures it was July twentieth Timothy was shot,' Lovejoy told him. 'The night before Joanne's birthday.'

'I said so all along,' Blair said. 'Except I thought that they'd taken off about that time. I did Timothy an injustice. Did you hear the results of the autopsy, ma'am?'

'Yes, I was up at the Greens' place.'

'It was all Joanne's fault.' Blair was harsh. 'It was bound to happen; you could see it coming miles off. She played around. Timothy was shot in mistake for her.'

Lovejoy and Rose wouldn't look at him. Miss Pink sipped her beer, thinking that this was obviously not the first time that they had discussed the subject, that there were differences of opinion. 'Why didn't you phone them when they didn't turn up for the party?' she asked.

'We did,' Blair said. 'There was no reply. We did wonder if maybe the phone wasn't working –' He looked distressed.

'You didn't think to go up there?'

'Well, you see –' Rose began, and stopped. She went on slowly: 'It wasn't the kind of situation where you jump in a car, go and drag them down to a party. I mean, if they didn't come it had to be something important happening up there, didn't it? We hadn't known Timothy long – for Heavens' sakes, they hadn't known each other long; in theory I guess she was still living with Vogel.' She spread her hands. 'We didn't know what the situation was.'

'No one wanted to go up there,' Blair said. 'None of us three. There was no telling what you might walk into.'

'You can say that again,' Rose said darkly.

'Yes, well, we weren't to know, were we?' Blair's tone cut like a knife.

'But it was the night before the party that Timothy was shot,' Miss Pink pointed out, and saw Blair stiffen.

'The bandage!' exclaimed Lovejoy. 'You realised what it meant.'

Blair said bleakly: 'You're thinking the same as the police: that it might not have been Vogel fired that shot.'

As if he'd been waiting for a cue Lovejoy plunged in: 'If it was Vogel he was one hell of a good actor: going along with us for weeks pretending Joanne and Timothy had gone away together. And we *knew* Vogel; he was laid back, but he wasn't an actor. He couldn't have kept it up.'

They were all staring at her. She said thoughtfully: 'So you think Timothy was shot in mistake for Vogel, that the gunmen thought Vogel escaped and crashed in the Jeep, and later, when they discovered he was still alive, they came back and did the job they'd bungled two months before. You're saying both murders are the work of one gang.'

'That's what the sheriff's thinking now,' Rose said.

'And it's the best theory we heard yet,' Lovejoy said. 'But will it stand up to –'

There were steps outside and all eyes were on the door as it opened to admit Charlotte, very colourful in a pale jumpsuit, an emerald bandana and dangling silver earrings. Carefully groomed, her hair a flaming aureole, in the dim light of the Queen she looked lithe and considerably younger than her years. She greeted everyone gaily, sparkling at Miss Pink and hoping she'd enjoyed a good trip despite the heat. She perched on a stool. 'My old boy's coming over,' she told the partners. 'Can we eat here? I'm taking the night off.'

'Sure,' Blair said. 'You'll all have to eat the same; it's a salmi of duck.' Over murmurs of appreciation he retired to the kitchen. Miss Pink asked Lovejoy for the wine list, and for sherry in the interim. Rose and Charlotte ordered martinis. They made a convivial group: the three women in their trendy casual clothes (even Miss Pink was in designer denim), Lovejoy attendant and attentive on the other side of the bar. 'Miss Pink agrees with the police,' he informed Charlotte. 'Well, I guess it fits?' He raised an eyebrow at her. 'That it was the same gang killed Timothy as killed Vogel.'

Charlotte gave the ghost of a smile. 'That's new?'

'You see?' He turned to Miss Pink. 'We all came round to that theory.'

'I didn't!' Rose was indignant, looking from him to Charlotte. 'I thought it was like the police said originally: Vogel killed Timothy, and a gang killed Vogel, no connection between the two. I never thought you were serious.' She glared at Lovejoy. 'I thought you were just kicking an idea around.'

Lovejoy shrugged and turned back to Charlotte. 'Did you realise that Timothy was killed on July twentieth?'

'No, I didn't.' She was amazed. 'How did you work that out?' He explained about the birthday party. 'I'd forgotten that,' she said. 'We weren't invited.' She turned to Miss Pink. 'So it was the twentieth? Fascinating.' She was being polite.

'His publisher wanted to know.'

'Of course. He would.' Charlotte sipped her martini. 'So you agree with the police.' She was lightly teasing.

'Well, actually –' Miss Pink was flustered, '– we could all be wrong; I only just thought of it – when I remembered the bandage. Of course it was obvious that the shot didn't kill Timothy, at least not immediately. I've had a feeling all along that the shooting could be an accident, something to do with a quarrel, a struggle involving a gun. From what people tell me, Joanne seems to have been a very *volatile* person. Suppose the gun was accidentally discharged, she could have bandaged him, then panicked and run, or rather driven away. On the other hand she could have thought Timothy was dead and she cleared out immediately, and Vogel came home within a day or two, found Timothy still alive and it was he who put the bandage on.'

'And he had to bury the body when Timothy died.' Charlotte was thoughtful. 'You mean, he guessed Joanne shot Timothy, or Timothy said she had, and Vogel was protecting her?'

'And with his record he didn't want the police around.' Miss Pink smiled, the picture of diffidence. 'Of course, it's all speculation.'

Lovejoy snorted. 'Like Julius's wild idea about Vogel having killed Joanne. All the same, it was −'

'Oh, no,' Miss Pink interrupted. 'Not Vogel; he'd come to accept −'

The screen door opened again and Julius Semple came in. The light transformed him as it did his wife. He was wearing a wide-brimmed hat and his ravaged good looks were further set off by a black bandana at his throat. 'High noon,' murmured Rose, but not loud enough for him to hear. He crossed the room, nodding to the occupants, and stood close to his wife. They made an extremely handsome couple of a certain age and Miss Pink reflected that, with those looks and a certain amount of team-work, they would make a success of any enterprise that might involve an element of showmanship, such as the museum.

'What had he come to accept?' Lovejoy asked of Miss Pink. 'We're talking about Vogel,' he told Semple. 'Miss Pink is giving us the rundown on how Timothy came to be shot, poor guy.'

Semple looked blank. 'Go on,' Charlotte urged. 'This is intriguing, even though you say it's all speculation.'

'I was going to say that he'd come to accept Joanne's promiscuity,' Miss Pink explained. 'And he had no more reason to murder her, I should say considerably less reason, than any other man who was her lover.'

'OK,' Rose said sulkily, 'but she didn't have − I mean −' she looked round the circle, '− when she was here she was

185

serious with only one guy: Timothy, right?' No one spoke. 'Wasn't she?' she asked doubtfully.

'Don't look at me!' protested Lovejoy.

'Well, wasn't she?' Rose asked of Charlotte.

Semple's expression was flinty. 'Give me a bourbon,' he growled at Lovejoy.

'I don't think Joanne was serious in the way you imply with anyone,' Charlotte said. 'Least of all Timothy. She was taking him for all she could get, and the only reason she was going off with him was because she thought he could get her a job in movies.'

'She had the looks for it,' Rose said, ignoring the rest of the comments.

Lovejoy said: 'That's a load of garbage, Charlotte! Joanne's a lovely girl, and completely innocent –'

'Innocent!' Charlotte glared at him, then softened as quickly. 'Innocent like an animal,' she amended. 'She was totally immoral –'

'She was loyal and loving and generous –' Lovejoy shouted.

The kitchen door opened behind him. 'You can say that again,' Blair said.

'What?' Lovejoy swung round.

'She was generous all right.'

'Now don't you start –'

'She was a walking bomb,' Charlotte said. 'In these days, with all the information pumped into us about Aids –'

Her tone was softly reasonable and Lovejoy's interruption cut through it like a rattler's hiss: 'So where was your old man on the night of the twentieth?'

There was an appalled silence. Semple gaped at him. Charlotte's eyes widened in shock, and Lovejoy took a step back so that he came up against the shelves of the bar. Blair looked frightened, Rose said weakly: 'That was gross, Earl.' Miss Pink's glasses flashed as she looked round them calmly.

Charlotte shook her head. 'Run that one past me again, Earl.'

Blair licked his lips. Lovejoy was embarrassed. 'Only a joke,' he muttered, moving forward.

'Sick joke.' Rose glanced at the Semples unhappily.

'Yes,' Charlotte said. 'I was getting there. It was a bit sick, Earl.' She glanced at her husband. 'Tell them, sweetie.'

He sighed. 'There's nothing to tell. I mean, hell, you steer clear of a woman like that – if you can.' He grinned shame-facedly. 'There isn't far you can go in Dogtown; I couldn't hardly jump in the pick-up and head for the back-country when I saw her coming, could I? I blame Vogel; he should have looked after her. Of course, I wasn't the only one –' he glanced at his wife, '– she was after anything in pants.'

'Difficult.' Charlotte sounded like an echo. 'She literally couldn't keep her hands off a man – even with me standing there! It was a compulsion, you know? A desperate need for physical contact, always having to touch people.'

'Even you?' Rose asked sweetly.

Charlotte's lips thinned. 'Whores are often lesbians,' she said coldly.

Rose gasped. Lovejoy opened his mouth to intercede but Miss Pink was there before him. 'When did Vogel come back?' she asked.

They were dumbfounded at the sudden change of subject. Rose recovered first. 'Some time after the twenty-first,' she said. 'After Joanne's birthday, must have been; they wouldn't have planned the party if he was going to be here. He didn't show in Dogtown for a while after, but that doesn't mean he wasn't at the ranch. He could go and come without anyone knowing: over Breakneck, down past Dogtown. You can't see the road from here.'

'You can see headlights at night,' Blair said.

'Only if you're looking.'

Miss Pink said absently, as if following a train of thought: 'On the night of the twentieth was there anything about, a truck or car – did you hear one – that you didn't recognise?'

They looked at each other. 'Not at night,' Charlotte said. 'We'd remember. On summer days there's usually tourists about: family parties, kids, like that –'

187

'They come over here,' Blair put in. 'We do hamburgers and hot dogs in the daytime.' He made a face.

Rose said: 'Everyone leaves the town by six, around there, when the museum closes – unless they eat here.'

'No one ate here on the twentieth,' Blair said. 'I was preparing for the party next day. I'd remember if I'd had to break off and cook for casuals.'

'We must have closed at six,' Charlotte said. 'We always do. I don't remember any strange cars after that, but then if someone was on the canyon road, we wouldn't see head-lights if we were indoors – and I don't see where else we could be. There's not a lot to do in Dogtown. Maybe we came over for a drink.'

'You didn't,' Rose said. 'But I did. I remember because Joanne had been down that afternoon and Earl and I were talking about her and the party next day: we were laughing about the menu she'd chosen: clam chowder, lobster salad and chocolate mousse – a kid's menu. Verne was making *petits fours* and I went in the kitchen to watch. I remember the night because it was all, like, preparations for the big event. And Charlotte was watching television when I went home and Julius was in the museum. I could see him through the windows. You were working at a bench,' she told him, 'so *you're* in the clear.' She stopped short. People looked at each other and as quickly looked away. The tension that had eased somewhat returned in force. Semple asked tentatively: 'What motive would they have had for shooting Timothy?'

'They?' Miss Pink looked bewildered.

'Well, anyone. You're considering everyone, aren't you?' He shuffled his feet, embarrassed.

'Miss Pink is,' Charlotte said drily. 'The stuff about strange trucks is a blind. You may as well come right out with it, say their names.' She looked meaningly at Miss Pink. 'We're all thinking the same thing. But Asa Fortune has never been violent – and Hiram?' She shrugged. 'Easy come, easy go.'

'Meaning he didn't care that much for Joanne?' Miss Pink asked innocently while Rose and the partners stared, and Semple looked sullen.

'Well, hardly a matter of *caring*.' Charlotte said. 'And so far as Asa is concerned, it's an enormous jump from robbing bodies to shooting people. Besides, if Asa'd suddenly come into a lot of money, wouldn't he spend it? You can be sure the sheriff's been asking in Endeavor did Asa buy a lot of luxuries in the last few weeks.' A pause as they digested this. 'Hiram?' she continued, still looking at Miss Pink. 'How did he react when you found Timothy's body?'

'I wasn't watching him but he had his hands full with the dog.'

'He could go up Danger Canyon without anyone knowing,' Semple said. 'Lorraine would know, of course –'

Rose said: 'If he told Lorraine he was in all evening on July twentieth watching TV, she'd say so, and she'd believe it. Lorraine's a zombie.'

'She's not as bad as that,' Lovejoy protested, 'but she could be brainwashed.'

'That would be what attracted Hiram to Joanne,' Charlotte mused: 'a girl with abundant energy – and there was the added thrill that she belonged to someone else –'

'She belonged to no one!' Rose flushed with indignation. 'You're talking like – like a Mormon! She was her own woman. Hell, you don't belong to Julius!'

'So what do you reckon?' Rose asked as they stood outside the Grand Imperial enjoying the stars. 'Do you still think it was one gang killed both guys, or do you think someone else fired that shot at Timothy?'

'Who would you think was responsible for Timothy's death?'

'Of the men in Dogtown? You're serious?' Rose turned away. 'There's a shooting star, it's fallen on the Argus Range. Asa? He steals but I don't see Asa shooting anyone – unless, of course, they were cruel to animals, but Timothy wasn't. Hiram? He had all the opportunity in the world and he was the kind of guy would be driven up the wall by a girl like Joanne. Julius. Well . . . '

'Yes.' Miss Pink too was thoughtful. The night was very

189

quiet. They could hear the murmur of the Semples' television set.

'I did see him on the night of the twentieth,' Rose insisted. 'I wasn't lying. He was working at a bench in the museum.'

They moved back from the hotel and looked up the street. There were lights in the museum. 'They're careless about electricity,' Rose said. 'They always leave the lights on. But I saw him; he was working on something with straps, like a bridle.'

'I believe you.'

'And you saw how he was terrified. You never met Joanne but she was one hell of a woman; if she did decide she wanted him, poor Julius wouldn't know what hit him.'

# Chapter 16

Lorraine Wolf was painting her nails. She stared helplessly as Miss Pink tendered a fifty-dollar bill in payment for petrol. 'No hurry,' Miss Pink said cheerfully, leaning against the counter to chat. 'Is Hiram about?'

'He's on the school bus. He's never here when you want him.'

'I didn't know he drove the school bus.'

'He don't. The driver's off sick so Wolf's standing in.' She spread her fingers and regarded her nails critically.

'That's an unusual colour,' Miss Pink said in admiration. 'Very fetching.'

Lorraine blinked and picked up the bottle. Her lips moved soundlessly. 'I can't read it.'

'Amaranth Lustre. It's good teamed with white.' Lorraine was wearing a white blouse with a plunging cleavage. Her eyes lit up and she gave Miss Pink a ravishing smile.

'You really think so? You're not just saying that? I didn't know whether I could wear it: purple and white. I liked it in the book —' she gestured to a magazine beside the cash register, '– but I don't have the looks.'

'Rubbish,' said Miss Pink lightly, and continued in the same tone: 'A nasty shock for your husband: finding Timothy's body.'

Lorraine showed no surprise at this. 'He didn't say much, just it looked bad for Brett Vogel. But Brett were dead then.'

'He'd be wanting to spare your feelings.'

'I dunno about that. He said the animals had been there.'

'What happened on July the twentieth?' asked Miss Pink in the same kind of tone that she might have asked what was on television that day.

'July twentieth?' Lorraine shook her head in amazement. 'That's two months back! How would I remember that long ago?'

'It was the night Timothy Argent was shot.'

'It was? So why ask me if you knew?'

'I put it badly. What I should have said was: did they call here for gas? or −' she glanced out of the window, '− did they turn off on the Dogtown road?'

'Who?'

'The people who killed Timothy. It wasn't Vogel.'

'Wolf said it was. So does the police.'

'Was Wolf here on July the twentieth?'

'I don't expect so. He's out most nights. Wolf likes a drink.'

'In Dogtown?'

'You're joking! That place don't have a proper bar, and he's got no time for − He don't care for the Queen. He goes to Endeavor. Oh, sorry, you want to pay for the gas.'

She made out a receipt and Miss Pink took her change. 'Is that your pick-up outside?'

'It's Wolf's. Why?'

'Should he leave a rifle in an open truck?' It was in a rack at the back of the cab.

'I don't expect it's loaded, and I keeps my eye on it.'

'I don't like seeing guns lying around in full view. There are strange people about.'

'That's why you gotta have a gun; you never know when you're going to need it, particularly out here.'

Turning away, Miss Pink checked. 'You mean that personally? You can handle a rifle too?'

'Of course, everybody out here does. Plenty of times a girl's on her own with her man off someplace till all hours. I keep the gun in the house at night − and I keep it loaded.'

'That one?'

'We only got the one.'

'Every night? Then that means Wolf is on the roads in the dark without a gun.'

'So what? He can lock the truck doors and he's a man

192

anyways. It's me needs the gun on my own in this place. I bring the dog in too but she don't even bark. The gun kills, don't it?'

'I was talking to Lorraine,' Miss Pink said. 'And she told me that the Wolfs have only one rifle and she keeps it in the house at night. So Hiram is out doing whatever he does unarmed.'

'Why you telling me this?' Asa Fortune was more interested in a white-headed woodpecker exploring a tree-trunk.

'If she's telling the truth it couldn't have been Hiram who shot Timothy.'

'What made you think it was?'

'Timothy was shot by mistake.' When he didn't react, she went on: 'The killer saw a shadow behind a screen in a lighted room. He didn't see the Jeep outside because Timothy had parked it above the cabin. He didn't care one way or the other about Timothy; it was Joanne he was after.'

He sketched a nod. 'So you worked it out. That wasn't difficult.'

'How many men would want Joanne to die slowly?'

'Or want her dead?' Now she had his interest. 'Why do you put it like that: dying slowly?'

'Someone hated her so much that when he thought she was in the crashed Jeep he made no attempt to go down into the creek and pull her out. She could have been alive and terribly injured.'

'You're guessing. There's no way of knowing what happened.'

She ignored this. 'Suppose Hiram did have a rifle that night and he did shoot Timothy, is he capable of leaving Joanne to die?'

'Hiram Wolf.' He chewed his moustache..A doe stepped out from behind a tree and regarded them gravely, its moist nose twitching. Fortune saw the deer and his voice softened. 'He can kill,' he said, 'but so do I; I go away from here where I don't know them. I kill strange beasts –' his eyes sharpened but his voice stayed low, '– difficult to say whether it's the same with people. It could work the other way round; it may be easier to kill folks as is close to you.'

'And she wasn't a stranger to him,' she said quietly.

'But she didn't care for him.'

'Did he care for her?'

'How would I know?'

'You might have been able to tell from his behaviour.' Without a pause or a change in tone she went on: 'In the tack-room, when you found the snake, the rosy boa, who was it came down out of the forest in Vogel's pick-up?'

He looked away and the deer, which had started to browse, jerked her head and stared at him, poised to run. 'Couldn't tell,' he said. 'I just saw headlights.'

'It was Vogel's pick-up,' she emphasised. 'The killer used Vogel's own truck to carry the body, even killed him with his own shovel.'

Fortune blinked. 'He were hung up with wire.'

'He was dead. The blow from the shovel fractured his skull.'

'Yeah, I guess he had to be dead first.'

'You didn't leave the ranch immediately.'

'I did so. A man like that, smuggler, he'd be armed, wouldn't he? I took off 'case he had a dog.' He looked sly. 'Hiram's bitch would have scented me, told him I were there.'

'But she didn't scent you. She wasn't there.'

'You don't know that.'

'You knew all along who was in that pick-up because you'd found the other truck before you reached the ranch.'

He shook his head. 'No.' The woodpecker started to strip bark and his eyes flickered. 'I didn't find no truck.'

'You hung around, you saw him park Vogel's truck and leave the ranch and return to where he'd left his own vehicle. You know who he was.'

'I went the other way, up Deadboy. I wasn't going down the meadow towards my place when he could come along

194

behind, lights blazing, and armed. Had to be armed, I figured, out at night, up to no good; poaching, I thought.' His voice strengthened. 'And it had to be Vogel. What else would I think? His pick-up comes down the meadow, turns in at the ranch where he lives. 'Fact, it probably was Vogel, no reason why not.' He avoided her eye.

The woodpecker stopped work and shuffled round the trunk. In the silence they could hear leaves tear as the doe browsed. 'I've talked to Joanne,' Miss Pink said.

He stiffened but he said nothing, waiting.

'She's well and happy, and careless as ever. I tried to persuade her to go away, to go into hiding. I wasn't successful.'

'Jesus,' he breathed. 'Is she close by?'

'Too close. And she's got a job in television. Soon everyone will know where she is –'

'No!'

'She has no idea she's in any danger. She laughs at the thought.'

'You gotta stop her!' His voice rose and the deer sprang away. 'She mustn't go on television,' he cried. 'Didn't you tell her?'

'Tell her what?'

'That . . . that –' He was mumbling and glaring, unable to find words.

'She thinks it was Vogel shot Timothy,' Miss Pink said earnestly. 'She's certain of it, and since he's dead she says there's nothing to worry about.'

'You gotta go back and convince her to leave. Where is she?'

'I'm not saying.'

He thought about that. 'Maybe you're right. How did you find her?'

She answered obliquely. 'It couldn't have been Hiram who shot Timothy, or if it was, his passion evaporated very quickly. Because he knows where she is and he didn't follow her.'

'Does anyone else know?'

'So you weren't bothered about Hiram either. And now

we both know who was driving the pick-up you found in the forest that night.'

'I don't. Sure I found the truck but I never saw the driver. I went up Deadboy like I said, but I did backtrack Vogel's pick-up, so I found his body. I'll tell you who the other truck belonged to if you take me to Joanne. I can convince her to go somewhere she'll be safe.'

'I know whose truck it was.' And she told him.

It was high noon in Dogtown. Windows and doorways looked blind, as they do in hot countries where fly screens shield open spaces. There was a moment, as the Cherokee came quietly up the wide bright street, when the place resembled a stage set: a plywood ghost town waiting for the gunfight, an impression heightened by a glimpse of Rose's horses dozing under a cottonwood.

The Cherokee itself shattered the illusion, and now the pick-ups were visible, although the Semples' was absent. Dust drifted away as Miss Pink came round and parked facing the Red Queen.

Lovejoy, stacking shelves, greeted her in surprise. 'I thought you said you were up to Palmer Meadows with Granville today.'

'I missed them. I've been working in Crazy Mule Canyon.'

'We're back to that, are we? Crazy Mule or Breakneck or Deadboy Pass. I guess it's a harmless occupation: a relief really after the past coupla weeks. Did you get your letter written?'

Blair came in with mugs of coffee, asked Miss Pink if she would join them, and went back to the kitchen.

'There are one or two loose ends,' she murmured, and turned to look out on the brilliant street.

'I never did get it clear −' he began, but Blair, reappearing with another mug of coffee, said harshly: 'Leave it, Earl. Everybody's had it up to here. And remember −' it was a warning, '− Miss Pink was intimately involved.'

'Sorry. Here's Rose coming over. Thirsty weather, this heat wave. She'll be wanting coffee too.'

Blair retreated. The screen door opened. Rose said: 'I thought you were out with the Westerners. What happened?'

'I missed them. There's no hurry. We can afford to take things easy now.'

'That's a change. And no police, no press; you dodged all that by taking off for LA.'

'It was too hot for interviews.'

Blair came in with coffee for Rose. 'This is nice,' she said with sudden appreciation. 'It's a bit dead – I mean, I feel as if something's missing; we gotta take up our lives again as if nothing happened. But something did happen – and it was shattering. So why do I feel a sense of loss?'

'Unfinished business?' murmured Miss Pink.

Blair made an impatient movement but Lovejoy's expression was questioning. Rose was still puzzled. 'We'll never know the truth,' she said helplessly, but the partners' attention had strayed to the street and the women turned to see Julius Semple walking through the sunshine, wearing a gun-belt with the butt of a gun visible in its holster. No one said anything, no one moved. Semple came in and clumped over to the bar in his high-heeled boots. Rose exhaled and said breathlessly: 'What on earth are you doing with *that*?'

His eyes were bright. 'Isn't it fabulous? The Colt's just to complete the picture, I have to find one the right period. I bought this gun-belt last week; don't you think it's a beauty?' He drew the pistol and laid it on the bar. Blair said: 'You know you can't bring a firearm in here, Julius.'

'It's not loaded.'

The partners stared at the Colt as if mesmerised. Semple unbuckled the belt and handed it to Rose. 'Look at the tooling on that holster; no one makes stuff like that today.'

Miss Pink picked up the gun which was, indeed, unloaded. 'A handy weapon,' she observed. 'Do you have a collection of firearms too, Mr Semple?'

'Julius, please. Who else does?' His eyes danced. A breath of spirits wafted towards them. Rose lifted an eyebrow and turned to her coffee. 'I'm off the hook today,' he informed them. 'My dear wife's at a sale in Endeavor.' He beamed: for him an unfamiliar expression. Usually he looked hag-ridden. Blair put a mug of black coffee in front of him. 'Drink that, Julius,' he said firmly.

Semple opened his mouth, caught the other's look and said: 'Good idea, Verne. Thanks.'

'Do you have other firearms, Julius?' Miss Pink's words dropped like water from a height: crystal-clear, discrete.

'Only a few,' he told her. 'But my collection's increasing all the time; that's my department: firearms, and harness of all kinds. Charlotte's specialty is the clothes. You came back early, ma'am; aren't you going up to Palmer Meadows?'

'I had to get some things straight for a report I'm working on for Timothy's publisher.'

'Like what?' Rose asked.

'I needed to know where the pick-up was concealed on the night that Vogel was killed.'

The import of this penetrated slowly. Lovejoy's lips moved as he repeated the statement, Blair blinked behind his spectacles, Rose's mouth hung open. Semple stared and said: 'What pick-up? They used his: his pick-up, his shovel to bury him –'

'Vogel wasn't buried,' Miss Pink said.

He laughed and shook his head as if to clear it. 'Of course he wasn't; I'm getting muddled with Timothy. But then I guess he had to be buried with Vogel's shovel because Vogel buried him, right?'

'Vogel buried Timothy, but he didn't shoot him. I was referring to Vogel being murdered; where was the killer's pick-up that night?'

Rose said: 'You're guessing. How could you know they had a pick-up and not, for instance, a car?'

'Because it was seen.'

'Oh no!' breathed Lovejoy.

'Who saw it?' demanded Semple.

'Why hasn't he come forward?' Blair was suddenly angry. 'Someone's having you on, ma'am.'

'There was a tip-off,' Miss Pink said vaguely.

'Anonymous phone call?' Blair jeered. 'Someone's got it in for his neighbour –' he looked uncomfortable, '– not a neighbour in Dogtown; probably someone in Endeavor trying to get in on the act.'

'People can be extremely spiteful,' she admitted. 'They can claim to recognise a vehicle, even to giving the registration number. The police get loads of false accusations after any major crime.'

'Which night are we talking about now?' Semple asked.

'Well, both nights really.' She sounded apologetic. 'There were two victims but only one murderer.'

'But the barbed wire!' Rose exclaimed. 'You're back to the same gang killing both of them?'

'There was no gang. Vogel's death was made to look like a gang execution.'

'Who was it?' Lovejoy asked, and everyone hung on the answer.

'There's no proof,' she confessed. 'It's just the word of one person, and Counsel would shoot her down in flames in court.'

'Lorraine?' Rose drew it out in disbelief.

'Joanne.'

'You mean,' Lovejoy said after a pause, 'Joanne would be a witness if they could find her? What you're saying is that she saw who shot Timothy?'

'If she did, she's in a hell of a dangerous position right now,' Rose said.

'No, she's safe –' Miss Pink began.

'He could kill again!' Lovejoy protested. 'Killing gets progressively easier, like with multiple killers. It's like a drug –'

'This man isn't that type; he's no longer aggressive.'

'How can you say that?' asked Semple. 'He could have found her already. She could be dead.'

'She's alive and I talked to her.'

There was an impression of impact, of a blow. They reeled, recovered, and threw questions at her. Then they stopped, aware of their own babble, only Rose trailing on

199

with: '— you have to tell us what she says happened that night.'

'We'd guessed most of it already,' she told them. 'Except that facts were lost in the welter of speculation. What happened was that Timothy was shot, Joanne thought he was dead and she escaped in the Jeep. At the same time she realised the tank was empty she saw headlights behind her so she sent the Jeep off the road and hid in the forest. The killer turned round above the crash and went back down the canyon. He never bothered to go down to the creek although the Jeep's lights were blazing.'

'Did she see the killer?' Semple asked.

Miss Pink looked at him thoughtfully. Lovejoy said: 'I hope she's got protection.' He was staring at his partner. Blair's body jerked as if he'd received an electric shock. All eyes came back to Miss Pink. 'He's driving the school bus,' she told them.

Someone gasped. Comprehension was followed by bewilderment. Rose said: 'I need a drink. Give me a brandy, Earl.'

'We all need a drink,' Semple said. 'Bourbon for me.'

'Why did he kill Vogel?' Blair asked. 'You did say there was only one killer. How did Joanne know what happened to Vogel? She was gone long before.'

'She didn't. Vogel was killed because he knew who shot Timothy. Obviously Timothy was alive after the shot and he told Vogel who was responsible. It had to be Vogel who came home and found him — well, had to be with hindsight. Vogel could have been blackmailing the killer.'

'You have to get on the phone to the sheriff,' Lovejoy said. 'He's out there, driving schoolkids: a double murderer!'

Semple laughed angrily. 'He's not going to start shooting kids, Earl!'

'The man's mad,' Blair said. 'He's a psychopath. He could take off soon's he finds out and go after Joanne.'

Miss Pink looked away and saw a swirl of dust drift past the windows.

'Now who's this?' Lovejoy asked.

Rose moved to the window. 'It's Charlotte,' she said. 'She's back early.' She went to the screen door and opened it. 'Charlotte! We're all over here; come and join us.' A question was asked. 'Yes, he's here too,' Rose replied. She returned to the bar. 'The police won't believe a word of it,' she told Miss Pink. 'I think you should take a run into town, tell them face-to-face. I'll come with you; I don't think you should be on your own till he's safe behind bars.'

'That's an excellent idea,' Miss Pink said as the door opened. Charlotte stepped inside and stopped short at sight of the company. 'Something's happened. Again,' she added drily. 'You're looking at me as if I came from Mars.' She regarded Miss Pink. 'You shouldn't be here. You're supposed to be out with the Westerners. I know: you've brought more bad news.'

'Only in a manner of speaking,' Lovejoy said. 'She's identified the killer.'

'In a manner of speaking,' Charlotte repeated.

'You shouldn't be here either,' Miss Pink observed. 'You should be at a sale in Endeavor.'

'They had nothing I wanted. What killer?'

'Vogel's and Timothy's.'

She moved closer to her husband. 'I thought they were a gang, the same gang. What are you trying to tell me?'

'It was Hiram,' Semple said.

Charlotte's hands closed on his arm. Her eyes were wild. '*What* was Hiram?'

'He shot Timothy,' Lovejoy said. 'Then he murdered Vogel.'

'Why?'

Lovejoy collapsed like a punctured balloon. 'You tell her,' he begged Miss Pink.

'Joanne was irresistible,' she said, enunciating clearly as if it was news to them. 'She was beautiful, adorable, completely unaware of the havoc she caused –' Charlotte's face was white and her nostrils flared as she inhaled. 'Two men have died,' Miss Pink went on, ignoring the effect on her listeners, '– another is going to stand trial for his life –'

'*Femme fatale*,' murmured Rose.

'No one was immune.' Miss Pink stopped and continued conversationally: 'This is how the media will portray her. Of course, that's a caricature; she's a normal healthy girl, a bit casual in her relationships, emotionally immature, but she exploded on this little community like a bomb. Everyone was affected by her –' her eye passed over Blair, '– more or less, but Joanne had no deep feeling, except perhaps for Timothy; she was just affectionate, and so careless she couldn't see that lovesick men might be dangerous. So the killer went up to the ranch one night, maybe with nothing more in mind than to visit her while Vogel was away – but he took a rifle. The feel of a gun in your hands when you're consumed by jealous rage must produce a terrible compulsion. He was blinded, he saw a shadow on the screen, and he fired.'

Wordlessly Lovejoy poured brandy and bourbon. The sound of liquid filling glasses was loud in the big room. A hawk's long scream came to them through the heat-soaked air.

'There's no man in Dogtown capable of a rage like that,' Charlotte said.

'How do you know?' Miss Pink asked.

'Not Hiram,' Rose said. 'Not really.'

'This is all circumstantial evidence,' Charlotte said. 'The police closed the case. They say it was a gang.'

'She's talked to Joanne,' Lovejoy said.

'How could – Where did you find her?' Charlotte's eyes were unfathomable in the gloom.

Miss Pink glanced towards the windows. 'In the desert.'

'And she told you who fired the shot?'

'More than that. And there were other witnesses. The pick-up was seen the night Vogel was murdered. The killer left his own truck concealed – as he did the night Timothy was shot – and he approached the ranch on foot, killed Vogel and strung him up.'

Charlotte said: 'Timothy's wallet was found in Vogel's cabin. You're saying that was planted?'

'Naturally. If Vogel had killed Timothy he would have burned it. The killer took the wallet the night he shot Timothy and kept it against a time when he might need to throw suspicion on someone else.'

'There's no proof of any of this,' Charlotte persisted. 'It's just what people say.'

'They are witnesses. Defence counsel would have to show that they're unreliable.'

'Exactly. And Joanne has no more credibility than any other cheap hooker.'

'The registration number of the pick-up is known,' Miss Pink said. 'The one concealed in the forest.'

'Concealed when?'

'Both nights. It's all over now; everything is known.'

Semple was shaking his head. Charlotte clung to him. 'What was the registration?' she asked.

'The same as yours,' Miss Pink said.

Charlotte relinquished her husband's arm and they drew apart. She stared at him and his eyes were expressionless. Someone said: 'It's not true.' It was Lovejoy. He added weakly: 'It's someone getting his own back. You got an alibi, Julius.'

Rose turned on Miss Pink. 'I saw him the night Timothy was shot, the night you say he was shot. I saw him in the museum. I keep telling you.' Semple looked at her but his eyes came back to his wife. 'So I saw him early,' Rose cried. 'So what? He went up there afterwards, but it was an accident, he was mad with jealousy –' She clapped her hand over her mouth, her eyes on Charlotte who had moved further away, as if dissociating herself from horror. 'What did you say, Charlotte?'

'What is it?' Miss Pink asked shortly

'I said, there's Vogel too.'

'Oh yes,' murmured Rose, trance-like. 'He can't claim Vogel was a mistake. There was the barbed wire.' She shuddered.

Charlotte shouted: 'Vogel was dead when he strung him up!'

'Oh, God!' Semple staggered, knocked over a stool, righted it and sat down. He eyed the pistol on the bar. Lovejoy signalled wildly to Miss Pink and she shook her head. They all knew it wasn't loaded.

'I'll have another bourbon,' Semple said, and grinned like a death's-head. 'The condemned man, you know? I'm running up a bill but my wife will pay.' He turned the ghastly grin on her. 'Won't you, sweetie?'

'Julius, it's going to be all *right* –'

'I'm sure it is. You're more than capable.' He tossed back the bourbon, put the glass down with a crack and looked meaningly at Lovejoy who brought his eyes round slowly to Miss Pink as if a sudden movement would result in violence. She nodded.

'Miss Pink gives her permission,' Semple said, and turned to Blair. 'You guys chose the best lifestyle; I never envied you until this moment, never saw any future in shacking up with a fellow – you needn't look at me like that, Earl, I'm not being offensive, just telling you how it looks from where I'm at.' He drank half his bourbon, savouring it. They watched him warily. He went on, still addressing the partners: 'You got it made, you two; the rest of us is in shackles. Women!' He smiled: a sad and reminiscent smile: 'There was Joanne: a gorgeous girl who don't give a damn for anyone – and then there's a lady like my wife –' He stopped, sucking in his cheeks, staring at her, ruminating. 'However, beauty's only skin-deep, isn't it, sweetie?' Charlotte turned her head away and all they could see was the mane of dyed red hair. 'And my wife,' went on the implacable voice, 'far from being careless, will never lose faith in me. If I'm going to fry in the electric chair, this lady will be protesting my innocence right to the very end, or at least saying I had provocation.' Charlotte walked unsteadily to the window. Semple raised his voice: 'Won't you, honey?'

She turned. She was haggard but she spoke firmly, with only the slightest quaver: 'I can't do that, Julius, but I'll stand by you – there's no question of that –' Her voice strengthened, she came back, put her arm on his shoulders

204

and stroked his hair. 'You're my old boy,' she said firmly. 'As if I'd ever let you down.' He pushed his glass across the bar. 'Should you –?' she asked.

'You go and pack my gear,' he said.

Their eyes locked. She gave the faintest shrug and turned to go. On her way to the door she paused and looked at Miss Pink. 'You destroyed my husband,' she said coldly, and walked out.

Semple smiled at Miss Pink. Lovejoy said: 'Don't take no notice; she's not thinking straight.'

'Oh, she's thinking straight,' Semple said, and stood up, taking the Colt from the bar. He strode across the room and pushed open the screen. They craned their necks to follow his progress down the street, his heels raising little spurts of dust. Blair lifted the counter flap, Lovejoy followed him and everyone moved across the room, but slowly as if frightened that he would turn suddenly and see them.

He came to the museum and stood against the wall outside the door. Facing the street, he lifted the pistol and took something from his pocket. 'Jesus!' Rose gasped. 'He's loaded it!'

Lovejoy picked up a chair and swung it at the window. The noise of shattered glass was shocking but Semple didn't flinch. He yanked open the screen door and leapt inside. There was a report, and another, overlapped by more, then silence.

'Someone had better telephone,' Miss Pink said when nothing happened, no one screamed or emerged from the museum and there were no more shots. 'Call for an ambulance, Verne, and a doctor.'

'What do we do?' Rose whispered. 'We can't go across.'

'Two people were firing.' Lovejoy was incredulous. 'Two!'

'They were firing at each other?' Rose asked. No one answered her. They listened to Blair telephoning in the kitchen. They waited, staring at the museum door.

The screen opened slowly and Semple emerged, looking as if a can of scarlet paint had been emptied over his shoulder. He held his forearm gingerly with the other hand

and started to lurch across the road towards the Queen. They hurried out of the restaurant.

'What happened to Charlotte?' Rose asked as they reached him. 'Who was firing?'

'We both were. I was the lucky one. She's dead.'

'Lucky!' Lovejoy repeated. 'You killed three people now.'

'No,' Semple said. 'Only one. She killed the others.'

'She blackmailed me from the first.'

They had dressed the wound and told him to stay quiet, to wait for the ambulance but, still shaking with shock, he couldn't stop talking.

'She had to tell me she shot Timothy,' he said, 'because I thought we had an intruder that evening. The television was on, I thought she was watching it. I'd been working late in the museum but I'd finished and I was drinking coffee in the cabin. I heard someone come in the back door and I went for my rifle – and it wasn't there. She came in the kitchen carrying it, and she told me she'd left the pick-up outside town, told me to go and fetch it. She didn't tell me the rest until I came back. By that time anyone looking would have seen me drive the truck home. She was in the clear.' He looked at them, seated round him in the partners' sitting room. 'What I never understood was, she didn't care for me much.' He shook his head. 'But she hated Joanne. She meant to kill that girl, she thought she had, or at least driven her to her death in the crashed Jeep . . . Then she killed Vogel.'

'So Timothy did know who shot him,' Lovejoy said. 'And he told Vogel.'

'No. He was unconscious when she got back to the cabin. That was when she took his wallet. She thought he was dead and she left him for Vogel to find. Vogel was the fall-guy. And he had to be killed before he could be questioned because he'd probably have an alibi for Timothy's murder. Even if he had to admit he was delivering a consignment of heroin, so long as it was a hundred miles away, that was preferable to a murder charge. So she killed him and planted the wallet in his stove.' His eyes closed and he slumped in his chair.

They moved away, talking quietly. 'That woman was a monster,' Rose said. 'She shot Timothy in mistake for Joanne, and then she followed Joanne to try again. She thought she'd succeeded. And yet Julius says Charlotte didn't care for him. What *is* this?'

'It wasn't sex,' Lovejoy said.

'Of course it was,' Miss Pink countered. 'But not directly. Julius wasn't having an affair with Joanne but Charlotte was possessive even if she didn't care for him, and she was insanely jealous of the girl's youth and beauty, perhaps most of all she was fiercely resentful of Joanne's total disregard of men's feelings.' She smiled wryly. 'Charlotte was no feminist.'

Blair said: 'Of course he was never frightened of Joanne, it was Charlotte who kept saying he was. What Julius was terrified of was his own wife; he knew what she was capable of.'

'She was setting him up,' Lovejoy said. 'He was to be the last fall-guy.'

'She almost won,' Rose said. 'He was behaving like he was beaten in here.'

'He knew he was no match for her.' Blair smiled thinly. 'Who would be?'

'Except he had the gun,' Lovejoy pointed out. 'And he had the magazine in his pocket.' He frowned. 'That don't look like he was prepared to be anyone's fall-guy. You know, I reckon those two hated each other.'

'He was carrying the Colt for self-defence,' Blair said firmly. 'He was married to a woman had killed one guy to silence him; it had to have crossed his mind that he was in a very vulnerable position himself. She'd killed twice – and she was about to kill again. He shot in self-defence. We all heard her fire first. There was the report of the rifle: the heavy boom, the shot that hit him, and then he fired, right?'

'Right,' they said.

*

'What do you propose to do now?' Rose asked later that evening as the Rattlesnake Hills smouldered above the shadow of the Sierras. 'Will you continue along the Joplin Trail from here or go back to the Missouri and start over? Or forget about them altogether?'

'I have to write the book,' Miss Pink said. 'It's the least I can do: to finish the job Timothy started. Besides, I'm attracted to Permelia Joplin.'

'Backlash! The virtuous pioneer women and their stalwart men forging westward against all odds: macho stuff.'

'They forged westward but the rest could be myth.'

'Oh, come on! The diaries aren't myth.'

'Diaries are written for posterity.'

'Are you suggesting that they left out significant bits, like bad relationships? You reckon there were women around as bad as Charlotte?'

'They've always been around.'

'Not on the pioneer trails!' Rose was incensed.

Miss Pink smiled. 'I suspect there was some form of balance in operation; public opinion would have put a curb on the ones who were merely naughty, like malicious gossips, but for women who were a serious threat to the community you'd need something more drastic.'

'Like a husband with a blazing Colt?'

'No. Other women probably, operating quietly and secretly, in the dark. Survivors don't go in for confrontations. High noon is for the men.'